DEADLY POLITICS

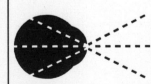This Large Print Book carries the Seal of Approval of N.A.V.H.

DEADLY POLITICS

MAGGIE SEFTON

THORNDIKE PRESS
A part of Gale, Cengage Learning

GALE
CENGAGE Learning·

Detroit • New York • San Francisco • New Haven, Conn • Waterville, Maine • London

LIBRARY OF CONGRESS CATALOGING-IN-PUBLICATION DATA

Sefton, Maggie.
    Deadly politics / by Maggie Sefton.
        pages cm. — (Thorndike Press large print mystery) (A Molly Malone mystery)
        ISBN 978-1-4104-5092-0 (hardcover) — ISBN 1-4104-5092-9 (hardcover)
    1. Political consultants—Fiction. 2. Young women—Crimes against—Fiction. 3. Washington (D.C.)—Fiction. 4. Political fiction. 5. Large type books.
    I. Title.
    PS3619.E37D425 2012b
    813'.6—dc23   2012028714

Published in 2012 by arrangement with Midnight Ink, an imprint of Llewellyn Publications, Woodbury, MN 55125-2989 USA.

Printed in the United States of America
1 2 3 4 5 6 7 16 15 14 13 12

I want to thank my agent,
Jessica Faust of BookEnds, LLC,
for believing in and supporting the
Molly Malone Suspense Mysteries
and for always believing in me.

ONE

Washington, D.C. lay spread out below me like a seductive old whore. White monuments and grassy parks — jewels on fine garment — only disguised what awaited this lover's embrace: the knife hidden in the folds of her gown. My breath still caught at the sight of her.

The passenger jet banked to the left as it began its approach to Reagan National Airport, and the forested subdivisions of Northern Virginia edged into view. Memories — bittersweet and painful rushed in. Home. Family and friends waiting for me. A grave sheltered on the banks of Rock Creek.

Descending, the plane dropped over that glistening ribbon of the Potomac as we approached the runway. From the corner of my eye, I caught sunlight reflecting off the Capitol dome, and other memories crept from the dark. Old enemies. They had prospered, while I'd run off to Colorado to lick my wounds.

Wheels touched down, and I joined the ritual grabbing of cell phones that now marked the end of every airline flight. Mine beeped into life, joining the shrill rings that bounced off the cabin walls, as we all scrambled into the aisles, laptops and briefcases slung over shoulders. Hurry up and wait.

Two missed calls. Nan and Deb both checking on me. My cousins and closest childhood friends, Nan and Deb had made me an offer I couldn't refuse. Free room and board while I started over.

Damn. I was tired of starting over. It seemed like I'd been doing it my entire life. I didn't know if I could start over again, especially here.

"Molly, where are you?" Deb's voice demanded. "I've driven around National three times already."

"We've just landed. I'll grab my suitcase and be out in front as soon as I can." Straightening the skirt of my interview suit, I inched forward behind my fellow passengers. "Let's hope the luggage isn't delayed."

"Okay, look for me. I've got the Jag. See

you soon."

"Deb, thanks again for doing all this. I mean picking me up and everything."

"Are you kidding? We've been dying to get you out here since forever."

"Well, thanks anyway, for being there, I guess."

"We're family, Molly. Besides, it's time. Time for you to come back home. See you in a few." Deb's phone clicked off.

I grabbed my carry-on from the overhead compartment and pondered what my cousin said. Time to come home. Denver had been home for over twenty years. Could I slip back in time, just like that? I didn't know. But I'd run out of options and excuses. I had nowhere else to go.

"Both interstates are clogged, so we'll take the parkway," Deb said as she merged into traffic. "Besides, that'll give you a chance to enjoy the view of the city. Kind of re-acquaint yourself. You've been avoiding it so long, dummy," she added in an affection-ate tone.

"I already reacquainted myself as we were landing." I reached for the carryout coffee Deb had thoughtfully brought along. "Wash-ington is as beautiful as the last time I saw it. And just as treacherous, if you believe

9

the newspapers."

"Let it go, Molly."

Deb. Always keeping us on track. Nan and I used to call her the "policeman" when we were little kids and getting into mischief. As much mischief as was possible in sleepy Arlington, Virginia, a suburb in the early 1960s. Whenever one of us suggested something too far off base, Deb would always rein us back in.

"I'm trying, Deb. But it's going to take me a while." I watched the green of East Potomac Park roll by across the river. The George Washington Memorial Parkway dipped and curved into the deep shade, the Potomac peeking through the trees. How many times had I driven this road?

"Take as long as you need, Molly. You're doing the right thing by coming here, you know. This is the Land of High-Priced Consultants, and you've got the background. You've been working for that Denver developer for years. You'll nail this job, I'm sure. You're perfect for it."

I wished I felt as enthusiastic as Deb. "I hope so. There's enough in the bank to get through this month, but it's not my bills that are worrying me. It's Patricia. Her salary's due at the end of the month." I stared into the blue sky above Lincoln

Memorial as the road curved. "That's a lot of money."

"How does your mom like Patricia?"

"She loves her, especially the Irish accent." Remembering the lilting voice of the woman I'd hired as my elderly mother's companion, I congratulated myself again. I'd hired her on gut instinct alone. References were great, price was, well, not great, but it was in the ball park with all the other senior companions. My gut, as always, was right. My mom loved her. Of course, Mom wasn't exactly sure why she needed Patricia, but she enjoyed the company.

"Boy, I can't believe what they charge."

"Yeah, it's a growth business, from what I've heard." Spying the familiar riverside outlines of Georgetown and Key Bridge edge into view, I checked my watch. "We're getting a little close with time. Maybe I should call Parker's office and let them know we're on the way." I dug for the cell phone at the bottom of my purse.

"Good idea. If the parkway is clear, then we should be in Fairfax in half an hour." Deb brushed her rust-colored hair over her shoulder before taking a sip from her travel mug.

Deb's hair was still a gorgeous rusty red. Silver-gray might be intruding, but she didn't care. As for Nan and me, we kept trying to fool Mother Nature — Nan with her blond hair getting blonder every year and me with my shorter frosted cut. Hide as long as you can.

I thumbed through the cell phone's directory for Parker's number. Jeff Parker and Associates. Commercial developer extraordinaire.

"Nan's making her special peppercorn-encrusted tenderloin in celebration."

I punched in the number. "Let's hope we have something to celebrate."

"We've got to do something about your self-confidence, Molly. You never used to talk like that."

"By the way, Karen may be coming over tonight. She called while I was leaving the airport. Wanted to wish me luck."

"It'll be great to see her. She still working for that congressman from Nebraska?"

"Yep. Six years now —" I heard Parker's office receptionist on the line. "Yes, this is Molly Malone. I've got a three o'clock appointment with Mr. Parker. My flight was a little delayed, but I'm on the way now. I should be there in half an hour."

"Ms. Malone? Mister Parker asked me to put you right through if you called. Hold on, please."

12

Something in the receptionist's tone of voice set my instinct buzzing. Why would Parker need to speak to me right now? The cold sensation that had become my constant companion for the last month settled into my stomach once again.

"Ms. Malone, Jeff Parker, here," a high-pitched tenor voice came on the line. "I was hoping you'd call. We've had some bad news."

Oh, God. Please, no. I braced for what I was about to hear.

"We just heard today. Our financing fell through. It's been a bear, Ms. Malone. Money's been tight this year as you know. I cannot tell you how sorry I am. I assure you, we had every expectation of bringing you on as head managerial accountant for this project, but we've had to put everything on hold. It's chaos right now, Ms. Malone. We've made commitments all over, and . . ."

"So, you won't be needing me?" I managed to say, putting the coffee cup in its holder before I spilled it all over the Jag's interior.

"What!" Deb sputtered, choking on her coffee.

"No, no, we won't. In fact, we may have to let people go. I'm sorry, Ms. Malone, believe me, we've heard nothing but glowing reports about you, and we were looking forward to having you join our team . . ."

I held the phone as Parker went on about nightmare delays and permits that didn't materialize and payments to subcontractors, and money drying up. His nasal voice droned, insectlike, while my old companion Cold claimed me completely. *Oh, my God. What do I do now?*

"Son of a bitch. Give me that phone." Deb didn't ask. She grabbed. "Jeff, what the hell do you think you're doing? Molly's come all the way here from Colorado for *your* project! You were drooling at her credentials three weeks ago. Now, you're ditching her? You can't do that. It's not ethical."

I only halfway listened as Deb chewed out Jeff Parker for firing me before I was even hired. Meanwhile, I concentrated on trying not to throw up.

"I don't care if that project went down. Plug her into another project. I know real estate, Jeff. You can do that."

Deb was good, but not good enough. Even loyal friends couldn't change the facts. Parker and Associates were strapped for money right now. Overextended. No way could they pay my salary, or rather, the salary I needed.

"Jeff, I'm not going to forget this," Deb

14

threatened, before she snapped off the phone and tossed it into my lap, her face puckering in a frown I recognized from childhood. Deb was fiercely protective of her own. "He'd better not ask Nan and me to do another one of his parties."

"Deb, it's not him, it's the money. He doesn't have it." At least the accountant inside was awake. The rest of me was going numb as the deep green of the parkway enveloped us, tall trees shading the road beside the river.

"Wait'll I tell Nan. She'll hit the ceiling."

"Better call and tell her to save that tenderloin for another time."

"The hell we will. We're still going to celebrate your homecoming," Deb said defiantly. "Then we're gonna brainstorm and find you another job."

"Can you pull over first? I've gotta throw up."

Deb steered into a scenic overlook. "Okay, tourists on the left at nine o'clock. I'll distract 'em. You're good to go on the right."

I didn't even wait for the car to stop before I opened the door.

"Just got off the phone with one of my clients. He confirms everything that Parker told you, Molly. Developers are taking a big

15

hit right now," Bill Anderson said as he settled into the patterned cushions of the white wicker garden chair. "Damn. I thought commercial was heating up again."

"So did I," Deb said as she placed a plate of fresh Camembert on the round table in the center of our little circle.

Nan, Bill, Deb, Deb's husband Mike, and I were seated in one of the many patios surrounding Nan and Bill's gorgeous colonial home deep in the woods of Vienna, Virginia. From here, traffic was a distant memory. This patio was crowned by a white lattice wood arbor, wisteria and climbing roses dangling through the top and along the sides. It looked like a photo spread for *House Beautiful.* Nan's flowerbeds dotted the backyard, shady and sunny, ready to burst into bloom. Since it was mid-March, the daffodils and crocuses were already out, flaunting their royal colors.

I reached for a wedge of Camembert, which was beside an overflowing antipasto tray and another platter of cheese and nuts. God forbid we starve. "We're not going to have any appetite for that tenderloin," I said before sipping my Cosmo.

Mike Beringer scooped up a handful of cashews. "Don't worry about the beef, Molly. Besides, you need something to absorb that vodka. We're still brainstorming." He gave me a wink.

"Well, storm away, but don't you dare fill up," Nan warned as she balanced her martini glass on the chair arm. "That tenderloin is perfect."

"I don't understand. There are shopping centers going up all over the place, all the time," Deb said, rattling the ice cubes in her empty glass. "You can't tell me they don't need someone with Molly's experience."

"Sure they do. We simply have to find the firms that are still hiring," Bill said in the declarative tone of a successful corporate attorney. "Let me refill that, Deb."

Deb wordlessly handed the glass to her brother-in-law as he headed for the outside bar, which was only slightly less stocked than the inside bar.

"Meanwhile, you can stay here as long as you want, Molly," Nan added. "The downstairs has been empty for ages."

I took a big sip of the martini, then smiled at my friend. "You mean the French Suite? I'm afraid to set a glass on the furniture. You've got antiques down there, for Pete's sake. It looks like a guest house in Provence."

"It should. She redid the whole room after

she read that book," Bill said, putting a vodka-filled glass in Deb's waiting hand. "You don't want to see the bills."

Nan gave a disparaging wave. "Don't believe him. Deb and I got great deals at the antique shops in Leesburg."

"Plus, we use a lot of the furniture for clients, depending on the event. Some hostesses want a special look. And we provide it, for a price, of course," Deb said with a knowing smile. She was the one who kept the books of their successful business.

"Boy, that hobby-turned-business has really blossomed. I'm so proud of you two." I held my almost-empty glass high. "To the Babson Sisters, Entertaining by Design." I tossed down the rest of the Cosmo and felt the vodka tingle through my veins. I didn't even bother to reach for the cheese.

That was the nice thing about relaxing with old friends. You could drink and get silly or sentimental or angry or whatever — and they still loved you. Thank God somebody did.

I'd grown up in Nan and Deb's home as much as my own. Since I was the only child of older parents, Nan and Deb were the closest thing to sisters I ever had. Daughters of my father's younger sister, we all lived in Arlington, Virginia, across the Potomac from Washington, D.C. Arlington was our backyard, and Washington was our playground next door. A stone's throw across the river. Arlington was quiet and sleepy then, not the crowded urban suburb it was now. In those days we could play anywhere, even ride our bikes through Fort Myer all the way to National Cemetery, waving at the smiling Army soldier guarding the gate. If we tried that now, we'd probably be shot on sight.

We played together nearly every day outside in the spring, summer, and fall; inside in the winter. We learned how to argue and fight fair, how to make up, and how to make each other cry. We confided our dreams, our secrets, and our current crushes. We practiced rolling our hair in curlers while gorging ourselves on popcorn and Coke at sleepovers, giggling ourselves senseless and scaring each other with ghost stories when the lights were out. We grew through every phase of childhood and girl-hood side by side, stumbling through awkward adolescences together and emerging as young women.

Bill and Mike entered the picture in college, when Nan and Deb married their college sweethearts. I married my college sweetheart, too, but lost him after ten years.

Nan and Deb were lucky. They still had theirs.

"You need another Cosmo, Molly," Bill said, rising from his chair again, ever the considerate host.

"Why not? No interviews in sight, so if I get hung over, it doesn't matter."

Another nice thing about being with old friends is that you can rejoice when you're happy and complain when you're not. And whine. Tonight, I opted for whining.

"I should never have left Colorado, you know that? I should have stayed with that Denver developer and found a second job. Sold my car. Sold something." Bill placed the icy glass in my hand, and I took another large sip. *Whoa.* He'd made it stronger this time. What the hell. The better to whine with.

"Might I remind you, Molly, you didn't have anything left to sell," Mike said, placing a large wedge of cheese on the cocktail napkin in front of me. "Your portfolio was damn near totaled by that broker."

"Asshole," Bill pronounced.

"Can't you get anything back?" Deb asked.

"Nope, he's repenting in an ashram in Boulder. Besides, it's my fault anyway. At the beginning of this year, I told him I needed money, and I needed it fast. When he suggested those other investments, I said to go for it."

"Damn, you didn't." Bill shook his head.

"Damn, but I did," I admitted, then took another large sip. Confession was good for the soul. "Commodities futures are a gamble. If you guess right, you're rich. If you're wrong, well, you go mooch off your friends."

"You're not mooching," Nan chided. "We've wanted you here since you divorced Frank."

"Asshole number two," Bill intoned behind his glass.

"You're simply starting over again, Molly, and this is the best place to do it. Here with us." She gave an emphatic nod.

There were those words again. This time the vodka egged me on. I snatched the yummy wedge of Camembert. Add a little cheese to my whine. "The thing is, Nan, I feel like I've been starting over all my life. When Dave died, I had to start all over again, all by myself, with the girls in Colorado. And I started over again when the girls left home. And then again when I married Frank. Sold my house. Gambled everything on a new relationship, and then the relationship died." I gestured in frustration.

"That weasel," Deb scowled.

I had to laugh. Deb was nothing if not loyal. "Well, he wasn't a weasel, just weak."

"And he couldn't keep his pants on."

"That, too."

"And he practically threw you out of your condo!" Deb was working up a righteous wrath, with help of the vodka.

"It was *his* condo, remember? He was letting me rent it until I decided where I wanted to buy. But this thing with my mom wiped everything off my radar screen. Time and luck ran out. The point is, I had to start all over again after the divorce two years ago. And now I'm doing it again." I released an aggravated sigh. "Damn, I'm fifty-six, and I'm still going in circles."

"Something will turn up," Mike said, giving me a reassuring smile. "I can feel it. By the way, how's your mom doing?"

I pictured my mom sitting with her old friends from Washington, laughing and playing cards in the garden of the gracious retirement community. "She's doing great. I called her on the way over and told her I'd visit tomorrow. She was really happy that I was back in town."

"What will you tell her about the job?" Bill asked.

"I'll think of something. It won't really

matter what I tell her because she won't remember it. After thirty minutes, she'll forget I even said it. I'll have to tell her all over again the next day," I said with a shrug.

Our little group fell silent, all of us no doubt pondering if we would wind up like my mother relaxing in some pricey retirement oasis, playing cards and visiting with friends, repeating conversations over and over, blissfully unaware of the mental deterioration. I wondered, did vodka kill brain cells?

Mike hunched over his glass of Scotch. "Molly, have you thought about moving your mom into an assisted living place? I know she loves it there in McLean, but it's damn expensive. That would solve your money problems, because you wouldn't need to pay a companion."

I leaned my head back and closed my eyes. "I hear you, Mike, and you're right, it would solve the money crunch. But I just can't do it. She's so happy there with her friends. These are women she's known from those old days when they were all senators' wives together. They've been best friends for a lifetime. It would break her heart to leave. I can't do that to her."

"Well, if her memory is going, maybe she wouldn't care," Nan suggested.

"Maybe she wouldn't even notice," Deb ventured as she selected from the cheese tray.

"Oh, she'd notice. I actually tried to suggest it, in a roundabout way, after she'd wandered off from the Kensington for the second time. I was getting worried, and the director reminded me that they have a 'three strikes and you're out' policy."

"But your mom is still there, and she went walkabout a third time," Nan said, handing her glass to Bill, who was making another trip to the bar.

"Only because I begged them to let her stay and promised I would hire a companion immediately." I snagged other slice of Camembert. "Thank God I found Patricia that next week. She'd finished one assignment and was ready for another."

"You know, Molly, there will come a time when your mom will have to go into assisted care." Bill paused at the arbor's edge, his deep baritone voice somber. "Remember, my dad had to go after my mom died. And I've seen it happen with other friends' parents. It seems to be a natural progression."

I stared at the stone patio, each block irregular, and shook my head. "Yeah, I know, but until that time I want her to be where she's happiest. She had such a look of shock on her face when I mentioned the idea of moving to a 'safer' place. I don't want to do that to her. Not yet. I'll know when it's time."

"Okaaay, then," Mike clapped his hands together, the successful chief executive calling the meeting to order. "Let's get back on point. Finding you a commercial development job. It'll turn up, I can feel it. You may have to go south. Down I-95. The commute will be God-awful, but it's another option."

I drained my glass and set it aside. Let the vodka float take me. "I'll do whatever it takes, guys."

"Can we do the rest of this brainstorming over dinner?" Nan suggested, rising from her chair. "That tenderloin is perfect."

"What, and absorb all that vodka?" Bill teased. "Molly's finally relaxing."

"Did you say Karen is coming?" Nan asked, finishing her martini.

"I called her after I heard from Parker and told her not to drive over tonight. She can wait until I snag a real job." Remembering my niece's disappointment over the phone, I added, "She's such a sweetie. She said she'd 'find something for me.' I told her I'd be okay. She's busy enough in that congressman's office. I don't want her taking time from her career to worry about me."

"She cares about you, Molly," Deb said, leaning back into the chair. "Ever since her mom and dad died, you're the only family she has left."

I stared out into the garden, dusk fast claiming the light. "You're right. She calls me every week to talk. I guess I do feel like she's another daughter."

Suddenly a familiar voice called from the side yard. "I rang the bell, and when no one answered I figured I'd find you all out here."

Talk about conjuring. There was my thirty-six-year-old niece, Karen Grayson, looking demure in her navy suit as she walked past the azalea bushes and rhododendrons. Despite the vodka cloud, I leapt to my feet. "Karen! You didn't have to drive through that nasty traffic tonight. I could have met you in D.C.," I said, rushing to give her a welcome embrace.

"No way I'd miss your homecoming, Molly," Karen said, giving me a big hug before she turned to embrace the rest of her extended family.

"Hey, sweetie, good to see you. Sit down and join us in a drink before dinner," Nan said, hostess taking precedence over gourmet cook for the moment.

"Actually, if you've got one of Molly's

Colorado beers in your fridge, I'll take that," Karen said when she'd finished receiving a circle of hugs. "Boy, I really needed all those hugs. It's been a tough week."

Bill headed to the bar once again. "One Colorado microbrew coming up."

"Here, sit down and relax for a while," Mike said as he patted an empty chair. "How many crises have you averted in Nebraska this week?"

Karen laughed as she settled into the chair. She brushed her shoulder-length ash-blond hair off her forehead in a gesture I'd watched from her childhood. "No crises so far in Nebraska." She held up crossed fingers. "Just the regular election-year anxiety."

"But we had an election last year. Why so early?" Deb asked, draining her glass.

"There's no such thing as 'early' for a congressman. We're in perpetual election mode," Karen said as she accepted the beer. "Thanks, Bill. I need this." She tipped back the bottle with the colorful label and drank. "Wow, I forgot how good these taste."

"Is Congressman Jackson going to have some real competition this time?" Bill asked.

Karen shrugged, then took another long drink. "Actually, I'm tired of talking about Jackson," she said with a mischievous smile.

"I came to talk about Molly."

"We've already beaten that horse to death," I joked. "I want to hear about you."

"But I've got news. Good news. Remember I said I'd ask around about jobs for you? Well, I found one. And I think you'll like it. In fact, I think you'll love it."

I blinked at Karen through the fast-evaporating vodka cloud. My mouth dropped open, but no speech came out.

Mike was quicker on the trigger. "What? You found something on the Hill?"

"Not on the Hill, but close. She'd be working for a senator. Just like she did years ago in Colorado." Karen reached over and patted my arm. "You're a natural, Molly. Politics is in your blood. It's time you got back to your roots."

I stared at Karen again, but this time I closed my mouth. The vodka had released an ocean of memories from long ago. They flooded through me. Returning to Colorado with my little girls, heartbroken, bitter, and needing a job. Old Governor Lambert taking pity on the young congressman's widow, giving me a position in his Denver office. Then, years later, Senator Hartman hiring me for his Senate staff. Both of them helping me create a new life in my husband's home state. My home ever since. *Roots?* I tore them out when Dave died.

I came back to the present, and the past scurried into the bushes. "*What!* Who would be crazy enough to hire me? I've been out of the loop for ages."

"God, Molly . . ." Mike shook his head.

"Either get her more vodka or some black coffee. She's losing it," Deb said.

"The new Independent senator from Colorado, that's who," Karen said with a sly grin.

My mouth dropped open again. John Russell had cut a swath through the Colorado landscape last year like a tornado over the High Plains. Russell's message of "fresh ideas" and a strong, independent voice in a fractious Senate resonated with enough Colorado voters to hand him the victory. Of course, the nonstop bloodletting of his Democratic and Republican opponents weakened any threat from them. Russell was a millionaire business success story who'd built a small local trucking firm into a national transportation powerhouse. A true visionary turned philanthropist. That track record combined with his dynamic personality and mesmerizing speaking style had handed John Russell a crucial swing seat in the United States Senate.

"You're kidding," I said when I found my

voice again.

Karen chuckled. "Nope. Apparently he's a huge fan of your father. Peter Brewster, his chief of staff, said the senator wants to model his Senate career and service after your father's. You know, a moderate senator from a conservative state, helping to make a difference."

I stared at Karen once again, memories enticing me to slip back to that golden time. It was another day, and that day was gone forever. Passed away with my father. Acrimony and dissension ruled our national debates now. There was no place for politicians like my father in today's Senate. No room for statesmen. Even iconoclastic, dynamic, mesmerizing millionaires like Russell. I shook those memories back into the bushes with the others.

"Karen, you can't be serious. I haven't worked in politics for years now. There's no way I'm qualified to work for any United States Senator again. Even this Russell. Especially not here in Washington. I couldn't do it. I just couldn't. I was able to in Colorado, but not here."

"You wouldn't be near the Capitol, Molly," Karen replied, a reassuring tone in her voice. "You'd be working in the senator's Georgetown residence. As a consultant.

Don't worry. I told Peter how reticent you were about working in Washington, and he understood completely. Believe me, he's anxious to meet you."

I tried to process what I'd just heard but couldn't. "What? I'd be working at his *house?* Doing what, for God's sake?"

"Who *cares?*" Mike exploded. "He wants to hire you!"

"But it doesn't make any sense . . ." I stammered.

Too late. My friends erupted in a chorus of "Damn, Molly!" "Are you crazy?" and "Grab it!" "Say yes, dummy."

Karen had mentioned the magic word. *Consultant.* King of Metro Washington Careers. All hail, billable hours.

"This is nuts," I muttered. "Let's stop the nonsense and have dinner. Didn't I see a yummy Bordeaux on the counter? Let's open it before Nan's fantastic tenderloin is ruined —"

Nan fairly leapt from her chair, empty martini glass in one hand. "Nope. Not a drop. You're interviewing tomorrow."

"What? For some glorified mascot or symbol or whatever this deluded senator wants?" I gestured dismissively. "No way."

"Yeah, way. You need a job, dummy," Deb chided.

"You don't have a choice, Molly," Bill added. "Your mom's retirement bills are mounting, even as we speak."

"Time to let go of all that Evil Washington crap you've been carrying around for years. This senator wants to hire you. What are you waiting for?" Nan threw in.

Good question. I didn't have an answer, or at least, a new one. They'd shot down everything else. But I tried to weasel out of it anyway. "Guys, I don't want to get close to Washington politics again. You know that. Too many bad memories."

There was a momentary silence, and I held my breath. Nothing like old baggage to stop a conversation — or a conversion — short.

Then Mike weighed in. "Molly, may I remind you of your promise made only minutes ago?" He folded his arms across his chest. "When I suggested job-hunting down I-95, traffic and all, your reply was, 'I'll do whatever it takes.' "

Damn. I had said that, hadn't I? Trapped by my own words. I hated it when that happened. I looked around at the triumphant grins surrounding me and threw in the towel.

The closet was stuffy and hot. He was

sweating beneath his Goretex jacket and pants. His cotton tee shirt clung to his skin.

C'mon, old man. Get outta the john and go to bed.

He pulled back the edge of his leather glove and checked his watch. 11:32. Later than anticipated. *Where had the old fart been tonight?*

Running water sounded and a toilet flushed. Then a cough, deep and congested, the rattle of long-ago smoking still audible. The bathroom light flicked off.

At last. He peered through the slanted louvers of the closet door, watching the elderly man in pajamas walk toward his king-sized bed. The flickering light of the television was the only illumination in the room, throwing odd shadows across the walls.

The elderly man threw back the quilted covers and climbed into bed, then pulled the comforter to his waist. A tired sigh escaped as he settled back onto the pillows.

That's it. Relax, watch the news, close your eyes, and go to sleep.

He checked his watch again and deliberately counted ten minutes go by. *Time enough.* He pushed the slightly ajar closet door open and stepped into the darkened bedroom. Slowly approaching the bed, he paused and watched the old man's breathing. Slow and even. He drew to the edge of the bed and reached across.

Suddenly the old man opened his eyes and blinked up in surprise. "Who . . . who the hell are you?"

"No one you'd know, Senator," he said in a quiet voice. Then lithe as a cat, he sprang upon the bed, straddling the surprised old man. He had the bed pillow over the senator's face before the old man could call out to the sleeping housekeeper below.

The senator struggled frantically, his arms flailing, his whole body writhing beneath his attacker. But his fingers slid down the slick jacket, unable to grab hold. Just as his cries were muffled. Smothered beneath fifteen hundred thread count Egyptian cotton. Within a short time, the old man's struggles ceased.

He lifted the pillow and checked for a pulse. There was none. An already weakened heart had helped finish the job. He climbed off the bed and returned the pillow beneath the senator's head, then straightened the bedcovers.

There shouldn't be any questions. Not with the old man's bad heart. Everyone will assume he died in his sleep. Odds were good that whatever D.C. cop showed up to investigate wouldn't even work homicide.

He paused at the bedroom doorway and glanced back once, checking the room again. The old man looked positively peaceful. Then he slipped down the stairs, pausing only to enter the security code before he quietly left through the front door. The same way he came in.

Two

"I'm going to gamble and double-park for a few minutes," Karen said as she switched off the ignition of her Honda sedan and opened the door.

I exited the passenger side and surveyed the narrow residential street in front of Senator Russell's Georgetown home. "The parking looks as bad as I remember."

"Pretty much. Fines are steeper, too," Karen agreed as we crossed the sidewalk leading to the senator's impressive white brick mansion, which rose behind tall brick walls bordering the property.

I followed behind Karen, nervously smoothing my black suit pants and jacket, arranging the collar of my white silk blouse. I'd decided to go with the sober, serious interview suit. Suitable for serious accounting positions or funeral directors. This morning's drive through long-forgotten streets had done nothing to calm my apprehension. Memories pricked like tiny needles.

Karen held the wrought iron entry gate open and gestured to the wide paved path leading to the front steps. The three-story mansion was a beautiful example of the Georgian style architecture that could still be found in Georgetown. "You look marvelous, Molly. Stop worrying."

Stop worrying? She had to be kidding. I'd been up since three o'clock in the morning, worrying. Wondering if I'd lost my mind. How could I let my family talk me into interviewing for this job? I had to be crazy, didn't I? Or, desperate. That was it. I was desperate. Desperate times called for desperate measures, right? Well, I had to be desperate to allow myself to be talked into getting within a mile of a Washington politician again. *What was I thinking?*

"I'll introduce you to Peter then I'll head back to the Hill," Karen said as she rang the chimes. "Relax, Molly. You'll do great. Remember, he needs an accountant." She gave me another encouraging smile.

I did my best to return her smile, but pre-interview jitters plus doubts about my sanity for even being here joined with old memories that begged to be unleashed. Dave and I had lived in a smaller townhouse only blocks from here for six years. Our kids played in the playground at the end of the block. Could I walk these streets without seeing ghosts?

Then, from somewhere inside, I felt another sensation. Excitement. Faint, but still there. *Where the hell had that come from?* It must be the insanity. I was sinking fast.

The crimson door opened and a gray-haired, matronly woman gave us a huge smile. "Ms. Malone, Miss Grayson, please come in. Mr. Brewster is waiting in the library."

We stepped inside the spacious foyer, polished walnut floors stretching ahead. I glimpsed crystal chandeliers, antiques, and Oriental carpets peeking from the formal rooms opening to the hallway.

"The senator is very excited that you're thinking of joining the staff, Ms. Malone," the woman said as she gestured down the hall. "He greatly respects your father's work in the Senate years ago. He's spoken of your father for as long as I've known Senator Russell."

If that was meant to reassure me, it didn't work. Instead, I was even more convinced that Russell wanted me on board as a glorified mascot. *Had I no pride?*

"How long have you been with the senator?" I asked as she paused in front of a polished wooden door.

"My husband, Albert, and I have been with Senator Russell for nearly thirty years now," she said, her pleasant face creasing as a smile spread. "Albert is the chauffeur, and I'm the senator's housekeeper, Luisa." With that, she knocked lightly on the door, and it quickly opened.

Peter Brewster practically sprang from the doorway, grabbing my hand in an enthusiastic handshake. He was tall and slender, his blond hair stylishly cut, surrounding a boyish face. *Good God, he's just a kid,* I thought.

"Molly Malone, I cannot tell you what a pleasure it is to meet you," he said, giving my hand a parting squeeze. "I couldn't believe it when Karen told me you were in town looking for a position. What perfect timing."

Karen smiled warmly as she gestured my way. "Well, I recalled the last time we'd had coffee on the Hill, you were moaning about losing the managerial accountant you'd brought from Colorado, and when Molly was suddenly available, well, it seemed a perfect fit."

"Perfect is right," Brewster agreed, his blue eyes alight. "The senator was beyond

excited when I told him you might be joining us."

Oh, brother. I felt the noose tightening, so
I opted for total honesty in hopes it might
be off-putting. "You're very kind to say that,
Mr. Brewster, but it's been several years
since I worked for Senator Hartman. I'm
afraid what political expertise I once had is
woefully out of date."

Instead of looking dismayed, Brewster
seemed amused by my comment. He
glanced to Karen and grinned. "Is she
always this self-effacing?"

Karen eyed me sternly like a big sister.
"Peter's got your file, Molly, so you can lose
that modest routine right now. He knows
where you've worked and what you've done.
Now, I'll leave you two to talk business. I
need to return to the office before Jed starts
screaming."

Karen's boss, Jed Molinoff. Congressman
Jackson's chief of staff. A hyper, Type A,
overachiever, according to Karen. "Maybe
you shouldn't have taken time off to bring
me here, Karen," I said, feeling guilty. "I
don't want you to get into trouble."

Karen glanced down. "Don't worry about
it, Molly. Jed's been on my case all week, so
a little more irritation won't matter."

"Tell him I asked you to bring Ms. Malone

40

by at the senator's request," Brewster said with a grin. "Jed's been sucking up to us ever since the senator came to town. That'll keep him quiet."

Karen's smile returned. "Peter, you are diabolical. See you later," she said, heading for the door.

"Later, Karen," Brewster called after her.

Watching her leave, I tried to get my head around what Karen said a moment ago. *I had a file?*

"Come into the library and relax, Ms. Malone. I use it as my office when away from the hill."

He gestured me inside the dark-paneled room, rich woods gleaming in furniture and floor-to-ceiling bookshelves. I could smell the lemon oil. The entire library was straight out of a Dickens novel. I chose a burgundy velvet armchair while Brewster settled in comfortably behind the polished walnut desk.

Unable to restrain my curiosity, I had to pry. "You have a file on me, Mr. Brewster?"

He grinned boyishly over the open folder. "Everyone has a file, Ms. Malone. And please call me Peter." He lifted the folder. "Thanks to Google, we can run, but we can't hide. May I call you Molly?"

I nodded, still processing. "That's seriously scary."

"Isn't it, though?" He tossed the file on the desk. "You're welcome to take a look if you like."

I shook my head. "Not on an empty stomach." I knew what was there. I didn't need to see blurry copies of newspaper headlines again. Those black-and-white images were already burned into my brain.

Brewster leaned back into the leather chair. "You surprise me. Most people would grab that folder."

"I already know what's there. I've had my fifteen minutes of fame, and then some. I have no need to relive those days."

He studied me, his boyish smile faded. "Karen says you blamed Washington for your husband's suicide. Is that why you haven't been back all these years?"

Boy, Karen really did tell this guy everything. I'd have to speak with her. "Actually, I do return to the area. I just fly into Dulles. After all, my elderly mother lives in a retirement home in Northern Virginia, and I have other family here in addition to Karen." I deliberately dodged the rest of his question. "Actually, yesterday was the first time I've flown into National in over twenty years."

He smiled at me. "How was it?"

"Wrenching. And heartbreakingly beautiful."

"You still blame Washington for what happened? That's a long time to hold a grudge, Molly."

Boy, this guy was like a laser, and I was clearly the target. I could feel the red dot warming my forehead. Sensing that subtle subterfuge and evasion wouldn't work with Brewster, I decided on total honesty. *What the hell?* I didn't want this job anyway. I may need it, but I sure didn't want it.

I glanced over his shoulder to the tall windows behind, draped in burgundy velvet. I spotted a garden outside. "I don't blame the city anymore," I confessed. "It's what it does to people. To politicians or anyone who works within smelling distance of Capitol Hill. The lust for power consumes them after a while. And they'll do anything to keep that power. Destroy anything or anyone that's in their way." My voice had hardened as I spoke. Old habits.

Brewster pointed to the folder. "It sounds like your husband wasn't consumed by it. Apparently he helped pass some significant legislation. Environmental protection. Education."

"You're right. Dave accomplished a lot in his six short years." I was surprised at the pride I still felt saying that.

"It must have been heady in those days. You two were the young couple to watch. The Golden Pair. The brash young congressman from the West, cutting through Washington red tape, carving a path. A rising star, the clippings say."

Resigning myself to this stroll down memory lane, I nodded. "He was all that and more."

"And there you were, right beside him," Brewster grinned. "Senator Malone's beautiful, politically savvy daughter, who cut her teeth on Washington politics, orchestrating every move in her talented young husband's career."

Whoa. I met Brewster's steady gaze. "That's flattering, but it's a gross overstatement. I simply helped Dave . . . live up to his potential, that's all."

"The word back in Colorado is you were the force behind David Grayson, Molly. You can feign modesty and deny it, but everyone I talked to both here and in Denver agrees. You were the politically savvy one, not your husband."

That dart grazed my shoulder as it passed. This guy was one hell of an interviewer. His comments were getting way too close. And dredging up way too many ghosts. Deciding righteous indignation would deflect his aim, I lifted my chin and replied, "Wrong, Mr. Brewster. David Grayson was a charismatic and caring congressman. His strength came from his ability to relate to people, not from me. That's why he was so effective. He genuinely cared about the people he represented."

Brewster sat silent, watching me, so I continued. "Unfortunately those same qualities were seen as threatening to some other people. Powerful people. He was in their way."

I clamped my mouth shut so I wouldn't say any more.

"Then why did he kill himself? Why didn't he stay and fight the good fight?"

Bullseye. Long-suppressed emotions rushed out, engulfing me for a moment. I fixed Brewster with a wry smile.

"You are something else, Peter, you know that? In all these years, no one has had the balls to ask me that. Did you come up with that question all by yourself, or is the senator behind this interrogation?"

His deceptively boyish grin returned. "The senator is way too polite to be so insulting. That's my job."

"To insult people? You're doing great so far. I'm going to need therapy after this session. You must have been a psych major, that's why you're attracted to politicians. They're all crazy."

He laughed softly. "Nope. Political Science and Economics from Northwestern, then M.B.A. from Stanford."

"Classy credentials," I admitted. "How'd you get here?"

"After grad school I started working on some California state campaigns, then graduated to congressmen. I discovered I had a knack for helping a candidate stay on message and get elected. I'll give you my résumé, if you like, but let's get back to you."

I shook my head in grudging admiration. "Damn, you're relentless. What else do you want to know? Go on, Brewster. Bring it."

This time he laughed loudly, clearly enjoying my abject surrender. "Enough of the past. Let's get up to speed. Present day. Why didn't you get involved in the last Colorado election? You'd been a player from the day you arrived from Washington. First, with Governor Lambert, then with Senator Hartman. The Democrats could have used your help. The Republicans took over some key congressional seats and the state legislature."

I threw up my hands. "Now, with the guilt, he starts. Don't even go there, Peter. My absence was insignificant. Those candidates lost that election all by themselves. They cut their own throats with that name-calling and mudslinging. I almost had to force myself to vote last November. Besides, your guy is an Independent. So all their mudslinging helped get him elected."

"Point taken. But you didn't come to *any* candidate's events. Not even the senator's. And my sources told me you personally supported his candidacy, even though he ran as an Independent."

It was my turn to relax in my chair. I was beginning to enjoy this banter. Getting my chops back, I guess. "Tell your sources they can screw themselves. I sent a check."

His eyes lit up as he laughed. Brewster clearly was enjoying this conversation. If I couldn't be gainfully employed, I might as well be entertaining.

"And tell them they're getting sloppy. If they were really good, they'd have known that I was divorced at the beginning of last year, and I was trying to put my life back together. Both economically and emotionally. The last thing I needed was a daily dose of the negative campaigning that today's politicians revel in."

"Actually, they told me about your divorce and your reluctance to get involved. I just wanted to see how you responded."

I studied Brewster, all relaxed demeanor and boyish pose on the outside, while that intense Boy Scout gaze probed, searching for weaknesses.

"Interesting interviewing style you've developed, Peter. You insult the job seekers so you can watch how each performs, am I right?"

His grin turned sly. "Spot on. Didn't take you long."

"Flattery will get you nowhere, Ace," I replied, surprised how comfortable I felt at the moment. "Tell me, why does Russell need an attack dog like you? What's he afraid of?"

Direct hit. Brewster shifted in his chair. "Senator Russell's not afraid of anything, Molly. That's the problem. I have to be afraid for him."

I wasn't expecting that response, and it must have showed because Brewster continued.

"I need to know that anyone who works with the senator can be trusted to keep everything they see or hear completely confidential. The senator is being approached daily, hounded almost, by senators from both sides of the aisle, congressmen, lobbyists, reporters. Everyone's trying to pick his brain to see if they can figure out a way to gain his allegiance. It's all I can do to schedule him some time for himself, he's being courted so heavily —"

I couldn't resist a wicked grin. "Like a virgin at a frat party."

Brewster gave a surprised, explosive laugh, then relaxed visibly. "Damn, Molly, I like you, and the senator will love you. You'll make a great addition to the team."

My ass. "Not so fast, Ace. Right now, you're 0 for 3. You've insulted my late husband's memory, sent your minions in Colorado mucking about in my personal life, and spent the last half hour baiting me. You've annoyed the living crap out of me. Why the hell would I want to work for you?"

"You'd be working for Senator Russell, not me."

"Don't hand me that. I know how this business works. You're the chief of staff, and you run the show."

"You want to know why Senator Russell and I want you for this position?"

"Let me guess. A mascot? A political symbol of some long-ago time when a few good men could actually make a difference in the Senate?"

To his credit, Brewster didn't even blink, let alone respond to the bait. "Actually, what we really need is an accountant and financial consultant. The household and entertaining expenses are fairly complicated. Plus, you'd be overseeing some real estate holdings as well. I'm afraid the complexity of it all was too much for the original accountant who came with us from Colorado. That and homesickness. She missed the mountains."

I glanced out the window again but saw no brooding mountain ranges, only box-wood hedges. "That's understandable. I miss the mountains, too." And yet, here I was sitting with a consummately political animal if ever I saw one. I eyed Brewster. "So, it sounds like you really do need an accountant."

"Did you think we only wanted you as a . . . what did you call it? A mascot?"

"The thought crossed my mind."

"I can see that. Tell me, how much was that Virginia developer offering you? Karen told me he's cutting back right now. Not surprising. The entire Metro Washington real estate market is still risky."

I had to admire Brewster's ability to stay on target no matter how much distraction got in the way. "Here, see for yourself." I withdrew a folder from my over-the-shoulder briefcase. "My last head managerial position is outlined there. Duties, salary, total compensation package. And the offer for the recently evaporated position with Jeff Parker and Associates is there as well."

Brewster accepted the folder with a bemused expression. "You're letting me see both? You surprise me, Molly. Do you usually interview this badly?"

"Nope. But in this case I decided to put all my cards on the table."

"Why's that?" he said, spreading the folder on the desk.

"Because I'm betting you can't come close to matching Parker's offer. Household and entertaining accounts don't need that level of management."

"Don't forget the financial consulting. Lots of real estate there," he said, perusing the neat columns of figures I'd prepared.

"I still wouldn't break a sweat. Face it, Brewster, I need more than you can pay."

"Plus, other duties as assigned," he said, glancing up with a grin.

"What? The senator wants me to wash his car? I don't think so."

"The longer I talk with you, Molly, the more I like you," he said, examining the pages.

Damn. Here I was, trying my best to be annoying, and instead, Brewster was

51

charmed. How did I manage that? Did that mean whenever I tried to be charming, it turned out annoying? Hmmmm. I should look into that.

"You're right, Molly. We can't match Parker's offer —"

Ha! Part of me exulted inside. I'd escaped the political snare. Tweaked the legislative lion's beard and gotten away. Victory was mine! Why, then, was there a slight feeling of disappointment inside?

I slipped my briefcase over my shoulder and started to rise from the chair. Make a fast getaway. "Well, Peter, it's been grand. I can't tell you when I've had this much fun. Although my last root canal comes to mind."

Still immersed in the columns of figures, Peter held up his hand. "Not so fast, Molly, I wasn't finished yet. As I was saying, we can't match Parker's offer, but we can get you the cash flow it appears you need every month."

Huh? I hovered over the chair. Brewster's hand waved me down again. "Does it involve wearing disguises and delivering packages in the middle of the night? If so, I'm not interested."

"Nope. Strictly legal. Want some coffee Molly? I'm dying for a cup." He suddenly pushed his desk chair over to an antique tea cart complete with china coffeepot and saucers.

Startled by yet another abrupt change in direction, I hesitated. Then the caffeine lobe of my brain began to throb. *When didn't I want coffee?* "Uh, yeah, I could definitely use a cup. I purposely avoided the caffeine rush this morning."

Brewster turned an incredulous gaze my way. "Good God, you mean this is you without caffeine?"

"Sober as a judge. Scary, isn't it? Black, please." I pointed to the cup he was pouring.

"Why am I not surprised?" Brewster walked over and handed me the delicate china cup and saucer. "I shudder to think what you're like wired."

"It's not pretty. Another reason not to hire me," I said, trying not to slurp the dark nectar in one gulp. It slid down my throat with that delectable burn, smooth and harsh at the same time. *Ahhhhh.* Nerve cells were coming online.

Brewster simply laughed as he poured coffee for himself. Clearly, my repeated refusals only heightened his interest. Just like a teenage boy in the back of his parent's Buick. The more his girlfriend said "no,"

53

the harder he tried. *Men.* Where do they learn this? In the cradle?

"Now, where were we . . ." He set the coffee cup on the desk and grabbed a pen. "Cash flow. Let's see what we can do." Brewster proceeded to scribble all over my neat columns of figures. "As they say, there're two ways to raise income. Either increase revenues or decrease expenses. What if we decrease your housing expenses to zero, Molly? Take a look and tell me what you think." He slid the open folder across the desk.

My curiosity aroused, I reached for the folder and examined what Brewster had done. He'd checked my budgetary requirements and neatly eliminated the housing expense. He'd also eliminated the commuting expenses. *What was this guy smoking?* Even if I moved into Nan and Bill's house permanently, I'd still have to get into Washington every day. And this section of Georgetown was not on the Metro line. I'd have to drive. A rental car at first, until I could bring my car from Colorado.

I gave the poor deluded boy an indulgent smile. "These are nice numbers, Peter, but they're totally unrealistic. There's no housing expense and no commuting expense. That's ridiculous. I will not move into my cousin's home permanently. I may not have much pride, but I have a shred or two left. I plan to rent an apartment, probably in Virginia, which means I'd be commuting."

Peter sipped his coffee. "What if free housing was available to you? Subject to your approval, of course. Would you be interested?"

That got my attention. "I'm listening."

"The real estate portfolio you'd be managing is mine. That's why I need your expertise. And that's how I can offer you more money. Your duties would be spread between the senator's domestic accounts and my business accounts. I have properties in several states and some in the D.C. Metro area as well. One of them is vacant. It's here in Georgetown. Only three blocks away, over on P Street. It's a modest two-story brick townhouse. Small, but nice."

Nice? *Nice!* A modest townhouse on P Street in Georgetown? It would have to be infested with rats not to be nice. And Brewster was offering it to me free when he must have scores of eager Washington wannabes clamoring to pay at least three thousand a month to live there. Now I *knew* he was on something.

I managed not to laugh in his face, but I did smile. "Peter, you can't be serious.

You're offering me free rent on prime Georgetown real estate? Washington has rotted your brain already, and you haven't been here a year yet. You need to see a doctor."

The sly grin returned. "It's my property, Molly. I can rent it to whomever I choose. And it's not free. Your residence there will be as property manager. Remember 'other duties as assigned'?"

He was serious. *Oh my God!* I sat back in my chair and stared at him. "You're willing to take a loss to let me —"

"I'm not taking a loss. It's vacant, remember?"

"Yeah, but you could rent it in a heartbeat for three or four thousand a month."

"It's okay. My other properties are rented. You don't have to worry about me, Molly." He grinned. "That's my CPA's job. You'll be working closely with him, needless to say."

Well, he had me there. I wasn't Brewster's CPA or his mother. If he wanted to give me a Georgetown townhouse to live in, who was I to say no? Meanwhile, an uneasy feeling in the pit of my stomach caused me to pause. Who was I to say *yes?* Could I actually live in the midst of all this again? Here in Georgetown? Memories were around every corner. Ghosts roamed the streets.

Could I do it?

Out of nowhere, a voice I hadn't heard in a long time whispered, *"Make new memories."*

I recognized that cheeky voice. Ever since Chaos took over my life. Crazy Ass, I called the voice, because it always brought the wild, out-of-nowhere, go-for-it suggestions. Good old Crazy Ass. I'd missed it. The voice of the opposition, Sober-and-Righteous, had been ruling the roost for weeks now and had sent Crazy Ass scurrying into the bushes when Chaos appeared. Virtuous, but boring as hell, Sober was strictly steady as she goes, nose to the grindstone and full of other guilt-producing clichés that could be counted on to keep me on track.

"Make new memories." Hmmmmm. There was a thought.

"You're considering it, I can tell," Peter observed.

"Damn right. I'd be crazy not to." I stared through the window at the boxwood. I hadn't smelt boxwood in years. By June, the scent would be heady. My nostrils twitched.

Sober-and-Righteous asserted itself into my imaginings. *Hold it! Everything's moving too fast. This guy is worse than a carnival barker hawking teddy bears. You need time to think.*

I had to agree with Sober. Things were moving way too fast. This offer, the money, the house, the idea of living and working in Georgetown — I did need time to think.

I looked Peter in the eye. "This is a lot to digest. The money, this whole job offer, the house, all of it. I need time to consider everything, Peter."

"I understand. Think about it all you want. This afternoon. Then call me with your answer this evening." He reached into his coat and withdrew a card. "Here's my cell."

"You need an answer tonight?" I said, not even trying to hide my surprise as I took the card.

Now it was Brewster's turn to be sober. "The senator needs someone fast. Those accounts are piling up. If you say 'no,' then we have to go back to square one."

Guilt. Works every time. "Okay, I'll let you know by this evening." I gathered my things and rose to leave.

Brewster came from around the desk, all boyish charm again. "Would you like to meet the senator?" he tempted. "Luisa beeped me that he's returned from his breakfast with constituents. He's got a few minutes before he heads to the Hill."

Shocked, I found myself stammering.

58

"Oh, that — that's not necessary, I — I don't want to delay him —"

"No delay, Molly. He's been anxious to meet you."

Brewster proceeded to escort me from the library and into the hall, ignoring my protestations. I looked down the hallway, and there was Russell, walking straight toward us. I gulped. No time to get away.

"Senator, I've done my best to sell Molly on the position. I'll leave it to you to close the deal."

Brewster handed me off to the senator. Russell clasped my hand in a hearty bear-paw handshake and leaned forward, his eyes gazing into mine. "Molly Malone, I cannot tell you how delighted I am, we all are, that you're thinking of joining our efforts here in Washington. I'm honored that you'd consider us," he said in that resonant basso voice I remembered from campaign news highlights.

The senator was even better looking in person. Although he was seventy, he still looked trim and fit in his expensive tailoring. Tall, silver-haired, handsome in a distinguished way, and mesmerizing as all get-out. I gazed up at the senator and felt the full force of his personality wash over me in a wave. *Whoa.* No wonder this guy won the election. Those other guys never had a chance.

I broke the cobra-mongoose stare long enough to reply. "I'm the one who's honored to be considered for the position, senator, but I'm not sure my past experience is adequate to its demands."

Russell looked astonished. If he was acting, he was skillful. "Adequate? Surely you're joking? We know your credentials, Molly. You're over-qualified for this position, and you know it. I've followed your career in Colorado for years. You're a dynamic addition to any politician's team."

Damn. Everyone's read my file.

"She suffers from a surfeit of modesty, Senator," Brewster observed.

"Washington will cure you of that soon enough. You've been away too long, Molly," Russell said, still clasping my hand. Suddenly his grin faded, and he placed his other hand on top of mine. His gaze turned sad. "Let me say, first off, that I am completely aware of your reluctance to return to this swamp of dissension that marks our Capitol City, and the reasons for it. The early loss of your husband was tragic, indeed. He was a brave, idealistic young congressman who had only the people's interests at heart. We need more like him in Congress."

The senator's earnest and passionate statement took me by surprise. "That's . . . that's very kind of you to say, Senator. Thank you. David tried to make a difference while . . . while he was alive." I didn't trust myself to say more.

Russell patted my hand in a fatherly fashion before he released his grip. "He was simply following in your father's footsteps, Molly. In fact, that's what I'm hoping to accomplish while I'm here in Washington. To be a voice of reason and reform in that rancorous chamber. Follow your father's example and try to reach out and build bridges. Be a moderate voice for change and reform, and I'm hoping to inspire others to join me. It's time our politicians stopped worrying about themselves and concentrate on the needs of the people who elected them. We're the people's congress, after all. We serve at their pleasure. Your father knew that, believed that, and conducted his entire Senate career toward that end. Serving the people. He was a true statesman. A giant in the Senate."

I stared at Senator Russell, conviction shining from his eyes, and was captivated despite myself. Captured by his obvious sincerity and optimism. Russell had gone straight for my Achilles' heel. *Idealism.* Call it a residue of the Sixties, whatever, it never really left, no matter how many curve balls life threw my way.

I decided to see if I could throw him, just for the hell of it. "You are one sly fox, Senator. If you read that notorious file of mine, you knew that I was a sucker for idealism."

Brewster stifled a laugh, but Russell didn't even bother to hide his reaction. He burst out laughing, a huge basso roar that bounced off the walls. Sort of like Falstaff without the fat. "Can you blame me, Molly? Peter and I have been scheming how we could get you on our team ever since we learned you were available."

"Senator, I appreciate the flattery, but I'm simply a managerial and financial accountant."

"This modesty doesn't serve you, Molly. Your financial skills are valuable, yes, but you've got other skills too, which would be quite helpful for an incoming senator, new to Washington and its wily ways." Russell took my arm, escorting me down the hallway, but not toward the front door. He headed toward the living room, which opened to a formal dining room. "I've started entertaining; nothing extravagant yet. Mostly receptions to let the politicians see that I'm not a lunatic or a wild-eyed revolutionary, despite what some of my opponents said in the election." He paused in the archway of the dining room. A gleaming, crystal bowl filled with daffodils and crocuses sat in the midst of the polished mahogany table.

"What I really want to do is arrange small, intimate dinners with various senators and their spouses. Strategic entertaining, I call it. That way I can get a feel for the men and women I'm working with. See where their real passions lie, away from the television cameras."

Intrigued once again, I studied Russell. "Shrewd move, Senator. Get a feel for the players. I'd recommend it highly, considering your position as the swing vote."

Russell gave me a cagey grin. "I figured you'd approve, considering that's precisely what your father excelled in. 'Getting a read on the players,' he called it, right?"

I returned his smile. "Right you are, Senator. And I can tell where your mind is going. You think that I can somehow channel my father's brilliance in that respect. All apologies to my beloved father's memory, but I cannot recreate his magic."

Russell steered me away from the dining room and down the hallway once more. Toward the door this time. *Thank heavens.*

I didn't think I could take anymore of this intense courtship.

"I'm forced to disagree with you, Molly. I think you inherited it," Russell said as he led me to the open doorway, Luisa standing beside. "If I'm not mistaken, you performed the same sort of magic during your husband's congressional years. Governor Lambert said the same thing. And you did it for Senator Hartman as well."

I eyed Russell. "Totally different scenarios, Senator. I haven't been in Washington for over twenty years. Any fairy dust I might have possessed years ago has dried up and blown away."

He chuckled. "I'd still appreciate any insights you might have — suggestions, whatever."

"Senator, to be honest, I'm not even sure I want this position. I've told Peter that. So, if it's magic you want, you need to start looking for another Tinkerbell. I've turned in my wings."

Russell threw back his head and let loose with another infectious belly laugh. Peter joined in this time as I stepped over the threshold and made my getaway at last.

THREE

My mother and her new companion Patricia waved goodbye while I hurried from the stately retirement home and escaped into the parking lot. Visiting with my mom and talking politics had taken the entire afternoon. When I'd told her my new job with Senator Russell would be as an accountant with no political involvement, her reply was succinct:

"Nonsense, dear. You're in Washington, remember? That would be like going to France and not drinking the wine."

I had to smile. When it came to politics, my mother was still sharp as a tack, recalling names and dates and behind-the-scenes maneuvering from long ago. But ask her if she had taken her morning medications . . . well, that was another thing. The question was met with a blank expression, then a worried frown while she tried to remember. Strange thing, memory loss.

Noticing the sun's downward angle, I checked my watch and decided to call Brewster while I drove back to Nan's house. Tell him I was accepting the position. I'd weighed the job offer over and over as I rode the Metro back to the Park-n-Ride where Karen had picked me up this morning. Now that I'd visited my mother and seen Patricia in action, I was certain of my decision. The logic was inescapable.

Patricia O'Toole was perfect. Competent and caring. My mom needed her, and the only way I could pay Patricia's salary would be to accept Senator Russell's job offer. I had no choice. Both Russell and Brewster were willing to throw money at me. Okay, then. I was in.

I slipped into the sporty Acura Nan loaned me and revved the engine, listening to its throaty purr as I flipped open my cell phone and punched in Brewster's number. He answered as I headed toward Chain Bridge Road, going west to Vienna.

"Peter, it's Molly," I said, noticing the rush hour buildup in traffic. "I thought I'd call and let you know that I'm accepting your offer. Yours and the senator's, that is."

"That's great!" Brewster crowed over the phone. "Molly, I cannot tell you how pleased we are you'll be joining us. I can't

66

wait to tell the senator . . . oh, here he is now."

"Peter, wait! I don't need to talk —" Too late. I could already hear Brewster informing Russell, as well as the senator's enthusiastic response.

Then Russell's voice boomed into my ear. "Molly! This is fantastic news! You'll have to come over right away, so we can celebrate. I'm having a reception tonight, and it would be a perfect time to announce that you're joining our staff."

What? Was he kidding? I was halfway to Vienna, heading west, miles and miles of cars behind me. Traffic was God-awful. "Senator, that's not necessary. Besides, I'm way out here in Virginia, almost to Vienna —"

"I insist. It's an ideal time for you to take a look at our entertaining."

He was serious. *Oh, my God.* "Senator, traffic is horrible. It would take me forever to get back into Georgetown through rush hour right now," I said, hoping to change his mind.

"That's no problem at all. Albert will come right out. Why don't you park at the nearest shopping center and Albert will pick you up. No need for you to endure this wretched traffic."

"What? Senator, that's . . . that's too much of an inconvenience," I countered, still trying to weasel out of it.

"Nonsense, Molly. Albert considers this traffic a challenge." His voice turned from the phone. "Luisa, could you please tell Albert he needs to fetch Molly from Virginia."

No! No! No! The last thing I wanted was to be thrown into a room full of politicians tonight. It was too soon. Besides, I was trying to fly beneath the radar, and Russell was thwarting me at every turn. "Senator, no, please, I'm . . . I'm not dressed for a reception. I'm still in my funereal black suit."

Russell chuckled. "And a lovely suit it is, Molly. You'll be radiant, I'm sure."

My God, this man had more blarney in him than my late uncle Jack. He had to be Irish. I started to sweat. Great for the lovely black suit. "Senator . . ." I wiggled again. "I appreciate your generosity and your flattery, but . . . but I promised my friends I'd join them for dinner." Maybe obligation would get him.

Russell shot that down as well. "They'll understand, Molly. I'm sure they will. Now, I'm putting Albert on the phone. We'll see you soon."

Damn. He'd out-talked me again. Russell was as good as I was at getting around people. He was going to be a challenge to work for. Sort of like working for myself. That was scary.

"Ms. Malone? Where are you now?" Albert's voice came on the phone. "Where would be the closest and safest shopping area to park your car?"

"Uhhhhh, let me think," I struggled, running the major shopping centers through my mind as I maneuvered into the left lane.

Tysons Corner was down the road, but that was a traffic nightmare in the best of times. Where else? Remembering a drug store at a busy intersection I'd passed earlier in the day, I nosed the Acura into the left turn lane and waited for a break in traffic, praying I could execute a U-turn without causing an accident.

"Okay, Albert, how about the intersection of Old Dominion and Glebe Road? There's a drugstore there. I'll park in the back."

"I'm on my way," Albert said, in the tone of a man on a mission. "I've got your cell number. See you soon, Ms. Malone."

"Right," I said before tossing the phone into the next seat. I needed both hands for this turn. I whipped the Acura around the tight corner and roared off in the opposite direction, ignoring the sound of honking horns.

His cell phone vibrated. The familiar number flashed on the screen.

"We may need you this weekend," a man's scratchy voice said.

"Good thing you called. I was about to head for the Bay tomorrow."

"If affirmative, we'll text you a keycode for data files."

"Location?"

"Georgetown."

"Again? Who pissed off those guys this time?"

"No one you'd know. Just a congressional staffer who's gotten way too curious for her own good. Looking into things she shouldn't and asking questions. That makes those guys real nervous. Problem is, she's connected. Her father was that congressman from Colorado, Eric Grayson. You remember him, don't you?"

"Of course."

"They're worried her father might have told her something before he died. So, when Grayson's daughter starts asking questions, they don't like it."

"Well, you know the old saying. 'Curiosity killed the cat.' " He laughed softly.

"We'll be in touch." Then the line went dead.

No sense of humor, that one, he thought as he pocketed his phone.

Albert pulled off Wisconsin Avenue and headed down Q Street, deftly weaving around double-parked cars, before pulling into the gated driveway. At his touch to the visor, the black wrought iron gate swung open, and we drove into the garage area behind the house.

Outdoor lights and lanterns threw bright arcs over the tall brick walls. Light pierced the fast-approaching twilight and I felt my heart beat faster. Albert opened the car door, and the sound of muffled conversation rolled over me like a wave on the beach. My pulse began to race. Nerve cells snapped awake. Old habits were hard to break.

I caught myself. *What the hell was I doing?* I'd barely been in Washington thirty-six hours, and I was sucked in already. How'd that happen?

"We'll slip in the side door, Ms. Malone," Albert said, as he helped me from the car.

"Please call me Molly," I said, as he guided me away from the enclosed rear garden and around the corner of the residence. Luisa was standing at a back door,

71

smiling as she took my purse.

I glimpsed the catering staff bustling about in a brightly lit kitchen as Albert ushered me down a back hallway. There was a delicious aroma floating in the air, and I made a mental note to ask Brewster who the senator used as caterers. I might as well provide counter-intelligence for Nan and Deb while there.

"Here, you go, Molly." Albert ushered me through a door that led off another passageway. "Peter is keeping an eye out for you. Enjoy yourself." He gave a friendly smile as he closed the door behind me.

I noticed the closed door disappear into the molding. *Well, I'll be damned.* A secret door, I thought, as I stood in the senator's elegant foyer. I walked slowly down the hallway until I reached the expansive living room. There, I hovered on the edge and watched. The room wasn't crowded because almost everyone was enjoying the gorgeous spring weather outside.

Sometimes Washington would be blessed with a springtime for the Gods. Mild temperatures, low humidity, and flowers bursting into bloom everywhere you looked. It never stayed long, but it was glorious while it lasted.

I could see men and women outside in

the garden, laughing and talking and drinking and talking and flirting and talking. Old instincts urged me to join them, but I stayed put. Sober-and-Righteous was still on the job. *No mingling. Not yet. Too soon.* I turned my attention to the staff that was serving the crowd, wondering if they were part of the caterer's crew.

A short, gray-haired woman with an old-fashioned Dutch Boy haircut moved efficiently around the room, offering glasses of wine. A young man, college-aged, I guessed, wove through the crowd as well, offering appetizers. I searched for more staff and spotted the bartender in the corner of the room. I edged closer, and noticed he appeared to be middle-aged and worked with smooth efficiency as he prepared drinks.

Suddenly a low alto voice sounded at my elbow. "Would you care for some wine, ma'am?" Dutch asked.

I declined. "No, thanks, I'm fine."

"You'll look less conspicuous with some wine," she said, her gray eyes smiling at me as she offered a glass.

This time, I took it. "Thank you," I said as she backed away. There was something strangely familiar about Dutch. Maybe she'd worked my parents' parties. Or Dave's and mine.

Edging around the room again, I sipped the Chardonnay. It was surprisingly good, and I decided I needed to see Russell's entertaining expenses. The sooner the better. Nan and Deb could tell me where to get the best prices on . . .

The accountant in me stopped analyzing as I spotted someone else in the crowd, edging around the room as I was. A tall middle-aged African-American man with a graying buzz cut, wearing a dark suit. *Security.* Had to be. Former military, no doubt. Retired military were thick as fleas in the Washington area. Thicker even than consultants, if that can be believed. In fact, most of the retired brass *were* consultants. Those salaries were too tempting to pass up.

The blond college boy paused at my elbow, offering an appetizer. I took one, the better to absorb the wine. I hadn't eaten since lunchtime. He gave me an engaging grin before weaving through the guests again. I inhaled the small quiche and washed it down with Chardonnay.

A voice sounded behind me then; a voice from the past. "As I live and breathe. Molly Malone," the rich contralto flowed smooth as honey. "I'd given up hope of ever seeing you again."

"Eleanor MacKenzie," I said as I turned to see my elderly mentor and political confidante smiling at me. Still as tall and imposing as I remembered, silver hair coiffed in an upswept French twist, and attired in her signature peach silk. Designer peach silk, if I remembered correctly. Eleanor always wore couture. "Thank God you're still in town, Eleanor. Maybe I'll survive this homecoming after all."

"Molly, my girl, the sight of you truly makes my heart sing," Eleanor said as she drew closer. Her step was as lively as I remembered, even though she must be over eighty by now. She reached out to take my free hand, capturing it between hers. "I never thought we'd see you on this side of the Potomac again. I'd heard you visited your family in Virginia and that's all. Ignoring our cozy little nest of vipers in Foggy Bottom."

I laughed softly. Eleanor's wry sense of humor was still intact. "Well, I never thought I'd be here either, Eleanor, but my mother's declining health forced me to return."

"I'm so sorry, Molly," Eleanor said, her face radiating concern. "How is Ginny doing? Has she taken a fall or something?"

"No, no, not yet, thank God. She's simply

having trouble remembering things. Things like medicines, doctors' appointments, how to balance her checkbook, and more or less anything I tell her on the phone. It simply goes in one ear and drops onto the floor. It doesn't even get to the processing center."

Eleanor released my hand, the concern deepening in her sapphire blue eyes. "Oh, my, I'm so sorry to hear that. Have you moved Ginny to an assisted living facility? I'd heard she's been living at the Kensington ever since your father died."

"She's still there," I said with an ill-concealed sigh. "It would break her heart to move, Eleanor. All her friends are there, and I just couldn't do it. So I hired a companion for her. A wonderful Irish lass who's supervising the situation."

"Oh, dear, I've heard they're frightfully expensive."

"You heard correctly," I said with a rueful smile. "In fact, that's why I'm here. I've sold my soul to pay for it all. Senator Russell has offered me a position on his staff. As an accountant."

Eleanor's eyes lit up. "An accountant? Of course, dear, whatever you say." She laughed deep in her chest. "That's quite a coup for Russell then. Ah, Molly, I cannot tell you how much I've missed talking with you, my girl. You'll have to fill me in on all the particulars in private. But right now, my friends and I are heading home for the evening." With that, she turned to address the couple approaching. "Alan, Brenda, look who I found in that wily senator's employ. Molly, you remember Alan and Brenda Baker, don't you?"

I certainly did and turned to greet the senior senator from Indiana and his wife. They were one of the Senate couples who could be counted on to preserve a tone of civility and respect. I'd always felt relieved each election cycle to see that the voters of Indiana had the good sense to return this man to the fray. He'd sat on the opposite side of the aisle from my father, but then Robert Malone formed his friendships without regard to political party.

"Senator, Brenda, how wonderful to see you again," I said with heartfelt enthusiasm as I shook their hands. They'd both aged visibly, but their friendly smiles were still the same and still sincere.

"Molly, dear, how wonderful to see you," Brenda said, giving my hand a squeeze before her husband jumped in.

"My God, Molly, it's been twenty years at least," Alan Baker exclaimed, pumping my hand. "You are a sight for disillusioned eyes.

Don't tell me Russell has not only spirited you away from Colorado, but from the Democrats as well? The party must be wringing their hands back in Denver." He cackled, like the good Republican he was.

I had to join the laughter. Since I was working for an Independent now, I didn't care who was wringing their hands back in Denver. After last year's ugly election, I'd declared a plague upon both their houses. "Well, I doubt anyone is that concerned. I left the political scene several years ago for managerial accounting. It pays a lot better."

"Molly's trying to convince me John Russell has hired her to manage his accounts." Eleanor MacKenzie fixed me with a devilish grin.

Senator Baker guffawed. "That's rich."

I simply smiled and kept my mouth shut while old friends laughed at me. *Why didn't anyone believe me?*

"Molly, you'll have to come over for dinner with Eleanor and update us," Brenda said as the senator escorted her away.

"Meanwhile, give our love to Ginny," Baker said as they maneuvered through the couples in the living room.

Eleanor MacKenzie paused before following after. "Take care, Molly. I imagine we'll all be seeing each other again soon for a very sad occasion. Senator Karpinsky died last night from a heart attack. It just now came on the news."

The jovial mood evaporated. "Oh, no! He was the last one of my father's closest colleagues still in the Senate."

"The last Old Lion," Eleanor nodded. "He'd had his second heart attack after the holidays, but he recuperated quite well. We all hoped he'd be with us for a few more years. But it wasn't to be. His housekeeper found him this morning."

"I hadn't heard," I said, shaking my head. "What a loss."

I pictured the robust barrel-chested Karpinsky I remembered from years ago, holding forth in filibusters with his Vermont accent. The Senate's watchdog. He had the sharpest eyes of any legislator when it came to appropriations. Karpinsky could spot pork and waste a mile away. "I can smell it," he used to say.

"A loss for the Senate and the country," Eleanor agreed as she moved away. "Take care of yourself, Molly. We'll stay in touch."

I gave her a wave and noticed that Peter Brewster was heading straight for me. "Well, it didn't take you long to make contact with the movers and shakers. Excellent. Word of your return will be all over Washington by tomorrow afternoon. Eleanor MacKenzie will see to that." He gave me a sly smile. "Good work, Molly."

Good work, indeed. Brewster was right. Eleanor's network was formidable twenty-plus years ago, by now it must rival the Internet. "All over Washington, huh? Great. So much for flying beneath the radar." I released an exaggerated sigh before tossing down the rest of my Chardonnay.

"I noticed you were eying the staff before Mrs. MacKenzie found you. That's good. What do you think?"

"Well, I've only been here a few minutes, but they seem to know what they're doing. They move efficiently and unobtrusively. They seem friendly and pleasant. All good. I assume there are more servers outside. Are they employees of the caterer?"

He shook his head as he sipped what looked to be a glassful of Scotch. "No, we use a private staffing agency that provides experienced, discreet personnel." He winked.

"The frat boy over there doesn't look old enough to be experienced."

"He's in grad school. Going for his Ph.D. Believe it or not, he's thirty-three."

Changing the subject, I held up my glass. "Nice wine. Is it okay if I check your suppliers? You know, compare prices."

Brewster grinned. "Worrying about the Senator's expenses already. I love it. That's positively sexy, Molly."

I rolled my eyes. "You have got to get out of that office, Peter. If the senator's financial accounts are turning you on, you're in bad shape." I gestured to the ex-military who was heading out to the garden. "Security, right?"

"Good eye, Molly." His sly grin returned. "You want me to introduce you? He's divorced, too."

"I'm sure he's lovely, but I've sworn off men. Divorce residue. I'm sure you understand."

"You need to relax, Molly."

"Are you kidding? I haven't been in Washington thirty-six hours, and suddenly I'm standing in a room full of politicians. Something I swore I'd never do again. Every nerve went on red alert the moment I stepped into this room. My only hope is the senator will be so absorbed in some policy wonk's sales pitch, he'll forget about me, and I can sneak out the door in a few minutes. Once Albert crosses Key Bridge, I'll relax."

"Don't bet on it, Molly. The senator has a razor-sharp memory."

Rats. "I have an idea, Peter. You're young and single. Why don't you go put the moves on some nice unsuspecting girl and leave me to skulk around the room in peace."

"But I promised the senator I'd keep an eye on you," he said with that boyish grin.

I made a shooing gesture. "Go. Find girls. Any girl. As long as it's not my niece, Karen."

"Why's that?"

"Because you two might get serious, and I wouldn't want you as a relative."

Brewster snickered over his Scotch. "You don't have to worry about that. Karen's already got one serious relationship. I doubt she has time for another."

I stared at Brewster. It was obvious from the tone of his voice that he knew a helluva lot more about Karen's social life than I did. *Well, damn.* Every time I'd asked Karen if there was someone special on the horizon, she always smiled and said she preferred to play the field, swearing she had no time for a serious relationship. Somehow, it irritated me that Peter knew more than I did. Karen and I were close. At least, I thought we were.

"Really? I didn't know Karen had met someone new."

Brewster stared into his glass. "Why don't you ask Karen?" Glancing up, his smile returned. "But you'll have to do that later. Right now, the senator is headed our way, with the new congressman from New Mexico in tow. I told you the senator has a good memory."

Sure enough, there was Senator Russell aiming straight for us with a middle-aged couple close behind. Congressman and wife both had the slightly shell-shocked look of those who were new to the Washington social circuit. My hopes for a stealthy escape evaporated like cheap perfume.

"Congressman, let me introduce you to the newest member of our senatorial staff, Ms. Molly Malone," Russell announced as he approached. "Molly, I'd like you to meet the congressman from New Mexico's second district, Henry Baylor, and his charming wife, Mary."

Somehow I found a bright smile and shook their hands. "Congressman, Mrs. Baylor, welcome to Washington."

"Peter Brewster, Senator Russell's chief of staff," Brewster said, shaking their hands enthusiastically. "Glad you could join us tonight."

"Oh, it's our pleasure," Mary Baylor gushed, her eyes alight with adventure. Poor thing.

"Molly Malone? You're from Denver,

aren't you? What brings you away from the Front Range?" Baylor asked, sipping what looked to be a dark stout, à la Guinness. My mouth started to water.

"It's all Senator Russell's fault, Congressman. He twisted my arm so hard, I had to come out. Plus, I have family here, so it was an easy move," I lied, surprising myself at how easily I had done it.

"Molly's father was Senator Robert Malone from Virginia, so Molly may be new to our staff, but she's certainly not new to Washington," Russell added.

"Yes, yes, now I remember," Baylor nodded. "This must feel like coming home to you, Ms. Malone. How does it feel to be back in our nation's Capitol?"

"Challenging, Congressman. I'm still getting used to the traffic."

Baylor's kind face spread with another grin. "I hear you. Mary won't go into the city alone unless she can ride the Metro. She refuses to drive in Washington traffic."

We all laughed politely while Mary Baylor gave her husband a playful poke in the arm. I was beginning to feel sorry for the Baylors already. They looked like a nice couple. Too nice to last in Washington. Those who did had a harder edge.

Suddenly, a bright flash went off to my

left, startling me. A photographer. I whirled immediately and was caught by another bright flash. This time I jumped.

"Young man," Russell called to the photographer who was about to blend into the guests again. "Why don't you take a group shot? Welcome our newest staffer. Come along, Molly, Congressman, let's gather around."

I flinched inwardly. Tonight was just getting better and better. Hopefully this photographer worked for some obscure journal that would line birdcages. Despite my reluctance, I allowed Russell to include me in the semicircle with the New Mexico couple. Brewster, however, had stealthily slipped away. The dog.

The photographer, who appeared to be in his twenties, started clicking. My cheeks twitched after several shots. Finally, he stopped. "Thanks, Senator," he called as he turned to walk away.

"Which newspaper are you with, son?" Russell asked.

"Freelance," was all the photographer said before he blended into the crowd, which had grown as the temperatures had dropped outside.

"Peter, did you see any press?" Russell asked.

85

Brewster shook his head as he approached. "The only one I spotted was that gossip columnist who shows up everywhere. She may have brought someone with her. I didn't recognize that guy."

"Well, if you see the young man again, tell him to give us a warning. I think he frightened Molly," Russell said, in a fatherly fashion.

"I'm okay, Senator. Part of being back in Washington, I guess. I'll get used to it."

"If it's a good photo, we'll use it in the senator's Colorado newsletter," Brewster said with a grin. "Good way to let the folks back home know you've joined our team, Molly. That will rattle a lot of cages back in Colorado."

Brewster was having entirely too much fun at my expense tonight. "And you can't wait to rattle them, can you, Peter?" I retorted.

Senator Russell threw back his head and let loose one of those infectious belly laughs of his, so we all joined in. I decided this was as good a time as any to make my escape. I'd been trotted out, photographed, weighed, and measured. I deserved to relax in my stall.

"Senator, Congressman Baylor, Mrs. Baylor, I hope you'll excuse me. This has been my first full day back in Washington, and I have to admit I'm exhausted. If you don't mind, I'll make my way into Virginia now." I was hoping the senator would be too polite to twist my arm in public. I guessed right.

"Why, of course, Molly. We don't want to wear you out the first day. You go home and rest. Albert will drive you home right away," Russell said in a solicitous tone.

"You poor dear," Mrs. Baylor said with a maternal expression. "You must be exhausted. Washington is so . . . so very draining."

"Yes, it is, Mrs. Baylor," I agreed as I began to back away; go while the going was good. "I'd advise you two to take it one day at a time. And remember to breathe." Everyone laughed, which gave me my chance. I turned to leave. "Senator, enjoy the rest of the evening."

"Thank you, Molly," Russell said with a genial wave.

I was almost to the foyer when Brewster caught up with me. "Go home and relax, Molly. You've earned it. Tomorrow morning Albert can take you on a tour of the townhouse on P Street."

I paused at the foyer, noticing that Albert was already standing by the front door with my purse, clearly waiting for me. "How early should I come in to meet Albert? And when do you want me here tomorrow for the reception?"

Brewster gave me that boyish grin. "You and Albert can set your own schedule. He's an early riser. And you can arrive anytime after six tomorrow evening. In between, Saturday is all yours, Molly. The senator and I will be busy on the Hill. So, enjoy your weekend." With that, he turned to rejoin the partying politicians. Back on the job.

Better him than me, I thought with a relieved sigh as I hastened through the opened door. "Quick, Albert, head for the bridge before Peter finds someone else to introduce me to."

"I told you not to worry. I've got it covered." He took a drag on his cigarette, easing that irritating scratch in his throat.

"I know you did, Raymond. I trust you. We all trust you," the man's deep voice came over the phone. "We simply want to make sure there'll be no problems. No slipups of any kind. There may be some last-minute adjustments."

"I've told you before. This guy is a pro. He doesn't slip up. Nothing throws him."

"Good, good. This one came up suddenly, so . . ."

"No time to take it up with committee, right?" Raymond joked before taking another drag.

The man on the other end of the phone snorted. "Hardly. So tell him to be extra careful."

"He's *always* careful. That's why he's still alive and still in business. Stop worrying."

"Worry is how *I* stay in business."

Raymond gave a raspy chuckle. "Hey, are you going to Karpinsky's funeral?"

"I wouldn't miss it for the world."

"Now that he's eliminated, you should have a clear path with the Banking committee. Who's the new chairman?"

"Senator Dunston."

"Foresee any problems?"

"Not at all. He's already on board. He'll start shifting the committee's focus as soon as he takes the chair."

"Wasn't he the one you took to the Keys last year? Marlin fishing, as I recall."

"And Matzatlan and the Bahamas."

Raymond chuckled deep in his chest, stirring up an old rattle. "He likes those trips, doesn't he?"

"And the speaking fees. And the investment advice."

"Next, you'll find his wife a job."

"His son already started in the Stuttgart bank."

Raymond laughed out loud this time.

FOUR

I spotted Karen as soon as I entered the high-rise harbor-front café. She was seated at a table beside a huge wall of windows, reading a newspaper. I hurried over to the table. "Is that the *Washington Post?* I need to check the obits page for the location of Karpinsky's memorial service. I forgot to write it down."

"Sorry, Molly, I left the *Post* at home. This is just a local gossip rag," she said with a sheepish grin as she folded the paper and dropped it on the table.

I picked up the tabloid-sized newssheet with bold type. " 'D.C. Dirt. *You read it here first.*' Looks sleazy."

"Yeah, kind of. Don't pay any attention. Those people aren't real reporters, just wannabes."

I stared at Karen for a second, then at the paper, then back at Karen. There was something about this paper Karen didn't like, and that made me curious.

She reached across the table. "Don't bother with it, Molly. I'll throw it away."

That did it. The only reason I would care what was in this gossip rag was if I was in it. My heart sank to my stomach. "Karen, am I in this paper?" I waved it accusingly.

Karen winced but didn't answer.

"That bad, huh?"

So much for flying beneath the radar. Brewster was right. I was busted. And it wasn't even by Eleanor MacKenzie's classy social network. It was some sleazy newsrag instead. *Wonderful.*

"Actually, the picture's not bad," Karen said, clearly trying to console me.

Instead, my heart dropped all the way to my feet. *"Picture?"* I cried, then remembered the photographer wandering Russell's reception. "I don't believe this." I scowled at the flimsy paper as I sat at the table. Paging through the *D.C. Dirt,* I prayed for a small, insignificant . . .

It didn't take long to find it. I couldn't have missed the photo if I'd tried. It filled a quarter page. There I was, looking surprised as hell, immortalized in the photographer's flash. Right behind me was Senator Russell.

It wasn't bad, I suppose, provided you liked the "deer in the headlights" expression. That, plus my somber black suit made me look like a funeral director who'd just been told one of the corpses got up and left.

"Damn," I said softly, so as not to be overheard by the rest of the posh café's diners.

My gaze dropped to the blurb beneath the photo. *Molly Malone, former congressional wife and daughter of a former U.S. senator from Virginia, returns to Washington to work for the quirky Independent senator from Colorado.*

Quirky? The senator would love that, I thought. So far, so good. I almost hated to keep reading, but I couldn't stop myself.

Spies for the Dirt *tell us Ms. Malone used to be quite the hostess years ago. If she intends to help the senator, we suggest she get a new wardrobe. Her dowdy evening ensemble was better suited for a wake than a Washington reception. Our advice to Ms. Malone: Go shopping or go back to Denver.*

I stared at the words, reading them again to make sure I hadn't read it wrong. I hadn't. *"Dammit!"* I exploded, startling the waiter who was leaning over our table with the water glasses.

Karen motioned him away while I fumed, oblivious to the nearby diners' scowls.

"I cannot *believe* you read this trash," I

accused Karen, noticing a haughty look from an elderly woman walking to her table.

"Everybody reads the *DC Dirt,* Molly," she said apologetically. "It dishes. Lots of fun gossip."

"Not if you're in it," I retorted. "I haven't been in town forty-eight hours, and I'm already pilloried in the press! I knew I should never have come back. Never, never, *never!*" I lowered my voice this time. Either that, or the café staff might throw me out.

"Molly, calm down. It's not so bad. The picture is kind of cute."

"I look like a jacklighted deer."

Karen laughed and sipped her coffee while I pouted.

"She called me dowdy. *Dowdy!* I've never had a dowdy day in my life. On my worst day, I'm not dowdy. Who is that reporter anyway?"

"Don't pay any attention. She's just trying to get headlines, according to Nan. I called her after I read the article. Nan said she's heard the woman is some third-rate actress who wants to make it as a columnist. And someone told Nan she went to Mount Saint Mary's when you did. Before you went to that big Arlington high school with Nan and Deb."

I glanced below and, sure enough, right

under my photo was a gossip column and byline. I stared at the name. *Diedre Turner.* "You've got to be kidding," I said, as old memories resurrected themselves from the dusty past. "My old nemesis from Mount Saint Mary's. Now it makes sense. Diedre hated my guts in high school. I guess she still does." I dropped the paper onto the table. "What galls me is she's right. I do have to go shopping. I left most of my wardrobe back in Denver."

"There're lots of shops on Connecticut and Wisconsin Avenues, but even more scattered around the city now. And a great one near Capitol Hill. Check out these." She slipped a pen from her purse and scribbled a few names on a napkin.

I scanned the napkin before shoving it into my jacket pocket. "Excellent. Maybe I'll go shopping this afternoon."

"How did you like Peter's townhouse on P Street?" Karen asked, clearly trying to switch subjects to one less incendiary. "Your message said Albert was taking you for a tour early this morning."

"The house is beautiful, even filled with dust and shrouded furniture. Dark wood, antique carved moldings, brick fireplace, updated kitchen with granite counters, bathrooms are updated, too," I enthused.

"There's even a jacuzzi tub in the master bath."

The thought of all those little jets massaging away stress was almost enough to sell me on the place. However, it was the kitchen that sealed it. Bright and spacious, it had large east-facing windows that allowed the morning sun to spill across the kitchen table. I could picture myself sitting with a cup of coffee, reading the *Washington Post.*

But the best thing about the P Street house was that it didn't remind me of the townhouse where Dave and I lived for six years. The floor plans were entirely different. This house was larger, brighter, with more sunshine. It even had a small patio outside the dining room. Standing on the uneven moss-covered flagstones outside, I had breathed in the unmistakable scent of spring and traced the English ivy climbing the brick walls and chimney. Purple crocuses were already poking their heads from the soil, and daffodils ran riot in an overgrown flowerbed. The neglected garden, the shady little patio, the sunny kitchen, plus the Jacuzzi sealed it. I was hooked.

"That's great, Molly. I'm glad you like it. I was hoping you would," Karen said as the waiter cautiously approached.

Ordering a muffin and coffee, I noticed

that Karen had barely touched her omelet. "I'm glad you didn't wait for me to order breakfast." Pointing to her plate, I added, "Don't you like it?"

Karen shrugged, then sipped her coffee. "I'm not really hungry."

I watched my niece tear her English muffin into pieces instead of eating it. Something was bothering Karen. I figured that was why she'd left two messages on my cell phone last night, asking to have breakfast this morning.

Peter Brewster's remark about Karen having a "serious relationship" wiggled from the back of my mind, and I wondered if that was what was bothering her. I decided to roll the dice.

"Karen, you look preoccupied. More so than usual, I mean. Is there something on your mind?"

Karen's shoulders relaxed, and a smile worked the corners of her mouth. "You could always tell when something was bothering me, Molly. Even when I was a kid. I'm so glad you're back. Just sitting with you makes me feel better."

"Wow, I wish I had that effect on everyone," I said as the waiter set my muffin and coffee before me. "Now that I'm here, why don't we have breakfast every week. I've missed seeing you, too." I took a large sip of the dark brew.

"I appreciate your meeting me this morning. I know you're going to Karpinsky's memorial service later."

"Along with most of Washington. I plan to stay in the background if I can."

Now that I'd been outed in the *D.C. Dirt,* I was bound to trip over more people from my past. Lots of government types wound up in Washington. Probably why the traffic was so bad. Old wonks were clogging the roads.

Karen stared out the window beside us that overlooked the Potomac River and harbor walk area of Georgetown below. Saturday sailors could motor right to the dock, then walk up the steps and into any number of outdoor cafes that lined the riverbank. From our window seat in the cozy café above, the Potomac glinted deep green with reflected sunlight. Another gorgeous spring day.

"You'll be at the reception tonight, right?"

"Of course. How could I skip schmoozing with all those Midwesterners?" Karen said, as she returned from wherever she was.

"Are you still planning to come to Nan and Bill's with me afterwards?"

"Absolutely. I don't want to miss Nan's

famous Sunday brunch."

Now that she was more relaxed, I decided to probe. "Since you didn't answer my question the first time, I'll ask it again. What's bothering you, Karen? There's something on your mind. Is it personal or business? You know you can tell me anything."

She gave a rueful smile. "I knew I couldn't deflect you, Molly. Actually, it's both. Personal and professional. I've been sitting here wondering how to begin."

I poured more coffee for both of us, sensing this was going to take a while. "Start at the beginning, sweetie. It's always the best place to start. But not before you've finished your breakfast. Sounds like you'll need your strength to tell me."

Karen chuckled, but picked up her fork. I sipped my coffee and watched her polish off the rest of the veggie and cheese omelet, like she'd suddenly recovered her appetite. While she spread jam on the remaining muffin, I decided to prime the pump.

"Peter told me that you had a serious relationship going with someone, Karen. If that's true, I'm glad. You've been alone far too long."

"I'm afraid it's more complicated than that, Molly."

"Okay, time for you to talk now. I'm tired

of guessing."

Karen looked at me over her coffee mug. "The serious relationship is with someone in my office."

"Hmmmmm, that can be tricky."

"It's my boss, Jed Molinoff."

I made a face. "Not good, Karen. Not good at all."

She released a long sigh, as if relieved at the telling. "It was at the beginning of last year when we were in paranoid campaign mode. Working those late nights. Sleeping on the office sofas, eating cold pizza . . . I don't know how it happened. Suddenly we looked at each other, and it was different somehow. We just fell into it, I guess, and we haven't been able to stop since. God knows I've tried." She shook her head. "But as soon as I go back into the office, it starts all over again. Jed starts talking to me, and I get this yearning . . . I don't know what it is."

I knew what it was. And had experienced it myself in the heat of an intense, hard-fought campaign. Being thrown together with people like yourself, shared emotions, shared dreams, it was hard to separate the adrenaline of the action from a real attraction.

"I know what you mean, Karen. I've been

there. But even so, you've got to stop it. The sooner, the better. Gossip can do more damage than you know."

"It gets worse," she said from behind her cup. "He's married with children."

This time, I flinched. *Damn.*

"You've got to put an end to it now, Karen. Tonight. No more working late. No more spending time together. This affair is toxic to you and your career. Once Congressman Jackson finds out — and he will, everyone always finds out — he'll want you to leave. You know that."

She closed her eyes. "I know, I know . . . how could I have been so stupid! I know better. I never thought something like that would happen to me."

"Loneliness makes us do stupid things. I can attest to that."

"And you're right. Congressman Jackson would keep Jed because he's so dependent on him. Jackson depends on me, too. Even so, I'd be the one to go."

"Tell Molinoff today. Don't wait until Monday. It's good you're coming home with me. That way, if he tries to call and pressure you, we'll be around tomorrow for moral support." I reached over and squeezed her arm.

Karen stared at the tablecloth, her finger

tracing an invisible pattern. "I'm not sure if Jed would pressure me to stay or not. We had an argument earlier this week, and he's been acting differently toward me ever since."

"Sounds like a serious argument."

"Well, I didn't think it was," her voice still betrayed surprise. "But Jed reacted strangely, not like himself at all. It surprised me how upset he got about it."

"What was this disagreement about?"

"That's what's so puzzling. There was no disagreement. Not at first. I simply asked a question about one of the congressman's campaign contributors — what he knew about the group — and he brushed off my questions. Told me not to worry about them. He'd visited with the head of the group, and they were a private think tank, that's all. Then he reminded me the congressman needed all the money he could get for this upcoming race."

She drank from her mug, staring out at the Potomac again. "I thought that was strange. He'd never said that about any other contributor. That made me curious, so I pushed and asked exactly what kind of 'political think tank' they were. Why was this group different? I mean, I'm an analyst. That's what I do. I ask questions. That's when he jumped down my throat. Told me to drop it and get back to work. The congressman didn't pay me to bother donors to his campaign. Then he added that this group had been donating to politicians for years on both sides of the aisle." She paused and sipped her coffee. "You know, Molly, that hurt; his berating me like that. We've always been on the same page about everything. Of course, that made me even more curious about the group."

"What's their name?"

"The Epsilon Group. It's low profile. Invites distinguished professors, economists, politicians, and international figures to gather periodically and brainstorm different issues. That's what I've been able to find out so far."

"Sounds like a good idea. I'm surprised I haven't heard of them. Have any of their ideas gone any farther than brainstorming?"

Karen nodded. "Apparently, yes. I tracked several of their policy statements over the past two decades and found three or four that wound up in legislation; either national or in a state legislature."

I watched Karen as she talked. There was something she wasn't telling me. "Sounds like a great organization. We need more brainstorming and less politicking. What was it about the group that concerned you, Karen?"

She resumed tracing a pattern on the white tablecloth. I waved away the approaching waiter, not wanting to disturb Karen's concentration.

"I'd seen that name before, years ago. It was in my father's notebooks. I'd forgotten he'd mentioned it. I hadn't looked at those notebooks for years."

Now I was curious. Karen's father was Dave's eccentric older brother, Eric. Eric Grayson had been a successful district attorney in Denver when Dave died. Eric had taken Dave's death as a call to action, somehow. I had never fully understood, but Eric became consumed with the idea of "carrying his brother's torch." He was quickly appointed to Dave's remaining term and easily won the seat on his own that fall. "Continuing David Grayson's legacy of reform," he called it and moved his wife and teenage daughter to the nation's Capitol. He served in Congress for ten years until he and his wife, Cheryl, died in a car crash outside Washington.

"What kind of notebooks?"

"Dad used to take notes on legislation he was working on, research he'd done on each bill, stuff like that. We'd sit up late at night

104

and talk about all the bills before Congress. Dad had other notes there, too. Personal recollections, I guess you'd call them. That's why I read the notebooks after he died. It was kind of like having Dad sitting across from me again." Her voice had turned wistful.

"What did his notes say about the Epsilon Group? Anything bad?"

Karen shook her head. "No, not at all. But he indicated that he was researching them. That's why I didn't remember it until I noticed the Epsilon Group on the list of donors this year. Something about the name sounded familiar, but I couldn't place it at first. That's why I dug out Dad's notebooks and went through them."

"What were you looking for?" I asked, puzzled.

Karen turned her clear blue gaze to me. "Hard to explain, Molly. Something about the words my dad used made me think he was curious about the group and was looking into them. I knew my dad so well, we were so alike. I guess that's why I started checking them. It was like, if Dad was curious, I should be too."

I stared into her open, direct gaze. That was Karen Grayson. Her father's daughter, through and through. Mirror image of Eric

Grayson's dedication and sense of service. It made sense. Karen idolized her father. I sensed that by checking on this group, Karen believed she was continuing her father's work. In reality, I guessed it was more a way to keep her father's memory alive in her heart. Loneliness can indeed make us do strange things.

"That's understandable, Karen," I said. "But you might want to back off a bit. Especially considering your relationship with Molinoff. Your soon-to-end relationship, actually. You don't want him holding a grudge. That could get *really* ugly."

Karen nodded. "You're right, Molly. I think —"

Her cell phone rang then, and I knew our quiet breakfast was about to end abruptly. Well, at least I'd been able to give some maternal advice — for what it was worth.

Karen put her hand over her other ear and leaned on the table, listening intently to the caller. She answered in short, clipped replies, leading me to believe that the caller was none other than her boss, and lover, Jed Molinoff.

"I'll be over shortly. And, Jed, we're not going to your boat today. No. We need to talk." A long pause rolled by, then Karen replied in a firm voice, "Yes, today. We need to talk now, Jed. I'm coming right over. Bye." With that, she flipped off her phone.

"I'm impressed, Karen. You were strong and decisive. Good job. Now, go over there and tell him it's finished. Today. Don't let him talk you out of it. Some guys are wheedlers and they'll try all sorts of things to entice you back. I've seen it happen. If he does, don't be afraid to use guilt. Remind him of his wife and children. Sounds like he's conveniently forgotten about them. That should get his attention."

Karen stared out the window again. "I wanted you to know, Molly, for the record, that I have tried breaking up with Jed before. I didn't want you to think I'd completely lost my moral compass. It's just, whenever I tried, I couldn't finish. Jed would start kissing me and . . . and I'd fall right back into it again." She turned her clear blue gaze to me. "I promise you this time will be different. This time I will do it. No matter what Jed says or does."

The earnestness of Karen's gaze touched me, and I reached across the table and squeezed her arm. "I believe you, Karen. And I want *you* to know that I'm so very proud of you. Of everything you've done over there on the Hill during your career. You're a credit to your father and to the

107

family. Don't let this stumble cause you to doubt yourself. We're all human, Karen, and we all make mistakes. All of us. I just wanted you to know that. For the record." I smiled.

Karen's eyes started to glisten, so I glanced away and signaled the waiter.

The phone vibrated in his jacket pocket. He leaned back in the outdoor café chair and took a sip of his beer before answering. "Yes?"

Raymond's scratchy voice came over the line. "There'll be some additional arrangements needed tonight. Bring your camera."

"That's different. She must really have them spooked."

"It's complicated. Turns out Congressman Jackson's chief staffer Jed Molinoff had a thing going with this girl, while the wife and kiddies were back home in Omaha. Problem is, she and Molinoff just had a nasty breakup today. A big argument, according to him. Now she's quitting Jackson's office, and she's carrying a grudge the size of Nebraska."

"Molinoff sounds like a loose cannon."

"You might say that. So bring the camera. Text file is on its way. Call me after completion."

"Roger that."

He clicked off and went back to his beer and watching tourists feed the pigeons beside the Potomac.

"Baked Brie, Ms. Malone?" the grad-student waiter asked, holding a tray filled with the tempting selections in front of me.

"When haven't I wanted baked Brie?" I admitted as I chose one. "I remember you from the Senator's reception last night. What's your name?"

"Ryan, ma'am. Ryan Bonner," he replied with an engaging grin. "Take another, Ms. Malone. They're small."

I laughed. "Yeah, and they have no calories, either. Tell me, Ryan, do you work many of Senator Russell's parties?"

"Yes, ma'am. Bud and Agnes and I work all of the senator's functions, ever since he came to Washington."

He nodded toward the bartender and the older woman with the graying Dutch Boy haircut I'd spoken to at the last reception. She was offering glasses of wine to the crowd that filled Senator Russell's living and dining rooms. Noticing Ryan's buzzed short blond hair, I wondered if he might be in the Reserves. Maybe that was how he was paying for his education.

"Which agency do you work for, Ryan?"

"Preferred Professionals, ma'am," he said, moving away from where I stood. "Mr. Brewster has all the contact information if you need it."

I'll bet he does. "Thanks, Ryan. And you can drop the 'ma'am', okay? Call me Molly."

"Yes, ma'am . . . Molly," he grinned before he turned toward the crowd again.

From my post alone in the archway, I spotted Bud, the bartender, efficiently offering drinks. Agnes was working her way back and forth between the thirsty crowd and the bar, effortlessly balancing her tray filled with glasses. It was good to have names. I could probe Nan and Deb about Preferred Professionals and see what they knew about the agency. Now that I was the senator's accountant, all expenses came under my scrutiny.

Glancing about the animated clusters of Midwestern politicians and staffers, I spotted Peter Brewster earnestly listening to an older, balding gentleman holding forth — as only a politician can — complete with finger-waving and head-wagging. Senator Russell was beside the fireplace, surrounded by several men I guessed to be junior congressmen. I noticed Russell was also holding forth, minus wagging head and fingers.

An attractive middle-aged woman approached, wine glass in hand. My instinct said "congresswoman," but I was damned if I remembered her name. I needed time to study that congressional directory.

"Ms. Malone," she said, extending her hand. "I'm Congresswoman Sally Chertoff from Iowa. I believe I spotted you at Senator Karpinksy's service earlier today."

"You're right, Congresswoman. I was there along with most of congressional Washington, it seems. That was quite a tribute."

"It certainly was. His death is a huge loss to the Senate. I once read that your father and he worked together on civil rights legislation years ago and were instrumental in getting it passed."

Shreds of old memories tugged at me. Proud memories. "Yes, indeed. They stood up and made a difference when it counted. The newspapers used to call them the 'two lions of the Senate.' "

"I never had the pleasure of knowing your father, but I'd say that was a pretty apt description of Senator Karpinsky," Congresswoman Chertoff said. "I had a chance to meet him last year when our House Financial Services subcommittee on International Monetary Policy was conducting a hearing. Senator Karpinsky asked to speak with us in a closed-door session. He was impressive, even at eighty-six."

"Isn't Congressman Randall Jackson on your committee?"

"Yes, he is. And Randall and I were talking a minute ago about how much we'll miss having Karpinsky as head of the Senate Banking committee. We were really looking forward to his guidance and support when our bill comes up before the House. Now that he's gone, we're not sure how much support we'll have for tougher language on regulation." She placed her empty wine glass on Agnes's convenient tray.

Another congressman beckoned across the room, and Chertoff excused herself. "It looks like someone needs to speak with me. Nice meeting you, Ms. Malone. I hope we can talk again."

"Call me Molly, Congresswoman, and stay strong," I said as she moved away.

I scanned the room again, looking for my niece this time, and saw her in the corner in her trademark navy blue suit talking to a tall slender man with light brown hair. Watching the anxious expression on Karen's face, I sensed the man she was speaking with was Jed Molinoff. He leaned toward Karen, talking and gesturing vehemently.

The mother in me wanted to casually wander by, in case Karen needed to escape. But I knew better. Karen had to break off this relationship herself for it to take. She didn't need rescuing.

"Chardonnay tonight, or some Pinot Grigio?" a woman's low voice came beside me.

I turned to see Agnes smiling at me, offering her tray of wines like she had yesterday evening. Her face showed sun wrinkles as well as laugh lines. Lots of laugh lines. Her smile seemed even more familiar tonight, as if my memory was sifting through faces.

"I'll try the Pinot Grigio this time, Agnes," I said. "Ryan told me your names. At least the three of you. Are there others the senator uses regularly?"

"Casey has also been with the senator from the beginning." Agnes gestured to the crew-cut, retired military type discreetly wandering the edge of the room. I recognized him from Thursday evening's reception. "Of, course, Casey is a permanent employee, while we're just temps."

"Security," I said before sipping my wine. Clean and crisp. "Better safe than sorry, I guess."

"Times have changed a lot since your father's days in the Senate."

This time, I turned and studied Agnes.

She stood calmly, with that amused smile of hers. "I knew I'd seen you before, Agnes. Were you at some of my parents' parties?"

"I was at most of them. Your father liked my sense of humor. And he liked that I could work around politicians whether they were drunk or sober or in full rant. He used to call me Aggie." Her smile spread. "I remember when you first started creeping around the edges of those parties. I also remember when you used to hide behind your father's library sofa, eavesdropping on politicians." She chuckled.

The name did the trick. Suddenly, a memory of Aggie spying me behind the sofa one evening — and not saying a word — crept from the back of my mind. "I remember! I held my breath waiting for you to squeal on me, but you didn't. Good Lord, Aggie, that's been years ago. I cannot believe you remembered."

"Ohhhhh, I remember a lot. Your father was one of my favorites. That's why I enjoyed working his functions. Plus, I sensed your father already knew you were hiding. And *you* knew he knew." She laughed softly. "He doted on you, Molly."

More memories wiggled free from the underbrush. "You're right, Aggie. Dad let me get away with murder. I also remember your working our functions. Dave's and mine. You were blond then, and your hair was longer."

Aggie nodded. "I used to turn down other jobs to work yours. It was always a pleasure to watch you and your husband together. You made a great team."

"Yes, we did," I said, allowing some of those pleasant memories to surface and dance before my eyes. "That was a long time ago, Aggie. Another lifetime, it seems."

" 'Hace se luvia mucho,' as the Cubans say. A lot has happened since then," Aggie replicd, the Spanish tripping easily over her tongue.

That brought me out of the past quickly. "You must work a lot of diplomatic parties, Aggie. Your Spanish is quite good," I said, curious as to the Cuban reference.

"I had a Cuban boyfriend years ago. Back when I was a blond," Aggie said with a wink before she blended into the crowd again.

I sipped the light wine, watching Aggie ply the Midwesterners with drinks and keeping an eye on Karen and Jed Molinoff in the corner. I could tell by the set of Karen's shoulders and the expression on her face that she was getting angry. That firm Grayson jaw was set. Molinoff was gesturing again, leaning closer, and I sensed

115

the temperature of their conversation was increasing rapidly. Once again, I had to squelch all thoughts of rescue.

Then, all of a sudden, Casey the security man sidled up beside Molinoff and spoke to him. Molinoff looked slightly startled by Casey's appearance. That, plus the fact that Casey was a lot taller and broader than the slender congressional aide, seemed to get Molinoff's attention. I figured Casey had observed the stormy exchange and decided to tell Molinoff to keep it discreet. Politely put: *Back off.* I liked Casey already, and I hadn't even spoken to him yet.

Karen said something and started to walk away, but Molinoff reached out and grabbed her arm, clearly angry. I was about to leave my perch when I saw Casey put his hand on Molinoff's arm while he spoke. Storm clouds darkened Molinoff's face, but he released Karen. Karen caught sight of me from across the room and headed my way. Molinoff, meanwhile, glared after a retreating Casey, then grabbed a drink from Aggie's tray.

"You okay?" I asked when Karen drew beside me. "It looked like it was getting hot over there. I gather Molinoff didn't want to call it quits."

Karen took a deep breath. "God, no. He

hit the ceiling when I told him this afternoon, and he's still raging. He kept accusing me of letting him down, and all this garbage." She shook her head. "That's when *I* got mad. All I could feel coming from Jed was how I was messing up *his* life. So I told him how I felt. How I *really* felt. And he didn't like it."

"I could see that from over here. And so could security." I nodded toward Casey who'd gone back to patrolling the rooms again.

"That was probably after I reminded Jed of his wife and kids. I'd had it with his telling me I'd let him down. So I let him have it."

"Right between the eyes, huh? Good girl. Sounds like he deserved it."

"He was furious." Karen snatched a glass of white wine from Aggie's passing tray.

I noticed Molinoff glance our way, still scowling. I purposely caught his eye and sent him a raised-eyebrow "Do you want something?" look. He glanced away.

"Why don't you stay with me until the party winds down, Karen?" I suggested. "That way Molinoff won't hit on you again. I figure we can probably leave in an hour or so."

"Thanks, but I don't think Jed will give

me any more trouble tonight. The security guy really scared him. I could tell. Jed went white as a sheet when the guy showed up." Karen slipped her BlackBerry from her purse. "I'm going to go outside and make some phone calls, in my car if I have to. I need privacy."

"Who're you calling?"

She looked at me with that clear Grayson gaze of conviction. It brought back memories of Dave. "I'm quitting Jackson's office. I can't work with Jed anymore, and I told him so this afternoon. That's the real reason he's so mad."

"Whoa, that's a gutsy move, but shouldn't you wait until you can find another position on the Hill?"

"That's what I'm doing. Several friends have told me they would open a spot for me on their congressional staffs anytime I asked. Well, I've decided to ask. I need a position where I can move up. This experience has taught me that. Jed has kept me by his side for more reasons than the obvious. I made him look good." A frown darkened her face.

"Karen, I'm *so* proud of you," I said, delighted to see her spark return. "This is a sticky situation, and you're handling it with class, even if Molinoff isn't."

"Thanks," she said, a smile peeking out. "Give me a hug for good luck."

"Always." I wrapped my arms around my niece and squeezed, sending as many good thoughts as I could with my embrace. "You're so talented, Karen. Any congressman would be lucky to have you on staff."

Karen squeezed back. "I can't tell you how glad I am you're here."

Sensing tears in her voice, I released her before moisture weakened her focus. "Now, go get 'em. Make those calls. Casey and I will keep watch over Molinoff."

"Thanks, Molly. Maybe we'll turn Nan's brunch into a celebration tomorrow," Karen said before she headed down the hallway.

Glancing about the room, I noticed Molinoff staring after Karen. I sent an "I'm watching you" look his way. I wanted Jed to know that I'd observed his earlier behavior. Molinoff glanced away and left the living room.

I walked up to Casey, extending my hand to the middle-aged security guard. "Casey, I'm Molly. I want to thank you for noticing the heated discussion in the corner. And especially for intervening in it. That was my niece, Karen Grayson, who was trying to extricate herself from the congressional

119

staffer's sweaty grip."

Casey gave my hand a firm shake. "Just doing my job, Ms. Malone. Some folks get a little excited at times. Usually a quiet comment calms them down."

"Call me Molly, okay? We're all working for Senator Russell, so let's keep it casual. You work for Russell full-time?"

"That's right," he said before turning his attention to the room again. Back on duty.

"It's a scary world when a senator needs full-time security," I commented. "I'm guessing you're former military. Which service?"

Casey glanced my way again. "Marine Corps. Retired First Sergeant. And don't worry about your niece, Molly. I'll keep an eye on Molinoff." He glanced around the room again. "Where is she? She was with you a minute ago."

"She went outside to make some phone calls in her car. She needed more privacy than a room filled with paranoid politicians affords."

"Okay. I'll check on her in a few minutes. Meanwhile, I just spotted Molinoff on his phone near the patio doors."

I glanced down the long hallway. "Is there a gate or something from the garden that leads to the front? I'm still so new here I don't know the lay of the land yet."

He shook his head. "Don't worry. There's no gate. That way no one uninvited can get in unless they climb over a six-foot brick wall." Casey started to back away, back to the perimeter. "Enjoy the rest of the evening, Molly."

"Thanks, Casey, I will."

Ryan reappeared then, and I accepted another appetizer from his tempting tray. I was about to find something more substantial than appetizers, when Peter Brewster approached.

"The senator wants to introduce you to the Kansas contingent," Peter said, indicating a group of congressmen by the fireplace. "Oh, and great outfit, by the way. Looking good, Molly." He gave me a wink. "Don't let that reporter scare you."

I glanced to the multi-hued long silk jacket I'd found in the trendy shop near Capitol Hill. One of several "finds" from my afternoon shopping excursion. I prayed my salary would arrive before the credit card bill.

"Actually, it wasn't her that scared me, it was the photo," I said, accompanying Peter as we wove a path through the guests. "I looked like a funeral director." I checked over my shoulder. "Thank goodness, I haven't spotted any photographers tonight."

"I haven't either. They've probably gotten bored with our large receptions. No reporters will be around for the smaller dinners. The senator likes to keep them as private as possible."

"How many of these receptions has he done already?"

"We started earlier this month, so there's only been four so far. Mostly twice a week."

My inner accountant flinched at the thought. "Good Lord, Peter, I'm almost afraid to see those accounts on Monday."

He laughed. "Don't worry, we have a budget. Honest."

"Uh-huh." I looked around at the congressional staffers chowing down at Senator Russell's well-laden table. "Is he really planning to work his way through the entire Congress? How many more of these receptions are scheduled?"

"I'll have a folder on your desk Monday, along with the budget," he promised with that boyish smile.

"Can I at least take a peek at the list tonight so I can put the dates on my daytimer? Pretty please, Peter?" I spotted Russell glance our way.

"I love your work ethic. Okay, I'll put the folder on the desk in the library. Just leave it there when you've finished," he said quietly as we drew near the fireplace circle. Then, raising his voice, Brewster announced, "Gentlemen, let me introduce Molly Malone, our newest addition to Senator Russell's staff."

I looked around at all the new faces and called up my brightest "meet-the-client" smile. *Showtime.*

"Ryan, I'm dying for some coffee. Those Midwestern congressmen talked me dry," I said, snatching a sausage-stuffed mushroom from his tray. "Could you bring me some in the library, please? Peter left a list for me there that I need to go over."

"Sure thing, Molly. Be back in a sec," Ryan said, scurrying toward the kitchen.

I was about to head to the library when I spotted Casey coming from the kitchen. "Is there any real food left, Casey? All I've had is appetizers between politicians, and I'm starving."

"They're starting cleanup now, Molly. There may be something in the storage boxes. Lots of coffee, though," he said as he headed back to the fast-dwindling group of guests in the living room. Suddenly, he stopped and turned. "Oh, I checked on your niece outside half an hour ago, and she was fine. Talking on her cell phone in her car like you said. Earlier, I made it a point to walk Molinoff outside myself. Since you told me your niece was in her car, I wanted to make sure he didn't head in her direction. So I escorted him to the sidewalk and pointed toward Wisconsin Avenue in the opposite direction. It was obvious he was pissed I was standing there and telling him where to find a taxi. I watched him walk all the way down the street."

I had to smile. "That was really good of you, Casey. At least you got Jed away from Karen. Thanks for that." I looked around the room but didn't see Karen. Still making phone calls, I figured, as I checked my watch. Nearly eleven o'clock. "When will these people leave?" I whispered to Casey.

"Sometimes you wonder, Molly. I just had to help two staffers into cabs and another into the upstairs bathroom to throw up. Be glad you're just talking to them."

"Whoa, thanks for sharing," I said and laughed all the way to the library. Ryan caught up with me at the doorway.

"I spied a few cookies, so I grabbed those, too," he said as I gratefully accepted the ceramic mug of coffee. Steam wafted off the black brew, tickling my nose.

"Thanks, Ryan, you're a lifesaver," I said,

snatching the cookies as well. "When do you get to go home?"

"Oh, in another half hour, probably. See you later, Molly." He was already halfway out the door.

There was Peter's folder on the desk, so I took a deep drink of coffee and pulled my phone from my pocket. I stood, paging through Senator Russell's dinner schedule and munching cookies, while I dutifully entered the dates on my electronic calendar.

I did notice that, with the exception of this weekend, Russell did the majority of his entertaining during the week, clearly leaving weekends free for return trips to Colorado. I'd been impressed with his regular attendance to his home state and constituents. Smart man.

"We'll keep you busy, Molly," Brewster said, strolling into the library. "You'll be earning your salary for sure."

"I can see that, Peter. My dance card is practically full. I notice Russell leaves weekends open. Back to Colorado, right?"

Peter nodded, sipping from a square-cut crystal glass. It looked like Scotch. "Absolutely. Gotta keep in touch with the people who sent him here."

I flipped through the pages again, this time noticing the suggested guest lists.

Several names jumped out at me, faces appearing. More faces and names coalesced as I went through the pages. "You've done a good job of arranging these lists, Peter. Did you do it, or does Russell pick and choose?"

"A little of both. Incidentally, if you see any potential conflicts in the guest lists, I'd appreciate your input. We can always move people around in the interests of congeniality."

I smiled as I read. "Congeniality, huh? I never pegged you as an optimist." Spotting a couple of names, I said, "Now that you mention it, you might want to separate these two." I pointed to the names of two Western congressman.

"Why's that?" Peter asked, peering over the list.

"*He* had an affair with *his* first wife years ago," I answered, pointing to the names. "You might want to invite them to separate dinners. In the interest of congeniality."

Peter chuckled. "Thanks, Molly. See, you're a great help already. Senator Russell has a lot of plans —"

I didn't hear the rest of Senator Russell's plans. Another list had caught my attention and another name. I stared at this name. Congressman Edward Ryker. I didn't have to search for this face. It rocketed from the back of my mind and out of the past. The past I'd tried so hard to bury. Old memories seared through me, cutting off my breath. Finally, Peter's voice pierced the fog.

"Molly? Are you all right?"

I blinked, then shook off the past to meet Brewster's confused gaze. "I . . . I'm sorry. What were you saying?"

Peter peered at me. "Never mind. I'm more interested in what you saw that transfixed you so. You didn't even hear me."

"Old memories from the past, that's all."

"Old memories or old enemies?"

I held his gaze. "Both. I've got a lot of history in this town, Peter. And a lot of ghosts. It's only inevitable they start creeping around."

"If there's any function you don't care to attend, just let me know. The senator will understand. And so will I."

I saw that he meant it. "Thanks, I'll bear that in mind."

The insistent ring of a cell phone sounded then, and Peter reached into his pocket as he headed toward the doorway. "Excuse me, Molly."

"At eleven thirty, I hope that's a girlfriend," I said, following after him. I'd had enough of schedules and lists and names for tonight.

"Don't I wish," he said with a grin as he flipped his phone open. "Peter Brewster."

I drained the last of my coffee as I headed down the hallway and glanced about the nearly empty living room. No sign of Karen. Was she still making phone calls? *Good Lord.* That girl had one heckuva contact list. I glanced into the kitchen and saw a remnant of the catering staff finishing up. Wiping down the counters. The evening was wrapping up at last.

Spotting Casey assist a wobbly gentleman down the hall, I waved as I walked to the front door. "I'll be back in a minute, Casey. I want to let Karen know the party's over. Time to go home."

"Yes, indeed," Casey said, walking slowly to match the elderly man's stride.

Lamplight and lanterns cast enough light to illuminate the yard, and I raced down the steps, shivering in the chill spring night as I headed for the gate. Summer's heat had yet to come. My luscious silk jacket felt cold against my skin, and I rubbed my arms while I walked, wishing I'd chosen the new suit for tonight.

Reaching the outside sidewalk, I searched the narrow residential street for Karen's car, but most of the cars looked the same in the dark. I walked along the sidewalk, peering into the vehicles, expecting to see Karen sitting in her Honda, still negotiating on the cell phone.

Albert's voice startled me from behind. "Are you looking for your niece, Molly?"

I jumped around. There was Albert, escorting a middle-aged couple to their car. "Yes, I am. Karen was making phone calls in her car. Have you seen her?"

"About an hour ago. Her car's a little farther down, Molly," Albert said as he assisted the woman into the passenger seat.

I kept walking and peering into the darkened cars. Georgetown streets were treelined and shady. Great during the day, but dark during the night. Tall streetlamps cast shadows as well, tricking you into thinking you saw someone in a car when you didn't.

Finally I spotted Karen's car, and there she was, sitting inside. She must still be talking and negotiating. Talk about a work ethic. Just like all of the Graysons.

I waved at her behind the wheel as I approached. She didn't appear to be on the phone. Excellent. We could leave now. "Hey, Karen. We can finally go home," I called. "I'll be riding with you, since I didn't drive over here. Albert brought me."

For some reason she didn't answer me, so I leaned over and knocked on the window to get her attention. She was looking straight ahead.

"Karen, did you hear me? We can —"

That's when I saw it. The blood. Blood on her face. On her hair. On her clothes. I stared at the blood. At Karen. Sitting so still, looking out the windshield. I blinked. The night shadows were still playing tricks on me. That couldn't be blood.

I knocked on the window again. "Karen! Are you asleep? Wake up, honey," I demanded in a voice that didn't sound like mine.

Karen didn't answer. She just sat there, gazing out the windshield. I sucked in an icy breath and stared at the blood again. *No.*

I stumbled around the car, holding onto it, while panic closed in. *No.* She's asleep. She's sick. She threw up. She had a seizure. She . . . she . . . Then I stared at the windshield and felt my body go numb.

Blood. Karen's blood. Splattered on the glass. The driver's window was shattered, broken glass all over the ground. Blood on Karen's face and clothes. A horrible bloody wound in her head.

I staggered back from the car, away from the blood and gore, and felt myself sink into another place, another time. A gruesome scene where another loved one lay drenched in his own blood.

I don't remember screaming, but there was an awful sound that pierced the night air as I sank to my knees in the darkened street and retched.

FIVE

The rough pavement scratched my cheek. Grit embedded my palms. I barely noticed. All I could feel was the pounding inside my head, the shrill scream still echoing in my ears.

Suddenly strong hands were on my shoulders, lifting my face from the pavement. "Molly, are you sick? Do you want a doctor?" Casey's voice sounded beside me, piercing through the noise inside my head.

I tried to speak, but couldn't. I reached through the fog that wrapped around me and found a whisper. "No . . . no . . ."

"Then why did you scream?" Casey said as he pulled me to my feet.

Feeling the ground beneath me, I willed myself to stand. I would not collapse. I would not collapse. I raised a shaking arm and pointed to the car. "Karen . . ."

Casey whipped his head around and stared at the gruesome sight. *"Jesus Christ!"*

He released me and raced to the car. "Did you see what happened, Molly?"

"No, no . . ." I whispered. "I found her like that just now . . . oh, God . . ."

Casey bent down and peered into the bloody car. "Jesus," he muttered.

"Oh, God . . . she's been shot . . . she's been shot . . . I can tell," I managed, my voice stronger now.

"You're right," Casey said as he drew a handkerchief from his pocket, reached over, and opened the car door.

Karen's BlackBerry dropped to the street with a metallic clatter. Something about the sound penetrated inside. The fog enveloping me evaporated.

Casey leaned closer and peered into my niece's death-pale face. "She's gone, Molly. I'm sorry."

I stared at Karen's pretty face covered in blood and closed my eyes. But not before noticing Casey reach down with his handkerchief and pocket Karen's BlackBerry as he closed the car door.

"My God, who did this? Who would kill Karen?" I could feel blood pumping through my veins as an old comrade crept from the bushes at the edge of my mind. *Anger.* It hadn't been around in a long time.

"I don't know, Molly," Casey said as he

slowly walked around the car. He scanned the sidewalk, then opened the other door and leaned inside the car.

Suddenly Albert's voice called out as he rushed up, Peter right behind him. "Molly, Molly, are you all right?" Albert cried, then jerked to a stop when he saw the car. *"Madre de Dios!"* He crossed himself as he swayed on his feet.

"My God . . . is that . . . is that Karen?" Peter flinched in horror. "What . . . happened?"

"She's been shot," I heard myself answer in a quiet voice.

"And from close range," Casey said as he backed out of the car. "It could have been a mugging. I didn't see a purse on the seat. Did she carry a purse, Molly?"

I nodded. "And a briefcase." My voice came stronger. My old comrade had joined me now, no longer content to hover at the edges.

Casey peered inside the car again. "Nope, no sign of a briefcase, either. Whoever did this ran off with both." He shook his head. "Son of a bitch."

My breathing turned ragged as anger flooded through me. "You mean some drugged-out meth freak killed my niece for her *purse? Goddammit to Hell!"*

Albert reached out. "Molly, why don't you come inside —"

I pushed his hand away. "*No!* I'm not going anywhere until I find out what happened to Karen. Where are the police? Where are the goddamned police?"

"I'll call them right now, Molly," Peter said, backing away, grimacing at the car once more. "We'll find who did this, I swear we will."

Senator Russell's voice called from the sidewalk behind us. "Albert, Peter! Is everything all right?"

"Better get the senator back inside, Peter," Casey said, glancing toward Russell who was approaching on the sidewalk behind us. "I'll call the police. I have friends on the force." He pulled a cell phone from inside his jacket as he returned to the sidewalk beside the car.

"Are you sure you don't want to go inside, Molly?" Albert asked. "Away from . . ." he gestured, not finding words.

I shook my head and watched Casey, talking on the phone as he paced the sidewalk beside the car. "No. I want to be here when the police come. You go back to the house, Albert, and keep everyone away from here." I didn't ask. I ordered.

Albert looked at me with undisguised

concern, then nodded before turning away.

I stared at Karen while Casey talked on the phone. Her pretty face frozen in death, mouth open, blue eyes wide, fixed and staring, blood staining her face, her hair, as she gaped in surprise. Less than two hours ago she was alive and full of plans and promise, looking for a new job, full of hope.

"They're on their way, Molly," Casey said as he approached. "Are you sure you don't want to wait inside? You'd be more comfortable there."

I shook my head, my gaze narrowing on my niece. Anger banked for now, waiting. "I'm not going anywhere until I have some answers, Casey," I said in a cold voice.

Casey stared at me. "I'm not sure you're going to get answers, Molly. Crimes like this are usually random and drug-related. Smash and grab. Steal a purse. Usually muggers don't kill unless the victim fights back."

"Karen would fight back."

Casey nodded, watching me. "You're probably right."

"How long before the police get here?"

"Probably a few minutes more. Don't worry. My friend got right on it. The cops will be all over the car. If the guy left any prints, maybe they can match 'em. If he's got a record."

That comment sparked a thought. I pointed to the car. "I want Karen's keys. Would you get them for me, Casey?"

Casey peered at me. "I don't think we should remove anything from the car, Molly."

Once again, I didn't ask. I simply ordered. "I'll be damned if I leave my niece's apartment and office keys for everyone to paw through. Leave the car key. I'm keeping the rest."

Casey observed me a second longer before he went to the car. He returned and dropped a handful of loose keys into my open palm. "I left the car key on the ring so it wouldn't look strange."

I dropped the keys into the deep pocket of my silk jacket, then held out my palm once more. "And I want Karen's Black-Berry, Casey. I'll need it to call her friends."

Casey hesitated. "Don't you think we should give that to the police, Molly?"

I shook my head slowly, my gaze never leaving his, while I let my voice drop an octave. "It was between the car seat and the door. That's why it dropped to the street. The killer never saw it."

Casey observed me for a few seconds longer, then dropped the smooth black cell phone into my hand.

■ ■ ■ ■

I sipped the strong black tea Luisa had made for me while I watched the District of Columbia's finest scurry about Karen's car. Casey and Albert stood on either side of me. Two high-beam lamps sat on the sidewalk, bathing the car and the street surrounding it in a garish white light.

Bright yellow taillights flashed as the ambulance carrying Karen's shrouded body backed up, beeping its high-pitched warning sound before slowly driving away. The awful image of my vivacious and beautiful niece lying lifeless inside that body bag darted in front of my eyes, haunting me. I shut my eyes, willing it away, but the remnants of the image stayed on the back of my mind.

The police detective who had questioned me earlier was squatting on the sidewalk beside the car with another investigator. They both pointed at the bloodied windshield and interior of the car, the broken driver's window, the shattered glass spread across the street. Tiny shards reflected the harsh glare of the lamps.

"Schroeder is one of the best, Molly. He doesn't miss anything," Casey said as he stood with folded arms, observing the scene.

"Good. That means he'll catch the scum who did this." I replied, voice still cold despite the tea.

Casey glanced my way. "He'll try, Molly. I can promise you that. But these crimes are hard to solve. If there aren't any witnesses, there're no clues to go on."

"Maybe the neighbors saw something," I suggested, glancing over my shoulder toward the darkened windows of the sedate brick townhouses lining the street behind me. Barely a lighted window could be seen along the block.

Most residents were either asleep or did not wish to be involved. They opted to ignore the disturbance outside in true Georgetown cave dweller style. But I knew they were watching. Peering around draperies and peeking through shutters. They were there, all right. Discreetly observing everything.

Casey glanced around the block with the practiced eye of a security man who had already checked out the neighborhood. "Doesn't look like many neighbors are awake now, but the detectives will interview them tomorrow, I'm sure."

I watched Detective Schroeder stand up, still talking to the other investigator, and point across the street. Then pocketing his notepad, he headed our way. I waited until he was closer before beginning my own interrogation.

"Did you find anything, Detective? Anything at all?"

Schroeder looked at me with red-rimmed eyes. He could have been in his forties or fifties. It was hard to tell. His face was lined, either with age or witnessing too many gruesome scenes like this one. "We've just started investigating, Ms. Malone. Your niece's car will be taken to our police lot and examined further. We may get lucky and match some prints."

"You found the purse, right? I saw you holding a bag that looked like Karen's a few minutes ago."

"Yes, ma'am. One of our officers found it at the corner curb, thrown near the drain." He pointed down the street. "It was empty. Looks like the thief grabbed the wallet and anything else valuable and tossed the rest down the drain. There was only a lipstick and some tissues inside."

"You mean the killer," I said, clenching the mug tighter.

Schroeder nodded. "It looks to be a mugging turned murder. Some thug saw Ms. Grayson in her car alone and decided to make a quick score. Smash and grab. Maybe your niece tried to resist or something, and he shot her." His gaze turned sympathetic. "I know this may be hard to understand, but crimes like this happen. Like any big city, Washington has its share of criminals."

I fixed him with an ironic look. "You don't have to explain Washington to me, Detective. I grew up across the river in Arlington. I'm well aware of this city's violent side. All the monuments are deceptive. Washington can be ugly."

Schroeder arched a brow. "Well, then, ma'am, I don't have to tell you how easy it is for this to happen. Georgetown streets are dark and tree lined, which makes it easier for muggers to conceal themselves. And most streets lead either to parks or busy congested avenues, where they can slip out of sight. So it's easy to mug someone and run."

I pondered the smash and grab theory he'd proposed. "So, he took the time to climb into Karen's car to steal her purse and her briefcase. Yet he left her Rolex watch. I saw it on her arm. Why wouldn't he take that too?"

The expression in Schroeder's eyes shifted. "As I said, Ms. Malone. This was most likely a crime of opportunity. The mugger saw Ms. Grayson alone in her car and took the chance. When she resisted, he shot her. After that, he probably grabbed the closest valuables and took off."

I had to admit that scenario made a kind of brutal sense. I was about to ask something else, when the other investigator walked up to Schroeder. I recognized Karen's briefcase in his plastic-gloved hand. "That's Karen's," I said, pointing.

"Where'd you find it?" Schroeder asked him.

"Two blocks down Q Street. All that's left inside are pens, calculator, and some file folders," the man answered. "I'll give it to the guys to take to the lab."

He returned to a cluster of officers across the street, while Schroeder returned to his notebook, pulling it from his pocket. "You said earlier that Ms. Grayson definitely carried her laptop in her briefcase, right?"

"Always."

Schroeder peered at his notes, flipping through pages for a minute. "And the last time you spoke with your niece was approximately nine o'clock this evening when she went outside to make phone calls, correct?"

I nodded.

"Do you recall if your niece was upset or

anxious about anything, Ms. Malone? Was there anything bothering her?"

I paused, choosing my words. "Yes, Detective, there was. She'd just had a heated argument with her boss and planned to quit her job with Congressman Jackson's office. That's why she was outside in her car tonight, making phone calls. She was trying to land another congressional staff position." I glanced toward the strange play of shadows on the street, feeling the unmistakable bite of guilt. "She was waiting for me to leave a political reception. We were planning to return to Northern Virginia where I'm staying with family."

Schroeder scribbled busily. "Who was hosting this reception? Which home?" He pointed toward the surrounding houses.

"It was Senator John Russell's reception," I said as quietly as possible.

"And did this heated argument between your niece and her employer take place at that same reception?"

Damn. I didn't want to drag Senator Russell into this. "Yes, it was, but the senator was nowhere near —"

"Can we keep the senator's name out of the press, Detective?" Casey cut in.

Schroeder exchanged a glance with Casey, then returned to flipping notebook pages.

"We'll see what we can do."

Albert spoke up then, in a softer tone. "Are you nearly finished with interviewing Ms. Malone, Detective? Her family has arrived to take her back home." He pointed toward the shadowed sidewalk down the street.

I turned and peered into the dark, trying to see despite the harsh glare of the lights. Shading my eyes, I thought I spotted Nan and Bill standing to the side of some uniformed officers. I waved.

"Of course, of course," Schroeder said. "I know this has been hard for you, Ms. Malone, and I do appreciate your cooperation. Just one last question . . ."

"Certainly," I said, barely paying attention. All I could see was my family walking toward me, ready to take me away from the glare and the gruesome signs of murder. I could feel tears pressing inside, ready for release. I could hold them off until I was safe inside Nan and Bill's car. I had to.

"You said Ms. Grayson had argued with her boss. Was that Congressman Jackson from Nebraska?"

"No, no," I said, starting to back away from Schroeder. "It was Jed Molinoff, the congressman's chief of staff. He was Karen's boss."

Without another word, I turned around, ran to the open embrace of my family, and threw myself into their arms.

Six

"I probably won't find a place to park around here, so I'll keep driving around the neighborhood until you finish," Deb said as she turned onto Seventh Street.

I glanced around Karen's Capitol Hill neighborhood in Southeast Washington. Tidy brick rowhouses lined the street. Not a single parking space to be seen. Parking never changes in Washington.

"That's fine. I'll call you when I'm leaving her apartment. It shouldn't take me too long. I don't want to be up there any longer than I have to. It'll feel weird without Karen."

"Want me to find a garage and park so we can go up together?"

I shook my head. "Naw, I'll be all right. I'm just going to check her closet and find one of those dresses she wore to a White House dinner. It was a beautiful azure blue. Gorgeous."

"Oh, don't forget lingerie."

"Right, right. Thanks for reminding me. And I've got to check her desk for legal files. Get a copy of her will and other stuff. We'll need that."

"Poor baby girl," Deb fell back on the same phrase that she'd been repeating for the last two days since Karen's death.

I didn't say anything. I concentrated on reading the addresses of the rowhouses as we drove past. Getting closer. I spotted the trim beige brick rowhouse, planters filled with blooming yellow and red tulips. Late March's sunnier days and frequent showers had turned Washington into a garden. The entire city was in bloom.

"There it is." I pointed. "Pull beside that convertible and I'll jump out."

Deb deftly moved the Jaguar beside the parked cars. "Okay, I'll see how long I can hang out here before I start cruising the area. Keep your fingers crossed that neighbors don't think I'm a stalker or baby snatcher."

I grabbed the small suitcase I'd brought as I pushed open the car door. "Why don't you call that funeral home and make sure their office will be open tonight so we can drop off everything."

"Good idea," Deb said as she flipped open

her phone.

I fished inside my purse for the key ring where I'd put all of Karen's keys while I raced up the concrete steps. Curved wrought iron railings graced either side of the steps leading to the front stoop. I sorted through the keys until I found the one that opened the navy blue entry door.

I stepped into a foyer with a long hallway accented by two wide columns. Doorways were on both sides of the hallway, and a staircase led to the upper floors. Like many townhomes, this one had been remodeled for separate apartments. Karen's was on the second floor. Not seeing anyone around, I assumed the other residents were at work, dutifully toiling away at some governmental agency desk. How would the government run without them?

I started up the stairs, sorting through the keys until I found the one for Karen's apartment. As I rounded the landing, I glimpsed a man leaving Karen's apartment above. Startled, I darted back around the banister, out of sight. *Who was that?*

I peered through the railings and saw Jed Molinoff stuffing something into his jacket pocket before he closed Karen's apartment door. *What the hell is he doing here?*

The familiar sound of a BlackBerry buzz

caused Molinoff to pause in the hallway. I took the opportunity to stealthily back down the lower stairway.

"Hey, honey, what's up?" he said as his footsteps sounded above me.

I scurried away from the stairs and hid sideways behind one of the hallway columns.

"How'd Billy play last night?" Did he get a hit?" his voice came louder as he descended the stairs.

Son of a bitch. He's talking to his wife while he's still in Karen's apartment building.

"Second base? Hey, that's great. Tell him 'Good job!' I'll call after dinner, okay?"

I heard the entry door open and close with Molinoff on the other side. No more family banter.

I stepped from behind the column. *What was that bastard doing in Karen's apartment?* Hurrying up the stairs, I quickly unlocked the door and stepped inside.

Karen's apartment looked as welcoming and inviting as it always did. The warm tones of rich cherry American Colonial furniture, soft green and blue plaids, colorful accent cushions, and everything in its place.

A lump rose in my throat, remembering

the last time I'd visited Karen here. It was a year ago, and we relaxed and drank a good Aussie Shiraz while we talked. She recounted various "Hill stories" while I laughed. Politicians never changed, despite their promises. The good, the bad, and the ugly. Capitol Hill had them all.

I slowly walked through the living and dining rooms, looking for anything out of place. It didn't feel right being here without Karen. I pushed the bedroom door all the way open and glanced about the room. The Colonial style extended to her bedroom. A rich, red cedar chest sat in the corner of the room. All was neat and tidy, bed made with almost military-squared corners, nothing scattered about. Karen was a compulsive neatness freak. I spotted Karen's blue velvet jewelry box atop the maple dresser. Lifting the box's lid, I took brief notice of the jewelry inside then stored it inside the suitcase I'd brought along.

Checking her closet, I surveyed her wardrobe, going through hanger by hanger, until I found the beautiful blue gown. Karen had already safely stored it in a garment bag, neatly labeled of course. Remembering Deb's admonition, I returned to the dresser and searched through Karen's lingerie, until I found a luscious silken set. Stashing that

150

with the gown in the suitcase, I left the bedroom.

Glancing about the apartment again, I still couldn't see anything out of place. What was Jed doing here, I wondered? Maybe he'd left some of his belongings, clothing or toiletries. I was about to hurry to the front door when I remembered Karen's will and legal papers.

I settled at the Colonial-style desk and started checking drawers. The first two on the left side held file folders, personnel and work-related. The bottom drawer held computer supplies. Her printer and scanner sat lonely on the desktop. Useless without her laptop and files.

Then I opened the top drawer on the right side. A jumble greeted me. Bright yellow photo envelopes were turned upside down, sideways, and wedged haphazardly. The drawer was a mess. There was no way Karen Grayson could leave a drawer looking like that.

Now I knew what Jed Molinoff had come looking for. *Photos.* Probably photos they'd taken of themselves when they were together, here in Washington or on his boat in Chesapeake Bay. Proof of their clandestine relationship.

I checked some of the envelopes. They

held photos of family or friends, vacations in New England and back in Colorado. But there were also photos of my niece smiling at the camera, sitting at cafes and on boardwalks. Photos taken by someone else, most probably Molinoff. I straightened the packages in the drawer before closing it, that familiar lump returning to my throat, as well as a simmering anger at Jed Molinoff, who'd been brazen enough to come into his slain lover's apartment to remove all traces of himself and their relationship. *Bastard.*

Yanking open the bottom drawer, I finally found what I'd come for — an old-fashioned accordion-style folder marked "Legal Documents." Inside were her life insurance policy, apartment lease, deed on her parent's land back in Colorado, and a legal file containing my niece's Last Will and Testament. Those words gnawed at me inside. Much too young to die.

Checking the center drawer, I found Karen's passport, checkbook, and bank statements. I shoved everything into the suitcase, then headed for the door. The uneasiness I felt being alone in Karen's apartment had grown into a creepy feeling. Molinoff had been here too, which meant he had a key. He could come back again. Time to install a bolt lock.

Passing the kitchen, I noticed the telephone and answering machine on the edge of the counter. The answering machine had the number "3" lit up in red. Three messages. I hit "Play."

The first message was garbled, and I couldn't understand it. Another was from a solicitor, and the third was from a department store saying her order was ready. Ordinary calls except for one thing. The last call was received today, only two hours ago, yet it wasn't blinking as a new message. It had already been played. I stared at the bright red numeral "3."

Jed Molinoff. It had to be. Who else would be brazen enough to listen to Karen's calls? The landlord certainly wouldn't. What the hell was Molinoff playing her messages for? Had he left an angry message on her machine after their last argument on Saturday?

Suddenly my cell phone rang, startling me. I jumped. The total quiet of Karen's apartment was really getting to me. Creepiness creeping closer.

"Molly, are you through yet?" Deb asked. "I've been around these blocks so many times, the neighbors are gonna think I'm casing the houses to rob them."

"I'm on my way now," I promised, hurrying for the door. Homing in on Deb's voice like a beacon, I slammed Karen's apartment door behind me, checking to make sure it was locked. Then I raced down the stairs.

Raymond spotted the man the moment he entered the sports bar. His barely-seen-the-sun pale skin was a dead giveaway. Too many hours sequestered in Capitol Hill offices under fluorescent lights. Out of place with most of the weekend soccer and rugby jocks that filled the nearby barstools.

Motioning the man over to his booth, Raymond caught the eye of a passing waitress. "Can I get a refill?" he asked, pointing to the coffeepot in her hand.

"Sure thing, sir." The middle-aged woman poured a black stream into Raymond's cup, then smiled at the man who approached. "Coffee, sir?"

"No, thanks," the younger man replied as he slid into the other side of the booth.

"I take it you're Larry." Raymond checked his watch. "What took you so long?"

Glancing around the noisy sports bar, something that passed for a smile pulled the edges of Larry's mouth. "Do you know how many traffic lights there are on Route 50? I've been driving for nearly two hours. Whatever possessed you to pick Fairfax Circle?"

"I figured you'd enjoy a drive in the Virginia countryside," Raymond said sarcastically. "You guys spend too much time in D.C."

Larry gave a snort. "Countryside, my ass. It's shopping centers and condos all the way to Winchester. You should have found a place in Arlington. That way I could have taken the Metro and saved hours."

"Oh, sure. Like some coffee house in Clarendon or Courthouse Road? You forget those places are nests of condos stuffed with government workers. You'd be spotted before you got your latte." He reached inside his jacket and withdrew a white envelope, then placed it on the table between them. "Have you moved into the office yet?"

"I should be in this week. There's a rush on my paperwork." His smile turned to a smirk. "He can't get me there fast enough."

"Do you expect any blowback from fellow staffers? Considering your, uh . . . less-than-graceful exit."

The smirk disappeared. "Nothing I can't handle. In fact, part of my new duties will be to oversee personnel and take care of any problems."

"Watching over the straying sheep, huh?"

"Something like that."

"Talk about putting a wolf in the fold," Raymond laughed deep in his throat until that pesky cough kicked in.

Larry waited until Raymond stopped coughing, then pointed to the envelope. "Is that the language they want inserted in the bill?"

Raymond nodded, then took a deep drink of coffee. He needed to get outside so he could smoke. "Think you can get it done?"

The smirk played with Larry's mouth again. "For certain. I've been feeding Jed data all these weeks I've been away. Believe me, he's eating out of my hand."

SEVEN

"Goodness, Molly. We didn't expect you so soon," Luisa said as she stood in the open doorway. "We thought you'd be taking more time off to be with your family."

"They're all gone, Luisa," I said as I stepped inside the Russell mansion's foyer. Somehow the cool elegance felt welcoming, with its burnished woods and crystal chandeliers. I felt myself relax. "My two daughters and their families flew back to Colorado yesterday. Nan's and Deb's kids returned to their homes in North Carolina and Maryland last evening."

"The senator said there was a large turnout at the church service."

"Yes, I was surprised how many people came. It was truly heartwarming." I stopped myself from saying more.

Both my daughters and their families had gathered, along with Nan's and Deb's children. Cousins all, they'd grown up visiting each other in Virginia and in Colorado. Since Karen had grown up with my girls, she was considered one of the cousins, too.

"Peter said you were the only family your niece had."

"That's right. Karen's father, Eric, was my husband Dave's older brother. Both Eric and his wife, Alicia, died in a tragic auto accident several years ago while he was serving in Congress. Even the grandparents had already passed away. So, my cousins and I were the only connection to family Karen had left."

"Well, I'm so glad they were able to be with you, Molly. We need our families with us in times of loss," she said, looking at me with compassion.

I patted her arm and smiled. "You're right, Luisa. And we need time to heal. That's why I've come back to work. I'll heal faster if I'm busy. And I'm dying to see my office. Albert said it was being cleaned when all of this happened."

Luisa nodded. "Well, then, let me show you. It's all ready, but there've been a few additions since it was cleaned," she said as she walked down the long hallway.

"Additions? You mean computer equipment or something?" I followed after her, glancing into the formal dining room and living room as I passed.

"No, we had all of that. These additions are temporary, I'm afraid. They won't last long." She paused in front of a door at the end of the hallway. Light shone through a lace-curtained window. "I'm glad you returned to see them," she said with a smile as she opened a door.

I stepped inside the room, which was a miniature version of the wood-paneled library. Burnished mahogany shone on walls, bookshelves, and the desk. At least I think it was mahogany. It was hard to tell because my cozy wood-paneled office was filled with flowers. On the lamp table, on the bookshelves, and covering the desk. Even the corner file cabinet had a vase of flowers. Roses of every color, daisies, daffodils, lilacs, even sprigs of cherry blossoms.

"Oh, my God," I breathed, stunned by the beauty of it all. *Where did all these flowers come from?*

Eleanor McKenzie had sent flowers to Nan's and Deb's houses. As had Senator Baker and his wife. So had the few old Washington friends who knew I was in town. And all my Colorado friends had Nan's address. Even my ex-husband Frank sent a spray. I wondered, who would have sent flowers here?

I paused at each display and inhaled the fragrances, admiring the delicate and bold colors. Each tag was signed the same. "I was so very sorry to hear about the death of your niece. DD." *Who in the world was "DD"?*

"Aren't they beautiful?" Luisa asked from the doorway.

"They're gorgeous, Luisa, but I don't recognize the sender. Do you think there was a mistake?"

Luisa shook her head. "Not at all. The man who brought them said they were for Molly Malone."

I puzzled over who "DD" could be, running through all the names of acquaintances and friends in Colorado and Washington. No faces came to mind.

"That's so strange. I don't know anyone who goes by the initials 'DD.' "

"Maybe you have an admirer who followed you here from Colorado," Luisa said with a mischievous smile. "He was very handsome."

I had to laugh. "Believe me, I don't have any admirers back in Colorado who'd be besotted enough to follow me to D.C." I looked around the room, admiring the display again. "Well, wherever they came from, we'll enjoy them while they last. But we'll have to move some of them because I can't find my desk."

Luisa picked up two vases and resettled them on the windowsills. "I'll bring you some coffee, Molly, if you'd like."

"Oh, yes, please. That would be wonderful." Surely I had landed in accountant heaven. A gorgeous office, filled with flowers yet, and someone was bringing me coffee. It didn't get better than that.

I quickly familiarized myself with my surroundings, checking drawers and the computer, printer, and scanner. All ready to go, and so was I. I flipped the switch and listened to the reassuring hum of circuits firing up.

Technology had addicted us all. We were like Pavlov's dogs, waiting for monitor screens to come alive. We couldn't get information fast enough, so addicted were we to our many forms of instant communication. How did we ever manage before? Clearly, we'd forgotten how. Meanwhile, we were all dragging around an invisible electronic tether that required us to be constantly available. *We hadn't bargained on that, had we?*

Watching the desktop icons pop into view, I was about to click on one when my cell phone rang. Stifling my annoyance at being interrupted, I reached for the flashing screen.

"Ms. Malone? Detective Schroeder, here."

All traces of annoyance disappeared. "Yes, Detective. Do you have any news? Did you find any fingerprints in the car? Anything at all?"

"There were a lot of prints in the car, Ms. Malone, as you can imagine. Unfortunately, none of them matched any of our databases. Most of the prints belonged to Ms. Grayson. So, I'm afraid that's a dead end. However, we did find one neighbor who was walking his dogs that night. He said he was going down Q Street and saw a man get out of a car that was parked along the side. When he passed the car, he glimpsed a woman sitting inside, but he didn't take a good look at her. But he does remember that his dogs acted excited and started barking as he passed the car. That's why he remembered."

My heart skipped a beat. "Did he get a look at the man? Could he describe him at all?"

"Only from the back, I'm afraid. He said the man was medium build and was wearing jeans and a dark jacket with a hood covering his head. He also said the man walked away from the car very fast and appeared to be holding something under his arm."

"That had to be Karen's briefcase and purse."

"We thought so, too. I wish there was more to go on, Ms. Malone. But at least it seems to confirm our theory of a mugging gone bad."

I pondered that for a second. "But wouldn't he run away? I mean, he just killed my niece. Wouldn't he be scared and run?"

"Most criminals who prey on people like your niece are pretty cold-blooded. And they wouldn't run because that would arouse suspicion in a passerby's mind. Walking away fast looks more normal."

What Detective Schroeder said made sense, I had to admit. Even though there was probably no hope of finding that scum without an identification, I pressed anyway. "Is there any hope at all that you'll find him, Detective? Be honest."

Schroeder sighed. "Honestly, Ms. Malone, it's slim to nonexistent. Unless he brags about the score, and we get a tip. Or we get lucky and happen to arrest someone he hangs with who wants to cut a deal. Otherwise, we have nothing to go on. I'm sorry."

"I figured as much, Detective. Please let me know if you learn anything else. And thank you . . . for everything you've done. My family and I appreciate it."

"You're welcome, Ms. Malone. And condolences to you and your family."

Tossing my cell phone to the desk, I reached for the folders that lay beside the computer. I needed to get my head back where it belonged: working. Inside the folders I saw pages of budgets. Budgets and numbers. I needed those numbers right now. They were reassuring, soothing, somehow. I could disappear in them. Nothing like numbers to get me back on track.

I sank into my cushioned desk chair as I lost myself in the numbers. I barely even noticed Luisa bringing the coffee.

Something brought me out of the cloud of Senator Russell's accounts. Was that the doorbell, I wondered? The doorbell sounded again, and I suddenly remembered I was on "door duty" while Luisa and Albert were away on an errand.

Scrambling from behind my desk, I hurried from my office and down the hall, hoping the visitor was still there. What if it was a messenger from the Hill? How embarrassing if I left them standing on the doorstep my very first day at the office.

I yanked the heavy door open. No one was

164

there. Then I saw the spray of flowers sitting on the front step. Glimpsing a man at the front gate, I raced down the steps.

"Wait! Sir! Could you wait, please?" I called after him, determined to learn if the floral messenger knew who the mysterious "DD" was.

The man turned at the gate, looked at me for a second, then began to walk back. As I approached him, I realized he didn't look like a delivery man at all. He was too well-dressed. Casual, but expensive casual. His brown leather jacket looked soft as butter.

Now that I was closer, I also noticed that Luisa hadn't lied. He was definitely good-looking. Very good-looking. His dark brown hair had flecks of silver running through it, and his face was tanned with an outdoors kind of tan.

"Sexy," Crazy Ass whispered in my ear before Sober-and-Righteous smacked her.

"Did you deliver all those beautiful flowers this week?" I asked. "They're simply gorgeous."

The man smiled. "Yes, I did."

"I'm Molly Malone, and I wanted to thank the sender for being so thoughtful. This has been a difficult time for our family."

"I believe the sender wanted to convey his

165

deepest sympathy on the tragic death of your niece."

"Well, I sincerely appreciate his kindness. But I confess I'm confused. I don't know anyone named 'DD.' Do you know this person?"

His smile spread to his eyes this time. I stared back. *Where had I seen that smile before?*

"He's an admirer of yours."

I blinked. "You're kidding. I don't have any admirers who would send me that many flowers. Not in Colorado and certainly not in Washington." I gave him a skeptical look. "Who is this guy, and how'd he find me?"

He pulled a folded newspaper from inside his jacket and opened it, then held up the page with my jacklighted deer photo. "Picture doesn't do you justice, Molly. You're much prettier than that."

I stared at the *D.C. Dirt,* newspaper of infamy, and closed my eyes. *Great.* A stalker. A handsome stalker, but a stalker, nonetheless. And this day had started out so well.

I pointed at him. "You're 'DD'?"

"Yes, I am."

"And you're a stalker. Great. Now I know I should go back to Colorado. Nobody cared enough to stalk me there. I haven't been in D.C. two weeks, and I've been insulted in the press, and now I'm being stalked. Wonderful."

"I'm not a stalker, Molly. I'm an old friend."

"Oh, *really?*" I allowed sarcasm to drench my voice.

"It was a long time ago, Molly."

"Uh-huh." I nodded, clearly humoring him. Apparently my alluring photo had attracted a disturbed, good-looking stalker. *Where were all the sane men?*

"We went to high school together in Arlington."

I wasn't expecting that, and it must have shown, because he laughed softly while I remembered to close my mouth. Maybe he wasn't a stalker after all. "You went to Washington-Lee?"

"Well, I certainly didn't go to that prissy girls' school."

That made me smile. "Yeah, I don't think you would have passed the physical."

"You've got the same smile, Molly."

That made me feel good for some reason I didn't understand. Maybe because it had been a really tough two weeks. I folded my arms and looked him up and down, allowing my memory to slip into the past again.

"Were we in the same class or something?" I approached closer, studying his face, hoping I'd recall. So far, nothing.

"Yeah, English and History, I think . . . I only remember *you*."

I stared up into his face, knowing I'd seen that smile, that devil-be-damned look in those dark eyes before. A long time ago.

Suddenly — out of nowhere — a torrent of memories surged through my mind, images from that long-ago past flashing in front of my eyes, startling me with their intensity. The scent of cherry blossoms in the spring, a rust-colored setting sun reflecting off the Tidal Basin, a spirited argument on the steps of the Lincoln Memorial. Words of war and dreams. A kiss in the twilight.

My mouth dropped open again as I stared into his face. "Danny?" I whispered. "Danny DiMateo?"

The light in his eyes deepened. "You remember."

Boy, did I. The memories flooded through me now, bringing a strange sensation inside — a lightness I hadn't felt in a long time.

"My God, Danny . . ." I breathed. "It's been years ago."

"Nineteen sixty-nine."

I remembered it all. Years of fire and rage. And Vietnam. Danny and I had argued for over an hour beneath Abe Lincoln's statue.

Danny was joining the Marines right after high school graduation. I couldn't believe it. The war was tearing the country apart, and Danny couldn't wait to get there. His dad had fought with the Marines in the Second World War.

"Nineteen sixty-nine," I reminisced. "I was leaving for college, and you were leaving for Vietnam. How . . . how long did you stay?"

"Long enough. Two tours." The light in his eyes changed.

"Thank God you made it out alive."

"More or less."

Somehow I couldn't break eye contact. "I worried about you," I said without thinking. *Where had that come from?*

The warm smile returned. "Maybe that helped."

I could feel his smile reach inside, and it felt good. Way too good. I needed to back off. Things were stirring inside me that I hadn't felt for a long time. I glanced away for a second. "Do you live in Washington now?"

He nodded. "Ever since I retired from the Corps five years ago."

I stared at Danny again. Couldn't help it. "You were a career Marine? My God, Danny, the world's blown up since high school, and you've probably been right in the middle of it."

"Pretty much. Special Forces."

I closed my eyes and grimaced on purpose while he laughed. "Why am I not surprised? You probably went from Vietnam right into a nest of guerrillas in some jungle."

"Actually, they sent me to college after those two Nam tours. By the time I got my degree, the Middle East was on fire. The jungle came later."

I let admiration color my voice. "An officer and a gentleman. That doesn't surprise me, either. You did good, Danny."

"Thanks. So did you, Molly. That's why I'm not surprised to see you working for Senator Russell. I've kept track of your career over the years. I had a feeling you'd be back in Washington one of these days."

My mouth dropped open again. *Damn.* I had to stop doing that. "You kept track of *me?* My God, Danny, my life is pretty boring. You need a retirement hobby. Why don't you take your wife traveling?" *Now, why in the world did I say that?*

"Divorced."

That was why. Well, no points for subtlety. If Crazy Ass didn't stop messing with me, *I* was going to slap her.

"Ah, yes, happens to a lot of us. But, if

you've been keeping track, you already knew that."

"You're right. So I figured you might like a reliable escort to help you reacquaint yourself with your old hometown," he said with entirely too engaging a grin. "Since you've moved back, that is. Are you living in D.C. or Virginia?"

"Actually, I live just a few blocks away on P Street. The senator's chief of staff is letting me stay in one of his vacant townhouses. For free, believe it or not. It's a long story."

"Well, I've got the time. Why don't you let me introduce you to some of my favorite coffee shops around here. Or maybe lunch."

Just then, Luisa's voice called from the front step. "Molly, I'm back. Did you learn who sent the flowers?"

I gestured to Danny. "Turns out 'DD' is an old friend from high school."

"Well, isn't that nice. Why don't you two catch up over lunch," she said as she hastened down the steps. I noticed she was carrying my purse.

The images of accounts and spreadsheets danced in front of my eyes for a minute. "I really should get back to work."

"Nonsense, Molly. You've worked enough for your first day. You should take it slowly,"

Luisa said, handing me the purse. "Now, run along and enjoy this beautiful afternoon with your friend. Everything's under control here." She gave a little wave and smiled before hurrying back to the house.

"Sounds like good advice," Danny said, gesturing toward the gate. "I have a café in mind I think you'll like. It's only a few blocks away."

I fell into step with him as we headed out to the sidewalk. "I've wanted to wander down Wisconsin Avenue and explore but hadn't found the time yet. There's so much to do, moving in." I glanced down the quiet residential street and the overarching trees that had leafed out in lime spring green. Old memories poked through. "Some things look exactly the same as when I . . . when we lived here. And some things are totally changed."

After several seconds of silent walking, Danny's voice came quietly. "Molly, let me say right now how very sorry I am about your husband's death years ago. That was tragic. I know you were devastated. I could tell. That picture in the paper of you and your little girls nearly broke my heart. I won't mention it again, I promise."

Wow. This conversation was going where no man had gone before. And . . . it was okay. I was okay. I turned and studied Danny for a long moment, while he stood unperturbed by my scrutiny.

"It's okay, Danny. Time has passed." I shrugged. "We heal, if we're lucky."

Danny glanced down. "Yeah, we do. We heal or die."

I'd glimpsed empathy in the depths of those dark brown eyes. Even so, I deliberately chose a lighter tone. "Scars on the inside, right?"

"Oh, yeah." He started walking again. "C'mon, let's have lunch. You can fill me in on this new job with Senator Russell on the way."

"Well, I guess I can't beat a badass ex-Marine escort, can I? I ought to be safe from stalkers for sure," I said, joining him as we headed down the sidewalk. "Marines probably eat stalkers for breakfast."

"Marines eat sand."

It felt good to laugh. A stray thought wiggled from the back of my brain. Something Danny had said. "How did you see my photo in the paper all those years ago? Weren't you on duty somewhere?"

"Yeah, but I always had the *Post* mailed to me."

I spotted the increased traffic as we neared Wisconsin Avenue. "Dave died in 1983.

Where were you then?"

"Beirut."

I changed the subject as we turned the corner.

Swirling the Vouvray in my wineglass, I savored the delicate aroma while I gazed out at the tulip-filled flower boxes that lined the café's patio overlooking the Chesapeake and Ohio Canal. Tourists in souvenir tee-shirts strolled along the towpath below, their voices muffled by the overhanging trees and surrounding bushes.

We'd chosen to walk to the café, which took us along treelined Georgetown streets, across the crowded main thoroughfare of M Street, then down to the towpath that bordered the canal. I saw restaurants paralleling the canal that weren't there years ago. Clearly, I needed to rediscover my hometown.

Strolling along the towpath that barge-pulling mules once trod, I confessed my anger and frustration over the investigation into my niece's death. Police had nothing substantial to go on, so the mugger-killer would get away with murder. Danny expressed his sorrow again over Karen's death — in words this time, rather than flowers. As we joined the tourists enjoying the early

April sunshine, I explained my new position with Senator Russell as well as the triple whammy of events that had brought me back to Washington.

Conversation flowed as easily and as smoothly as the Potomac River, only a couple of blocks away. Talk turned personal at lunch. Danny admitted his reluctance to accept his last promotion, knowing that "bird colonels" were usually stuck behind a desk in D.C. He'd traded off one overseas assignment after another so he could keep the desk at bay for a while longer. Special Forces had spoiled him to the adrenaline rush of action. Washington was too slow for him, and Danny confessed he'd gotten married a second time out of boredom. Either that or the city had rotted his brain.

After I stopped laughing, I admitted my own poor track record at a second marriage. Maybe I hadn't remarried out of boredom, but loneliness was a poor excuse, too. I sensed that was closer to Danny's rationale as well. By the time we'd finished a delicate broiled salmon and the last glass of wine was poured, our conversation had settled into the comfortable, relaxed cadence of friends who'd been talking to each other for years instead of hours. Silence interspersed with sharing.

I glanced out at the canal flowing within its ordered locks, the towpath winding beneath the trees. Memories flitted through my mind again. I used to run along this towpath in the mornings when the kids were in preschool.

"Thanks for taking me here, Danny. This has always been one of my favorite places. Can people still run on the towpath? That would be a great way to start my day."

Danny set his empty wineglass on the table. "Yeah, but there are some places that are safer than others. Why don't you go running with me first, and I can show you a safe route."

"Go running with an ex-Marine? You'd leave me in your dust." I drained the last delectable drop of Vouvray.

"I'll throttle back. Besides, we can finish up at another favorite outdoor cafe for breakfast. You know Washington. This gorgeous weather will be gone in a heartbeat."

"True enough," I said with a sigh, as I drank in the colors surrounding me much as I had the wine earlier. "Is that offer of tour guide still good? It looks like I need to relearn this city."

"Absolutely. How's this weekend?"

"Saturday would work. Nan and Bill have already planned something for Sunday."

He withdrew his data phone. "Okay. I'll give you a call this week. What's your number?"

I rattled off my cell number, realizing that in so doing I was agreeing to see this man again. This man from my past. That surprised me. Of course, it delighted the heck out of Crazy Ass and sent Sober into a scowling pout, muttering that only a week or so ago I had "sworn off men."

I didn't care. I'd relaxed this afternoon, completely relaxed. And considering the traumatic events that had happened since I arrived in Washington nearly two weeks ago, relaxation was something I needed a lot more of.

"You've got my card. That has my cell. Call me anytime, Molly."

"Your card says you're consulting. Not surprising. Like most retired brass. Who're you working for, or can you say?"

"Mostly I consult for private clients."

I'd noticed he said 'mostly.' Intrigued, I pressed for more. Couldn't help it. That was my nature. "What the heck is operational logistics?"

"You know the old saying, Molly. 'If I told you, I'd have to kill you,' " he said with a smile.

"This is your idea of retirement? Sounds

like you're still skating on the edge of that scary stuff."

"I simply give advice and counsel."

"Uh-huh." I glanced at my watch and was shocked by the time. "Oh my gosh! It's after three o'clock! I should get back to the office." Sober gave me a jab.

"But we haven't had coffee yet," he said as he flagged down the waiter.

Watching the efficient waiter scurry off with our coffee orders, I remarked, "I'm amazed they've let us sit here so long." I glanced around the empty café. "We're the only ones here."

"I let them know that we'd be lingering over lunch and requested we be undisturbed. As I said, I'm a regular."

I laughed softly as I leaned forward, resting my arms on the table. "That had to be some tip."

"It was worth it."

"That's flattering as hell, Danny."

I could feel that bad-boy smile of his working the same magic inside that it had years ago. *Good Lord.* Was this a second childhood, or had I never left the first? *Beats me.*

"I'm glad you notice."

"Notice? How could I not? You're like a laser beam. And I thought *I* was focused."

"Can't help it, Molly. Old habits. Focus keeps you alive."

"Yeah, but it's kind of intimidating. I feel like there's a red light dancing on my forehead. Am I the one who got away or something?"

Danny laughed as he leaned back into his chair, allowing the waiter to serve our coffees. "Sorry, Molly. Didn't mean to spook you. I'm simply glad to see you after all these years."

I decided to see if I could throw him off balance, just for the hell of it. I settled back into my chair and sent him a wicked smile. "Danny, you live in Washington, D.C., where single women outnumber single men five to one or more. You can't tell me you've been lacking for female companionship."

Danny met my gaze and held it, while he laughed. "That's true. But you're different. You always have been. That's why I've never been able to forget you, Molly."

That felt *way* too good. So good I had to break off eye contact. Okay, he won that point. "Well, thanks to the *D.C. Dirt,* no one in Washington will be able to forget me." I sipped my coffee. Strong and rich with a hint of chicory.

"This day is too pretty to waste. Let's take the housekeeper's advice. My car's parked right down the street. Why don't we take a quick drive past the Tidal Basin?" he tempted with that smile. "For old memories' sake."

Despite Sober's admonitions, I let myself slip back in time to a late-March afternoon long ago.

Maybe it was the seductive spring weather that made me hand my books to Nan one day after school while I jumped on the back of Danny's cycle, leaving both Nan and Deb open-mouthed in astonishment. We roared away from Arlington and across Memorial Bridge toward the familiar monuments. Never before had I done something so out-of-bounds, so deliciously out of character. The wind blowing through my hair, the unbelievable sense of freedom, holding on to Danny for dear life while we flew through the streets winding beside the Potomac. We headed first to the Lincoln Memorial, then to the Tidal Basin and Jefferson's graceful dome. The scent of cherry blossoms, heady in the gathering dusk as we walked beneath them. The intimacy. And a kiss I still remembered.

Something of that memory must have shown on my face because Danny grinned at me. "The cherry blossoms are still in bloom."

I just laughed while Danny signaled the waiter.

EIGHT

"Are you all moved into the townhouse, Molly?" Albert asked as he poked his head into my office.

"Finally finished last night, Albert. I'm all set up," I replied, sipping coffee while checking emails.

"Okay, then, I'll pick you up from the townhouse tonight before the reception. And don't bother making dinner. We've got the Southern congressional delegation coming. So the caterers have come up with some specialties."

"Southern cooking, huh? That's always deadly. Thanks for the warning."

I finally felt like I was settling in. This week there was only one evening reception, so I was able to ease back into the socializing demands. Next week would be business as usual — two or three receptions each week for the rest of April and May.

Taking another deep drink of Luisa's rich

coffee, I skimmed through the last of the emails that had arrived since I'd logged off last night. Now that I was officially on the job, it was amazing the people who emailed me. I scrolled down, separating legit emails from spam. Not knowing a lot of these correspondents yet, sometimes it was hard to tell.

My BlackBerry beeped as it lay on the desk. Stopping the scroll, I checked my phone and found a voice mail. I swiveled my comfortable desk chair around and looked out into the senator's landscaped garden as I listened to the message.

"Ms. Malone, my name is Celeste Allard, and I worked with your niece Karen in Congressman Jackson's office. She was a good friend of mine. I wanted to have coffee with you, so I could tell you something. Something that's been bothering me ever since she died. Please call me back. I . . . I promise this isn't a prank call or anything like that. I really was Karen's friend. Thank you, Ms. Malone. I'll wait for your call."

I listened to Celeste Allard rattle off her cell phone number, wondering what on earth had inspired one of Karen's co-workers to call me. I stared out the open window, a slight breeze lifted the lace curtains hanging inside the velvet drapes.

The woman's request made me slightly uneasy, despite her assurances that it was not a prank. Did she simply want to meet me to share maudlin reminiscences about my niece? She said something was bothering her ever since Karen's death. What could that be?

I debated erasing her message, then paused. There was something about her voice. An urgency to it that reached through. I punched in her number and listened to it ring.

"Celeste Allard," a woman's crisp voice answered, not sounding unsure like the voice on the message.

"Ms. Allard? This is Molly Malone returning your call. You said you had something to tell me about my niece, Karen?"

"Oh, yes, can you hold on a minute, please?" Her voice dropped lower.

"Certainly," I said, returning to my emails.

After a few moments, she returned to the line. "Ms. Malone, I'm sorry to make you wait," she said. "I just didn't feel comfortable talking in my office. So many people around. You know how it is."

"Yes, I do, Ms. Allard. Now what was it you wanted to tell me about Karen?"

"I was hoping you and I could meet for coffee. Would that be possible? It's . . . it's a lot of stuff."

I wondered if I should have simply deleted her voice mail instead of returning it. Celeste was coming off a bit weird. I had enough random weirdness in my life. I didn't need any more.

"You know, Celeste, I'm really up to my ears trying to adjust to my new job here in Washington, and I simply don't have any spare evenings this week or next for that matter. Why don't you tell me on the phone, okay?"

"Well . . . it's a lot to tell, Ms. Malone . . ." her voice tentative now.

I decided to cut this off. "Celeste, I truly am not in the mood to listen to some office reminiscences about Karen. This has been a very difficult time for my family as you can —"

"It's not reminiscences, Ms. Malone. It's about Karen and Jed Molinoff."

I paused. "What about them?" I allowed an edge into my voice.

"I . . . I knew about their relationship and was worried about Karen. Jed has a wife and kids back in Omaha. I didn't want her to get into trouble. Gossip on the Hill can kill careers. Jed knew I was Karen's friend and had seen the two of them together. He demoted me right after her death. He switched my job from staff researcher to a drone job in Records."

I weighed what I was hearing, still dubious about Celeste's credibility. "Had you ever confronted Molinoff about their relationship?" I probed, wondering if I was dealing with a potential blackmailer. Maybe she'd threatened Jed. Promised to expose him to his wife and family back in Nebraska.

"God, no," Celeste said. "But he started treating me differently after Karen's death. Probably because I had seen other things."

I figured I'd give Celeste a little more rope and see if she hung herself. Or at least proved herself to be a resentful co-worker with a grudge. "And what sort of things did you see, Celeste?"

"First, he was going through her desk, looking for her daytimer and getting mad when he didn't find it. Then I saw him on Karen's computer, copying files. He caught me watching him, unfortunately. That's when he started interrogating me every day, asking what I was working on. He transferred me downstairs two days later."

I paused, considering everything she said. "All right, Celeste, you've got my attention. Meet me at the Marvelous Market Café on Wisconsin and P Street at twelve noon. I'll only have about thirty minutes, so make it

186

succinct and to the point. I promise I'll give you my full attention."

I balanced my coffee and settled at the café table across from the young African-American staffer. She'd obviously gotten there before me and found a table away from other customers at the outdoor café. I took a deep drink of coffee and used the moment to survey Celeste. She was petite with chin-length black hair that curved stylishly beside her cheeks. Her almond-shaped brown eyes stared out at me expectantly from behind large glasses. Her round face made her look younger than her thirty-two years. I'd made it a point to Google Celeste and check her in the Hill directory before meeting her. Just in case she truly was certifiable. Nothing startling had shown up on my brief records search. She seemed to be exactly what she appeared — a young congressional staffer, not unlike thousands of other staff workers who peopled the offices of Capitol Hill.

"Okay, Celeste. As promised, you've got my full attention. So, talk to me."

Celeste stopped picking at the cardboard sleeve on her takeout coffee cup and fixed me with an earnest gaze. "I want you to know that I'm not some disgruntled employee trying to get back at my boss. I've been working for Congressman Jackson and Jed Molinoff for five years now, and up to this incident, Jed had always indicated my work was exemplary."

"What exactly did you see him doing, again? Copying files?"

"Yes. It looked like he was going through her emails and copying certain ones into a folder. I got a good look from where I was working at the desk behind Karen's."

I sipped the dark brew. "You know, Celeste, it could be that there were some personal emails between Karen and Jed that he simply wanted to remove before the info-tech crew got to the files. That would be my guess."

"I thought so, too, Ms. Malone. That's why I came back later that evening and checked to see if anything had been deleted."

I looked at her in surprise. "Did you find anything?"

"There were several, but they all looked like regular office correspondence, not personal. You know, meetings, fundraising, stuff like that. I didn't understand why he'd delete them." She shrugged. "I would have looked at more files, but I heard some noises and figured someone else had come into the office to work, so I left. The next day, Karen's computer was gone."

"Maybe the tech crew came and took it away before you arrived for work."

Celeste shook her head with that solemn expression of Girl Scout innocence. Her round face gazed at me with earnest sincerity.

"No, I checked. They weren't even scheduled to come yet. But what really spooked me was when Jed started going through Karen's desk the next day. He was pawing through the drawers, slamming stuff around, and then yelled at another staffer, asking if she'd moved Karen's daytimer."

I watched Celeste carefully. My antenna was picking up some strange signals from this young woman. "Maybe he was trying to find an important phone number or an email that she wrote down."

"That's what I thought, but then I overheard him talking to someone on the phone and Jed specifically said, 'Her daytimer is missing,' " Celeste said in a faintly ominous tone.

That got my attention. "Any idea to whom he was talking?"

Celeste shook her head. "I don't know, but I do know where Karen's daytimer is. I helped her pack up her things that Saturday.

I kind of walked in when Jed and Karen were having a big argument. Jed looked furious, and he stormed out of the office after I came in. Karen was so upset. She asked me to find some boxes so she could clear out her desk. She loaded up three boxes."

"What was in the boxes aside from her daytimer?"

"Oh, files and folders, some personal stuff, music players, lots of books."

"Did she take them home, do you know?"

"She never had the chance. I helped her carry them out to her car. But Congressman Jackson came rushing into the office right afterwards and asked Karen to do a last-minute research project for him before the reception that night. He planned to drop by the office and go over it with her, then head straight for the reception. Poor Karen never had a chance to go home and freshen up or anything. She went straight to Senator Russell's house." Celeste's voice dropped. "She said she planned to tell the congressman she was leaving his office that following Monday." Her dark eyes focused on me. "Something else bothers me, too. Jed started acting different right after Karen's death."

"How different?"

"He's nervous, jumpy. I mean he's always

been hyper when we're working on projects, but this is different. He . . . he's way more impatient. He yells a lot. And he rehired this creepy guy that he'd fired only two months ago." She frowned. "When I asked him about it, he said he needed Larry now that Karen was gone. Thing is, Karen was the one who'd insisted that Jed fire Larry two months before. Karen caught him berating one of the new admin assistants. He had her so upset, she was in tears. Karen told Jed he couldn't allow that on the congressman's staff. Jed didn't want to let Larry go, but Karen insisted. And Larry threatened her before he left. I heard him."

I didn't like the sound of that. "What did he say to Karen?"

"He told her 'she'd be sorry.' "

I ran my finger around the rim of the coffee cup, considering what Celeste said. "How has this Larry guy been acting since he came back on staff? Is he behaving himself?"

"Yeah, so far, but he's always creeping around, watching everybody. I think Jed hired him to spy on everyone. I catch him watching me."

I finished off my coffee, wondering what to make of everything Celeste told me. Was she an astute observer or overly paranoid because she'd been demoted? I still hadn't made up my mind about her. Glancing at my watch, I rose from my chair. "I don't know what to say, Celeste. I appreciate your telling me all of this, but . . . I confess, I don't know what to make of it."

Celeste stuffed her napkin into her empty cup and rose as well. "I know it sounds strange, Ms. Malone, but I'm not crazy. And I'm not holding a grudge against Jed Molinoff. Honest. I just wanted you to know what was going on. Thanks for listening to me." Her young face registered disappointment.

I gave her a maternal smile and reached out to squeeze her arm. I remembered what it was like to be single and working in a crazed political atmosphere. "I don't think you're crazy, Celeste, not at all. I had the opportunity to watch Jed Molinoff in action once myself, and I know he can get pretty obnoxious."

I spotted a smile for the first time. "You're right about that, Ms. Malone."

"Listen, why don't you keep me updated on whatever's happening over there, particularly if you hear Molinoff mention Karen's name again."

"I'll be glad to. Hearing Jed say that on the phone really bothered me. Almost as much as that Larry guy creeping around, watching everybody."

"At least you're out of the office and down in Records."

"Yeah, but he comes down there regularly to check files. I catch him watching me."

"Well, you take care of yourself, Celeste, and let me hear from you, okay?" I said as I headed for the door.

"I promise. Take care, Ms. Malone. And thank you."

I gave her a good-bye wave as I sped from the coffee shop and headed up Wisconsin Avenue, walking fast. Walking was still faster than trying to find parking in Georgetown. As I walked, I let Celeste's comments play over in my mind.

What was Jed Molinoff up to? Going through Karen's emails. Rummaging through her desk. Maybe he simply moved any personal emails he'd sent Karen to another folder, getting them out of the files. Just like he'd gone through the photographs in her desk and removed the photos of them together. He wanted to leave no trace of their affair. *Bastard.*

But what was so important in Karen's daytimer? Who was he talking to? Was it Congressman Jackson? And why did he rehire the bad actor? Was he simply trying to replace Karen? The Fillmore guy's past history of bad behavior could cause more trouble in Jackson's office.

Turning onto Q Street, I angled down the shaded street, digging for my cell phone now that I was away from the noisier avenue.

"Hey, did you guys round up some packing boxes or do you need me to buy more?" I asked Nan when she answered.

"Don't bother. We've got plenty. Are we still on for tomorrow evening?"

"Yep. I checked with Peter, and he said it would be fine for me to leave early. I told him we needed to clear out Karen's apartment because the landlord has another tenant wanting it. So, why don't we meet over there at five, okay? By the way, I found an official message from the D.C. Metropolitan Police Department on my cell phone. Karen's car is ready to be picked up from the impound lot."

"Deb and I can go over to get it tomorrow morning. Shall we take it over to the dealership like you said?"

"Yes, but first check the trunk," I said as I approached the Senator's mansion. "Apparently Karen cleaned out her office that Saturday and there are several boxes in the trunk. I'll call the insurance guy and get

194

this process started. We'll repair it and donate it to charity, whatever. I never want to see that car again."

NINE

Ryan approached with a tray of wicked appetizers. "Get away from me with those things, Ryan. They're lethal." I shooed him with my free hand, before sipping my Sauvignon Blanc.

"Oh, but they're small, Molly," he tempted anyway.

I kept shooing. "Begone, before I snack again." This was the last time I would take Albert up on his suggestion to sample the caterer's fare for dinner. They had the most deadly array of calories and cholesterol spread out in the kitchen that I'd seen in quite a while. Deep Southern specialities, miniaturized. Cajun treats were dotted here and there to spice things up. I'd inhaled several of them before I caught myself.

Sipping my wine, I strolled down the hallway, away from the clusters of congressman and aides, staffers and hangers-on. I'd already done my conversational duty for the evening and then some. Peter had emailed that he and the senator would be delayed, so I reported for duty early, ready to meet the eager politicos. Sure enough, six of them showed up early, standing on the mansion doorstep. Luisa shepherded them my way, and I took over. First, I paraded them past tables laden with scrumptious delights, then I took them to the bar. Get them happy and well fed. That was my strategy.

More congressmen and spouses had trickled in, and I renewed old acquaintances while making new ones. The senator, bless him, was only a few minutes tardy and made everyone forget with his booming laugh and tirade on D.C. traffic. By the time Peter made an appearance, I'd chatted my way through seven states, discussed offshore drilling with two Louisiana freshmen over étouffée appetizers, debated the pros and cons of state gambling casinos with an old friend from Tennessee, commiserated with a Florida representative about the current real estate insanity, and celebrated Georgetown's showing in the NCAA Sweet Sixteen last month with a fellow alumnus. I'd had to tap dance around that one. Chaos had taken over in early March, and basketball never even got on my radar screen.

I walked down the back hall to the kitchen

and stood in the doorway. The caterers were starting to wrap things up. Coffee urns had sprouted on the counters like larkspur in my garden. Trays of cakes and other assorted high-calorie dessert treats sat ready to distribute.

Noticing it was nearly ten o'clock, I wondered if I might be able to slip out. Then I could get up really early and take a good run along the canal towpath. No need to wait for Danny to show me his special route. I'd run there years ago. It couldn't have changed that much over the years.

Once I started my running schedule again, I'd really feel settled. I hadn't had a spare moment to ponder personal stuff all day or evening. Running always provided a quiet time for me to be alone with my thoughts. I could think and work out problems.

My conversation with Celeste earlier that day still bothered me, particularly her comments about Jed searching for Karen's daytimer. Once I could retrieve the daytimer from Karen's boxes, I could take a look myself. See if anything jumped out at me.

Suddenly a memory surfaced. Karen's BlackBerry. I hadn't looked at it since I'd accessed her friends and co-workers' phone numbers for the funeral. There would be voice mails and call records. Maybe I should take a look and see what was there.

I checked my watch. Time to go home. Draining my glass, I retrieved my purse from Luisa's special cabinet, and headed for the door. Albert could hail a cab for me. During the day, I would walk the few blocks to my home, but at night . . . well, we all knew what happened in the nighttime. Different people prowled the streets. Dangerous people.

I wondered how long it would take to feel comfortable on the streets at night again.

The early morning sunlight angled through the trees bordering the canal, casting shadows amidst the light. Dappled sunshine sprinkled across the towpath and those of us out running or walking. Early morning sunlight was peaceful somehow.

I'd only had a few hours sleep. Late-night coffee and combing through Karen's Black-Berry sent sleep scurrying. I checked the incoming and outgoing call logs with my online congressional directory and found most of the calls either came from or went to other Capitol Hill colleagues and staffers. There were several out-of-area phone numbers I figured I'd check later.

But it was the voice mail messages that yielded the puzzles. There were several business calls from other staffers, a call from me, another from a friend who wanted to have lunch, a researcher from some European corporation, and two very different messages from Jed Molinoff.

Jed's first call was dated several days before Karen's death and sounded as if he was calling from the office, his voice chief-of-staff authoritative and confident.

"Look, Karen, I'm sorry if I barked at you this afternoon. It's just that . . . there's so much going on. Stuff I haven't talked to you about. It's . . . it's complicated. I'm trying to put something together . . . something with a new donor group. You know how much Jackson needs money. We need this, Karen, and I'm really working my ass off to put it together, so just cut me some slack for a while, okay? Listen, call coming in. Call me later."

I wondered what Jed was working on that he hadn't told Karen about? Which new donor group was he working with? Was it a political action committee? Ever since a law had passed years ago to curtail political campaign spending abuses, special-interest PACs had sprouted throughout the political landscape like mushrooms in the dark.

But it was the other call, dated the day of Karen's death, that gave me pause. This time Jed's voice was tentative, his tone pleading, as he begged Karen, "don't do anything you'll regret." There was an anxious note in Jed's voice that got my attention. It wasn't the cajoling tone of a rejected lover trying to wheedle his way back. I detected a tinge of fear in Jed's voice.

Shade alternated with sunshine up ahead and I spotted several more runners coming from the opposite direction. I heard the sound of running feet behind me, and I waited for the person to pass. Danny pulled up beside me instead.

"Hey, there. You're out early," he greeted.

"I had trouble sleeping. Too much stuff bouncing around my brain. So I figured I might as well check out this canal trail," I said, while trying to match my stride to his.

"Something bothering you?"

"Yeah, kind of. One of Karen's office friends called yesterday and asked to meet for coffee." I paused for a couple of strides, getting my breathing in sync. "She wanted to talk about Karen."

"Reminisce?"

"That's what I thought. But she started telling me how Karen's boss seems to be losing it, yelling at people. He transferred her downstairs to a drone job after she saw him copying files on Karen's computer."

"Sounds like a disgruntled employee to me."

"Yeah, I thought so too. Then she said he got mad when he couldn't find Karen's day-timer, then called someone about it." Trying to talk and keep up with Danny was proving a challenge. "It all sounds strange; I don't know what to think." Up ahead the trail fell into shadows again as it ran directly beneath Key Bridge, that wide thoroughfare which spanned the Potomac between Virginia and Georgetown.

Suddenly a man stepped out of the concrete shadows directly ahead of us. Danny's arm shot out in front of me as he moved ahead, putting himself between the man and me. The man darted a bleary look our way and scuttled up the grassy embankment away from us.

"As I said the other day, some parts of this trail are safer than others. Drunks sleep it off under the bridge at night. As the nights get warmer, there'll be more of them. You might want to turn around before you get to this point," Danny said as we ran along the darkened trail. The sound of rush hour traffic rumbled above our heads. Tires on asphalt.

I glanced around, saw empty bottles, trash, and smelt urine. Listening to the sound of traffic as we executed a U-turn, I checked my watch. *Uh-oh.* I'd been running longer than I thought.

"Hey, Danny, I'm going to take a shortcut and race home so I won't be late for work." I pointed to the stairs that led to the streets above the canal. "Meanwhile, I've got us down for sightseeing on Saturday. Call me later and we'll set a time, okay? See you." I waved, then made an abrupt turn and took off for the stairs before Danny could say a word.

TEN

"Thanks for coming out on your lunch hour, Celeste," I said as I pulled out a chair at the outdoor cafe and coffee shop. Only a stone's throw from the Foggy Bottom Metro station, I figured it would be easier for Celeste to meet me on short notice. Her Capitol Hill office was near the Metro line. No need for taxis on a research staffer's salary.

"No problem, Molly. I'm happy to come. I'll be glad to help you any way I can. What do you need?"

"I'd like you to check out Karen's emails for the last couple of months before she died. Your Records office must have them on file."

Her face turned solemn. "What are you looking for?"

"I'm looking for anything that would make your antennae go off. I know that sounds strange, but I've been thinking about what you said. Jed was going through Karen's computer checking her files, copying certain emails. I'm wondering if she was working on a special project or something, and now he can't find it. Maybe that's why he was checking her files. I'm curious."

"Is there something wrong? Have you heard anything about Jed or the congressman?"

I shook my head. "No, no, nothing at all. You can chalk this up to my own curiosity. I want to know if you see anything that sticks out or looks unusual. Especially if it involves money or fundraising. Check out the donors' list, if you can access it. I know this sounds strange, Celeste, but —"

"No, it doesn't. Karen was always working on stuff for Jed. I assumed it was for the congressman. But if you're curious, then that makes me curious, too." Celeste nodded solemnly, her huge brown eyes gazing at me.

I shrugged. "I don't know. Maybe I'm chasing shadows. But I figured, if Karen was working on a special project, surely there would be trace of it in the files."

"Don't worry, Molly. I'll take a look and see what jumps out at me. I've got good instincts. If Jed's got some special project going on, I'll find it. I promise I will."

He wiped his hands on the linen napkin, then took another sip of his Belgian beer before answering the cell phone's insistent buzz.

"What took you so long?" Raymond barbed, his scratchy voice revealing annoyance.

"I was in the middle of pan-seared scallops with butter and garlic." He deliberately took another sip of beer before adding, "You should slow down and relax more. Enjoy the scenery." He sank back into his chair and looked out over the Potomac flowing lazily along its banks beside the restaurant.

Raymond gave an annoyed snort. "New target. A small one. Observation, only. Text will follow."

"A rabbit, huh?" He speared another scallop, dripping with pan juices. "Sounds like fun." He popped the tender white delicacy into his mouth.

I drained my cold coffee. How long had it been sitting on my desk? I glanced at my watch. How could it be nearly five o'clock? I was only halfway through Peter's real estate spreadsheet.

Checking the angle of the sun through my office window confirmed the time. That was the thing about accounting. It could suck me in and hold me for hours. Solving puzzles, uncovering secrets. Then suddenly, the afternoon is gone.

I stood up and stretched. The Russell mansion had already fallen into a Friday-afternoon quiet. The senator, Peter, and Albert had already left for the airport and their weekend return trip to Colorado. Back home to the voters. Only Luisa stayed to keep the house running. And Casey, of course. Security never slept. It did, however, stay in place. When the senator traveled home, he had his local Colorado security team take care of him. Apparently, security guys were very territorial. Not surprising, since they were all former military.

Powering off my computer, I loaded my briefcase and stacked several files in my version of neat piles on the desk. They could wait for Monday morning. No emergencies in sight and no entertaining. I was free as a bird until Monday, not counting household chores and retrieving Karen's boxes from Nan's garage. Sunday, I planned to go through both the daytimer and boxes before dinner with my family. See if I could find any special reports or anything that jumped out at me. Saturday, I had already blocked out for sightseeing with Danny.

Locking my office door, I headed for the exit and home, trying to decide between frozen spinach casserole or a fresh spinach salad. I noticed Luisa at the front door, talking to someone. She turned to me with a big smile.

"Ah, here she is. I was just coming to get you, Molly. You have a visitor."

Danny stood on the porch, all suited up in sports coat, shirt, and tie. He certainly cleaned up well. "Hey, Danny. I thought we were on for tomorrow?"

"I dropped by in case you'd like to run through the itinerary over dinner," he said with an engaging grin. Luisa had retreated into the hallway, smiling like the Cheshire cat.

"We have an itinerary? Wow, that sounds daunting. Do I have to dress up? Guess I can't wear my Clapton concert shirt, huh?" I joined him on the porch.

"I thought you might enjoy starting our tour tonight at the waterfront. Are you in the mood for fresh seafood?"

When wasn't I in the mood for fresh seafood? Growing up this close to the Chesapeake Bay and the Atlantic Ocean meant fresh seafood was always available. My stomach growled in anticipation.

"You really know how to tempt a woman, don't you?" I teased, heading for the steps. "You're on. Which restaurants have survived? Any of my old favorites?"

"One or two. Some names have changed, but the restaurants —"

"Double D?" a voice called out behind us.

Danny whipped around as Casey emerged from the house and approached us.

Casey strode up to Danny, hand outstretched. "It's good to see you, sir. We served together in Beirut. I was in your platoon."

Danny stared at Casey for a few seconds, then I saw a flicker of recognition register on Danny's face. He clasped Casey's hand and shook it, then placed his other hand on top. "Casey. That's right. I didn't recognize you at first. It's been a while."

"Yes, it has, sir."

"How long did you stay in?"

"Career."

"Good man." Danny glanced back at the mansion. "What do you do for the senator?"

"Security."

Danny nodded as the two men released their handshake. Glancing to me, Danny said, "I guess I don't have to worry about you, Molly. You're in good hands with Casey on the job."

"You're right about that. Casey takes excellent care of us," I said, pausing by the steps, not sure if there was more manly bonding.

Casey backed away, raising his hand in a wave. "Luisa said you two are going to dinner. Enjoy yourselves."

"Thanks, Casey." Danny took my elbow, and we sped down the steps.

"You two served together in Beirut?" I ventured, curious. "Was that during those awful bombings?"

Danny's face lost all traces of a smile. "Yeah. Casey was one of those who survived. He helped me carry my men out of the collapsed barracks."

I didn't ask anything else.

The little oyster lay there in its shell, unsuspecting. I speared it mercilessly, waved it past the hot sauce, and gobbled it down. Danny simply slurped his oysters right from the shell. Sipping the clear, crisp Sauvignon Blanc, I reached for a fresh shrimp and savored its delicate flavor. Next, I opted for the Cajun-spiced shrimp.

Danny and I were seated at a corner table overlooking the waterfront. Boats were moored in a surrounding marina. We could look across the water and see Maryland. It was a beautiful view, but we barely noticed. We were too busy eating. Our table was laden with platters of oysters, shrimp *au naturel* and Cajun, and that delectable specialty of the Chesapeake Bay and all coastal areas: fresh crab.

I reached for the little mallet beside my glass and hit the crab claw on my plate. It only dented the bright red shell.

Danny snickered. "Gotta hit it harder than that. You've been away too long." He slid a morsel of crab from its shell and popped it into his mouth.

I sipped my wine again and waved the mallet at him. "Give me time. It's coming back." I gave the crab claw a solid whack, and it yielded. The tender white, oh-so-sweet shellfish delicacy was my favorite. Lobster was fine, but give me crab any day.

"See!" I crowed, waving the white morsel. I dipped it in the melted butter. Real butter, of course. I savored the succulent, sweet taste all the way down my throat. To-die-for delicious. "Oh, God, this is so good." I reached for an oyster. Start another round of decadence. "Even though my cholesterol is rising as we speak."

"Don't worry. You'll run it off." He

whacked the main shell of the crab and it collapsed. Pink and white flesh opening like a flower.

"I hope so. I'm putting all my eggs in that exercise basket." I speared another helpless oyster. Down the hatch it went, with its delicious slithery wiggle. I dug another morsel of crab from the stingy shell. Tasting it alone, I savored the sweetness while Danny finished his shrimp.

Relaxing in my chair, I surveyed the meandering branch of the Washington Channel that flowed past the waterfront, then on toward the Tidal Basin before joining the Potomac. Washington was almost entirely surrounded by water. Rivers, canals, creeks, channels. I sipped the crisp wine and watched the current move the boats past us.

"This is exactly what I needed tonight. Feasting on fresh seafood beside the water. These last few weeks have been hard. And strange."

Danny popped a Cajun shrimp into his mouth, then tasted his wine. "Why strange?"

A boat motored by lazily. "Well, for starters, when I went to Karen's apartment to pick up clothes for the funeral, I saw Karen's boss, Jed Molinoff, coming out the front door."

Danny looked up, surprised. "What was

he doing there? Did they live together?"

"No, but they were having an affair, so he must have had a key."

"That makes sense. What'd he say when he saw you?"

"He didn't. I spotted him first and hid behind a post until he left. But I did see him put something in his jacket pocket as he was leaving."

"Any idea what it was?"

I nodded. "Photos, probably. The photos in Karen's desk drawer were all jumbled together. Karen never would have left her desk like that."

"Can you tell which photos he took?"

"I can only guess he took photos that showed the two of them alone together. Trying to eliminate all traces of the affair. But that stuff never stays secret for long. Too many eyes are watching on the Hill. That staffer who called me knew they were having an affair. In fact, she walked in on their blow-up argument that Saturday afternoon."

I watched the current flowing past, pelicans and ducks floating by. "Molinoff's married with children back in Nebraska. I'd told Karen that Saturday morning she needed to break it off, and she went to the office right away and told Jed it was over. Jed didn't take it well. They were still arguing that night at the reception. Casey had to step in and tell Jed to cool off." I drained the last of my wine.

Danny didn't say anything at first, then he poured the last of the bottle into both our wine glasses. "Now that story makes more sense. Jed definitely had something to hide and felt guilty. Guilt makes people do strange things. He didn't want to leave anything that could get back to his family in Nebraska."

"Still, it was pretty brazen. Prowling through Karen's apartment. Rifling her desk. Listening to her phone messages."

This time, Danny folded his arms and leaned on the table. "How do you know he did?"

"I checked the messages when I was there, and the last one was left earlier that very morning. Yet the light wasn't flashing, which meant somebody listened to them. The landlord wouldn't. Only Jed Molinoff would do that. And that bothers me." I stared at the current. "When I saw Jed's tracks at Karen's place, I chalked it up to his guilty conscience. But now that I've talked to Karen's friend, I think I'll make some inquiries of my own about Jed."

Danny peered at me. "What're you planning to do, Molly?"

"Start asking questions. Check out Jed Molinoff with some of my old contacts and see what turns up. Gossip and rumor being what they are in Washington, I'm sure I'll learn something. I already asked Celeste to check the records for Karen's emails these last couple of months. See if something turns up. Jed's worried about something. Maybe there's some financial irregularity involving fundraising. Something that might reflect on Jackson. Maybe Karen found out and wrote Jed an email about it."

"That sounds like pure speculation, Molly."

I shrugged. "Yeah, I know. But my instinct is starting to buzz on Jed Molinoff. Something's up with him and it's not just hiding an affair. He's worried about something else. And I want to find out what it is."

I sipped my coffee while sitting on my secluded back patio examining the pages of Karen's daytimer. Karen made as many notations on the pages as I did. Along the side, over the top and bottom, scribbling on every date square. Focusing on the month of March — the month she died — I scrutinized every square, every notation.

"Jed meeting H." "H speaks tonight at 7

p.m." "H & J meet." "H & D meet." "H & R meet."

"J" could mean Jed or Congressman Jackson. There was no clue as to which one. And who were H, D, and R? I could only guess at the other initials. Karen's notes were cryptic, almost as if she were writing in code for herself. Dates were filled with meetings, calls, appointments. Email addresses and phone numbers were scribbled everywhere.

I tapped my finger on the daytimer. Was there anything else I could check? Anything I'd missed? I glanced to the box at my feet. Karen's personal files from her office. Setting my coffee aside, I sorted through the files. There were reports on agricultural subsidies, personnel files, another report on Nebraska fundraising. Then, a file marked "Miscellaneous."

Checking the sun's angle, I guessed it was approaching late afternoon. As I sipped my coffee, I paged through the file, noticing copies of emails sent to vacation rentals, social correspondence, and emails with scribbled phone numbers. Vacation ads for cruises were torn out of newspapers and interspersed with letters, invitations, and other personal correspondence. My heart squeezed knowing that Karen would never get to enjoy those vacations. Such a short life cut off so young.

I caught myself and pivoted away from the quagmire of loss. Pausing at one email, I noticed it was from a Hill colleague dated last year, offering Karen a tempting position at a higher level. One year ago. That was probably when she was first immersed in that affair with Jed. Her good judgment clouded. *Damn.*

Draining my coffee, I continued paging through the personal emails and letters. Then I found several emails held together with a clasp. Subject line: *Epsilon Group.* I noticed the dates and turned to the latest one, skimming them one by one. The first email dealt with Epsilon's contribution to Congressman Jackson's campaign. Another for Jackson's charity. Then a message about a speaker's forum. Ambassador Holmberg speaking on Global Markets: *Risk or Reform.* More emails on financial policy papers. More and more. Then one on Jackson talking points for a speech he made in Chicago. Another on the legislative subcommittee where Jackson served. Debating the language to be used in the banking bill being considered. Emails inserting and revising language for the bill.

Karen had apparently put together every email concerning Epsilon. Noticing that the next-to-last page had her handwriting, I paused. She'd circled a name in the email above. "Ambassador Holmberg." Then below, she'd written in her neat script, "Holmberg — met with Jackson twice. Met each member subcommittee. Contributions. Holmberg also with Senator Dunston." Senator Dunston was now the chairman of the Senate Banking, Housing, and Urban Affairs Committee. Senator Sol Karpinsky's old seat. A powerful position. I flipped to the last page. More notes on scheduled Epsilon forums since January.

I stared off into the garden from my shady patio perch. Now some of Karen's daytimer notes made sense. Was "H" Ambassador Holmberg? Was "D" Senator Dunston? And who was "R"? Both Karen's daytimer notes and her saved emails indicated she was keeping track of the Epsilon Group and its connections to Jackson and other members of Congress. I was left with lots of questions but no answers. Whatever was going on inside Karen Grayson's mind died the moment that 9mm bullet tore through her brain.

Glancing at my watch, I saw it was almost time to leave for dinner with my family in Virginia. I returned both the file and Karen's daytimer to the box. I'd have to check those numbers with Karen's cell phone calls. See if there were any matches. It was a safe bet that most of the Washington, D.C., area codes were fellow Hill staffers.

I also made a mental note to myself to copy down those out-of-state phone numbers. I could check them out later.

ELEVEN

"I'm so glad you were able to join us tonight, Molly. I know how busy you are over at the senator's." Eleanor McKenzie's bright blue eyes lit up. "He's still entertaining the congressional hordes, I take it."

"Right you are, Eleanor," I said as we strolled along the brick walkway that ran through the garden of her gracious Cleveland Park estate. "But I simply couldn't miss one of your soirees. They're such a highlight of the Washington scene. I'm so glad you're still doing them. The pianist was wonderful, incidentally."

"You've settled in remarkably well from what I observe and hear." She gave me her knowing smile.

Eleanor's Network. Still at work. "Lord knows what they're saying about me." I watched the guests milling about the oak tree-shaded gardens, grazing at the tables spread with catered delicacies.

"Don't worry, dear, I would tell you if there was anything unpleasant making the rounds." Eleanor looked over her gathering with an experienced hostess's eye. "I always look out for my favorites, you know that."

That I remembered. Eleanor took my dear friend Samantha Suffolk and me under her wing when we were both teenagers, growing up as senators' daughters.

Since our fathers were two of the most respected and influential men in the Senate, both our mothers decided they wanted another set of "eyes" supervising any outside social gatherings arranged for politicians' children. Eleanor McKenzie stepped in as watchdog. Widow of a prestigious senator and former secretary of state, Eleanor was uniquely qualified and experienced to keep an eye out for any unacceptable behavior. She missed nothing.

Of course, Samantha and I provided Eleanor a challenge. We both shared a devilish sense of humor and usually paired up at some of the terminally tedious social functions we had to attend in the late sixties. As senators' daughters, we were always under a magnifying glass. Still, Samantha and I would concoct bizarre pranks that couldn't be traced to us. Both our fathers would have grounded us until graduation.

Eleanor, however, had an uncanny ability to sniff out our plots before they came to fruition. She also would take us aside and give us her version of The Rules: "Never do anything you wouldn't want printed with photographs on the front page of the *Washington Post*." That was usually enough to keep us in line. Samantha and I called her the Queen Mother. And she always singled us out for special attention.

I laughed softly. "Thank God, Eleanor. It's good to know someone is looking out for me. Samantha and I depended on your good graces to save us all those years ago."

Eleanor shook her head. "Ahhhh, you girls were a pair. You really tested my wits. Both of you were as smart as whips and would see through any speeches that worked on the other girls. But you two, well, headstrong is a word that comes to mind. And rebellious. Qualities that are always risky, especially in Washington."

Memories crept from the edges of my mind. Samantha and I were both rebels at heart who couldn't risk overt rebellion. Rebels who had to be good. Fortunately, Samantha and I had an escape. College. Even senators' daughters were officially "let off leash" after high school. Once we checked into our respective universities, Samantha at Ole Miss and me at Georgetown, we discreetly cut loose. We'd get together on holiday vacations and share experiences over pizza and illegal D.C. beer. Virginia was as dry as a cornfield in July.

"Well, I think I got all of the rebellion out of my system long ago, Eleanor," I said, glancing over the garden and the string quartet that was playing.

"I wish we could say the same about Samantha." Eleanor brushed a fly away with her lemon-yellow silk sleeve. "She seems to have saved up most of her rebellion for this stage of life."

I smiled to myself. *Samantha's affairs.* They could fill a book. Ever since her powerful and elderly husband — the senior senator from Alabama — died, Samantha went from being the power behind the throne and model of wifely propriety to the Merry Widow. Emphasis on merry. She indulged in a series of "strategic affairs" as she called them. Samantha and I had seen each other twice in these last five years, so I was always belatedly learning about the various liaisons. Amazed at her brazen flouting of propriety, I'd once teased her about it. Samantha simply laughed and said she'd been "saving up" all those years. Now, she intended to spend it.

I'd always sensed Samantha's rebellion stemmed more from the broken heart that never fully healed. Samantha had lost her young husband, the love of her life, within the first three years of their marriage. Eddie Tyler, a dashing Annapolis Naval graduate, had gone straight from his graduation from flight school to his first assignment in Vietnam as a Navy pilot. His plane was downed over the Gulf of Tonkin months later, in an incident that was never fully explained. Samantha went into seclusion with her baby daughter in Mississippi and didn't return to Washington until 1977. That was the same year Dave and I came to town when he was appointed to a vacated Colorado congressional seat.

From the moment of Samantha's return, I saw that there was a part of my dear friend that was walled off. Unavailable. Of course, the always stunning and vivacious auburn-haired Samantha was still there, and it wasn't long before Washington swains were succumbing to her charms. But even I was surprised when she chose an old family friend and colleague of her late father as her next husband. Widowed Senator Beauregard Calhoun was a sweetheart of a man. Big-hearted, big-drinking, and one of the wiliest dealmakers in the Senate. He and

Samantha made quite the pair.

"I have to admit, I stopped keeping up with Washington gossip when I started working for that Denver developer a few years ago. What taboo has Samantha broken now? I thought she'd broken them all."

"Oh, the usual," Eleanor said with an airy wave of her hand. "Multiple affairs, usually with younger men. All of them junior members of Congress. With no regard to whether they're married or not." She tsked without making a sound.

"Ah, yes. I asked her about that a couple of years ago. I assumed it was because her husband had been so much older than she was. She told me she chose her conquests carefully. Each one was starting to make his mark. She said she was 'grooming them.' "

That comment brought a royal sniff from the Queen Mother. "Grooming them, indeed. Well, she'd best downplay her mentoring projects before they attract any more attention. She's been particularly blatant this past year." She looked me in the eye. "I wish you would have a talk with her, Molly. She'll be back in town soon. Apparently she's away on vacation to one of those spas she frequents. Why don't you visit her? Maybe you could convince Samantha that she's risking more than her reputation."

This time, I had to chuckle. "Eleanor, you know better than anyone that Samantha doesn't care about her reputation. She was the wife of one of the most powerful men in the Senate for over twenty years. In fact, she was the one who kept him going those last six years. She read the bills and conferred with staffers, and she was watching over his constituents and coaching him so he could say the right things on television. I swear, she should have held the pen when he signed legislation." I took a deep drink of my Pinot Grigio. "Talk about the power behind the throne. She *was* the power. So she's practically untouchable in this town now."

"No one's untouchable, Molly. Not in Washington. You know that."

Unfortunately, I did. "Have you heard anything?"

Eleanor glanced off toward the musicians and her guests. Someone waved, beckoning her to join them. Hostess duties never ceased. "Ohhhh, just a ripple of discontent. Rumors. Snide comments. It seems to have arisen more these past few months. Maybe because she was seeing Senator Karpinsky again. Going on holidays with him after his release from the hospital. Rumor has it she was with him the night he died." She tsked again.

I was searching for something to say, when a familiar voice boomed behind us.

"Wonderful pianist, Eleanor. And Molly, good to see you again. None of us can resist Eleanor's events, can we?"

I turned to greet my old friend, Senator Baker. "Good to see you, too, Senator. And you're right, Eleanor's events are one of the best things about returning to Washington."

"I'm going to leave you two to discuss the pianist's fine points while I return to the garden and my guests. I confess that catching up with Molly has made me forget my hostess duties." Eleanor swept away in a rustle of yellow silk.

"Molly, you're looking wonderfully well, considering what's been happening in your life recently. I'm so very sorry about Karen. She was a sharp, dedicated staffer with a lightning-quick mind. I had the pleasure of meeting her when Congressman Jackson and I were both supporting some bipartisan legislation on farm subsidies two years ago. It was a tragic loss."

"Thank you for your kind words, Senator. It has been a difficult time for all of us," I replied, then quickly changed the subject. I no longer wanted to dwell on the subject of loss. It was the gateway to a spiral that went only one way: down. "Tell me, what's happening on the Banking Committee now that Senator Karpinsky is gone?"

Baker chuckled. "Back on the job, eh, Molly? Accounting, my ass."

I couldn't resist a grin. "Just curious, Senator. Rumors float like pollen on the breeze here."

"Don't they ever? Well, you're right. It will be a different committee now that our watchdog is gone. We'll just have to wait and see how it goes with the new chairman, Senator Dunston. But I'm afraid his previous statements lean toward reducing oversight on financial institutions, not tightening it. And, of course, that could affect the outcome of Congressman Jackson's efforts with his Financial Services subcommittee bill."

Now that we'd meandered into the arena I wanted to discuss, I changed to the subject I had in mind. "Tell me, Senator, what's your opinion of Jackson's chief of staff, Jed Molinoff? Karen told me he was a mover and shaker. If he is, then I want to keep my eye on him. What's your impression?"

"Your curiosity again, Molly?" Baker grinned. "I'd say that Karen's assessment of Molinoff was right on. When Jackson and I met to talk about those farm subsidies, Molinoff was always Johnny-on-the-spot with reports, new research data, analysis. You name it, Jed seemed to have it in his hand. Or up his sleeve." Baker chuckled at his own joke.

I joined him, wondering how much of Jed Molinoff's quick response was provided by my niece, Karen. Suppressing my resentment, I added, "Thanks for your insight, Senator. I wanted to confirm Karen's opinion with an outside source. Just in case Senator Russell has any dealings with Congressman Jackson's office. Who knows? With the two of you trying to build bridges, the Senate might get some meaningful work done."

Baker guffawed. "Molly, when did you become an optimist?"

A middle-aged man I didn't recognize suddenly walked up to us and placed his hand on Baker's arm. "Sorry to interrupt, Alan, but I wanted to let you know that Ambassador Holmberg will be speaking next week at Dumbarton Oaks. Remember when we talked about him? He was the one who helped oversee the changes to the European Union's Central Bank."

"Well, if he's coming, then I definitely want to attend," Baker said. "When is he speaking?"

"I'll send you an email," the man said as he backed away. "I apologize for interrupting your discussion, Alan, I just wanted to tell you before I forgot."

"I appreciate it, Fred. Take care," Baker said with a wave. "Fred's a good man. He's with the Commerce Department, and we've found ourselves attending some of the same meetings around town involving global financial markets." He drained his beer.

"Who's that speaker again?" I asked, zeroing in on the name I'd seen in Karen's day-timer.

"He's Ambassador Holmberg, a finance minister at the European Union. He lectures all over the world on global finance. I first heard him speak at a symposium put on by the Epsilon Group last year." He shook his head. "It's a rapidly changing world, and I'm afraid our country will lose ground to the rest of the world if we're not careful."

At the mention of the name "Epsilon Group," my little buzzer went off. "I'm not familiar with the Epsilon Group, Senator. Who or what is it?"

"It's an organization made up of distinguished experts in finance. Some are past financial ministers or served on international corporate boards."

"And what does this Epsilon Group do? Give speeches around Washington or something?"

Baker smiled. "Well, they do give a lot of speeches. But they also publish policy papers on various subjects, trying to educate the public on this whole topic. We've been woefully neglectful of our role in the greater world economy, Molly."

"Well, you're right about that, Senator. Maybe I should check out that speaker."

"You should. You'll be interested, I'm sure."

"I'll check my daytimer and see what entertaining plans Senator Russell has on tap first. We've only worked our way through a third of Congress. We've got another two-thirds to go. That is, if I can balance the senator's budget so that we can afford to feed the congressional hordes."

Raymond took a long drag on his cigarette then blew out a stream of smoke. "You keeping track of everything?" he said into the phone. "Sounds like you've got a lot of pieces in motion."

"We're keeping an eye on it," the man's deep voice replied. "Oh, and thanks for the information. We're adding it to the file."

"Anytime. Let me know if you need further intel. That's his specialty."

"You can count on it."

TWELVE

I raced into my office, trying not to spill my refilled mug of coffee. My cell phone's familiar ring was sounding. Had to be a personal call. All business calls went through my BlackBerry. I was scrupulous about that. Better to keep personal and business separate. It saved a lot of problems.

The familiar beep sounded, indicating a voice mail, so I punched it in. Samantha Calhoun's magnolia-dipped voice came lilting over the line, bringing back memories. I stood at my desk, grinning and listening, while Samantha gushed her joy at my return and made a date to get together all in the same breath. Those Southern girls sure had a lot of hot air. She'd pick me up at five thirty tonight at the foot of Key Bridge on M Street. Look for a white Lexus.

What? In the middle of rush hour traffic? She had to be crazy. We'd be run over by a pack of irate drivers if she tried to stop there.

I was about to call her and negotiate our meeting place when my cell phone rang in my hand. Celeste's number flashed on the screen.

"Hey, Celeste. How's the search going? Have you found anything interesting?"

"Well, yes and no, Molly. I'm searching all the emails for the last three months, and so far nothing has rung my buzzer, even the ones concerning fundraising. I copied them all for you anyway."

Darn. I was hoping something would jump out. "Well, at least that tells us there wasn't anything underhanded going on."

"Was there any other area you'd like me to search, Molly? I agree that Jed is worrying about something, because that Larry creep comes down here to check on me several times a day. Every day, I swear to God. Always asking what I'm working on. It's pissing me off. I've started copying the files onto flash drives and doing my searches at home. That way, I have my regular work screen ready whenever the creep shows up. And I always cover my search tracks."

"Oh, Celeste, I don't want you to take work home." Now I was feeling guilty.

"No problem, Molly. It's become a quest."

"Now that you mention it. Would you do a search involving the Epsilon Group? See what comes up, would you? Apparently it's a think tank or something."

"Yes, I've heard of it. Sure, I'll go through the files and emails again. New target, huh?" Her voice sounded almost excited.

"Yeah, Celeste. New target. Let's see what we can hit."

"I hope you know I was nearly run over trying to get in your car just now," I said, settling into the leather of Samantha's snow-white Lexus as she drove across Key Bridge into Virginia. "Whatever possessed you to pick me up back there?" I gestured toward the black-and-white neon façade of Dixie Liquor, a decades-old landmark, fast fading behind us in the rearview mirror.

"Nostalgia," she drawled. "You remember when we used to sneak over the bridge with our dates on college break and try to buy liquor in Georgetown?"

I laughed out loud. Some memories were better left forgotten. "Don't remind me."

Samantha's burnished auburn hair shone in the stylish cut that brushed the shoulders of her expensive designer outfit. Even though Samantha had lost her girlish figure years ago, the extra pounds seemed to add to her voluptuous quality. It emanated from her like her trademark gardenia perfume.

"Looking good, Miss Thing," I said as we hurtled around Rosslyn Circle, horns honking around us. I braced for impact.

"Why, thank you, sugar," she gave me one of her dazzling dimpled smiles. Unfortunately, she was also merging onto Route 66 at the time, causing even louder honking of horns. "And you're looking fantastic, Molly. I swear, how do you stay so slender? It took me two weeks at the spa to lose five pounds."

"It's called stress. And I don't recommend it, even though it's effective."

"Well, we'll just have to work on getting you to relax while you're here. Nobody's called me 'Miss Thing' since you left town. It's so good to have you back, sugar." Samantha suddenly reached over and gave me a quick hug while changing lanes at the same time.

Talk about stress. I wondered if I'd survive the drive to the restaurant. I was about to say a prayer, then remembered that I'd stopped praying years ago. God didn't listen anyway, so why bother?

A midnight-blue Mercedes swerved out of our way, its horn blaring. This time I cried out, "For the love of God, Samantha, would you watch where you're going!"

"No need to invoke the Almighty, sugar.

You know I'm always in control." Samantha corrected her trajectory with the tip of her finger while she gave a dazzling smile to the guy she'd just offended. Red-faced and apoplectic, he flipped her off.

"People are so rude nowadays," she tsked.

"You probably gave that guy a heart attack, you know that?"

"Nonsense, he's just too stressed. Like you."

Samantha's gardenia-scented cloud wafted over me from her hug. I inhaled the seductive fragrance as we passed the Iwo Jima Memorial. "That gardenia scent still drawing the men?"

"Like flies."

"I tried wearing it once, but it gave me a headache. Maybe that's why I never had as many flies buzzing around me."

Samantha gave me one of her looks. "Oh, they were buzzing, all right, but you kept swatting 'em down. I declare, Molly, you ought to let a couple land once in a while. It'd do you good."

That made me laugh out loud again. Nobody talked to me like Samantha. Even Deb and Nan. "Well, I used to, but I've kind of sworn off flies since Frank."

"Well, we'll just have to see about that," she said as she steered the car down the

George Washington Parkway, the Potomac glistening alongside in the late afternoon sun.

I decided to deflect Samantha's attentions and honor Eleanor's request, for all the good it would do. "Speaking of flies, it sounds like you've been attracting more than your share. In fact, Eleanor McKenzie is concerned enough she requested I have a 'talk' with you. She's concerned about the, ah, how shall I phrase it, the pace of your recent liaisons?"

Samantha tossed me a wicked smile. "Did the Queen Mother call and ask you to check up on me?"

"No, I spoke with Eleanor at her musical evening a few days ago —"

"Those are so dreary. Only the booze makes them bearable."

"The music helps, too. Anyway, Eleanor must have gone on for five full minutes, she was so concerned about your recent activities with the younger congressmen."

Samantha snickered. "I imagine I've shocked the pants off the old girl."

"Pretty much, so I promised I'd mention it to you. Even though I told her it wouldn't do any good. You're not about to change your wicked ways, are you, Miss Thing?"

"Why, heavens, no. I'm having way too

much fun." She flashed another smile.

"Okay, off the record. How many are we talking about here? Eleanor made it sound like you're taking a roll call of the junior members of Congress."

Samantha hooted with laughter. "Oh, Lord, the old girl must be slipping. I've only taken a handful under my wing to groom, shall we say. Each one carefully selected, of course. They're all beginning to make their marks and about to move up."

"With your guidance, of course."

"Let's just say I have considerable expertise I can share with them. Help them avoid some of the early pitfalls. And I must say some of my earlier pupils have made quite a mark for themselves already."

I grinned. "Sounds like you've established your own intern program."

"I like to think I'm continuing my service to the Congress, in my own special way." She gave me a wink before she steered the car onto a shaded driveway off the parkway. I glimpsed the river up ahead and a gracious colonial miniature mansion sprawling beneath the trees.

"All right, I'll report back to the Queen Mother that you've established your own finishing school of sorts. See how that flies," I teased.

"Sort of a clandestine, undercover training program, you might say," Samantha added with a grin.

We both sat in the car and laughed until tears came to our eyes.

"Have you tried one of those fried oysters yet? They are scrumptious," Samantha said, sipping her signature mint julep. Signature in that it was made with her favorite bourbon.

I had disappeared into a seafood-lover's dream once again. I was back home near the water. Big water. And all the delicious little creatures that swam and burrowed within it. Bivalves, crustaceans, and all the fishes in the sea. The Atlantic was only two and a half hours away. And Chesapeake Bay a mere hour. Almost close enough to smell it. Meanwhile, I was eating my way closer to the shore.

"I will in a minute. This crab soup is unbelievable." I savored the creamy rich flavors. "I've been indulging myself in fresh seafood these last couple of weeks. Welcoming myself home, I guess." I took a sip of my Cosmo and admired the view through the windows overlooking the Potomac. The water sparkled with the rays of the setting sun.

"You could have knocked me over with a feather when I learned you'd come home and were working for Russell. After all those years of trying to stay away, you just couldn't resist that old siren call, could you?" She took a big sip from her julep and smiled at me.

I enjoyed another couple of spoonsful of soup before taking the bait. "Well, I kind of fell into it. That commercial development position evaporated in a real estate crumble the very day I arrived. Thank God, Karen found this position with Russell, otherwise I'd be in a world of hurt. Trying to pay my mother's bills and all."

Samantha swished the whiskey mixture in her glass. "I was simply stunned to hear about Karen. I'm so sorry I was out of town when it happened. I know how devastated you and your family were. She was a bright light on the Hill. Smart and principled. It's such a senseless loss."

There was that word again. I finished my soup, took another sip of my Cosmo, and changed the subject.

"Speaking of Karen, I was curious what you know about her boss, Congressman Jackson. She made it sound like he's really trying hard to forge some strategic relationships in Congress. If so, I'd like to keep an eye on him. For Senator Russell's sake."

Samantha raised an eyebrow. "I thought you said you were his managerial accountant and financial consultant. Sounds to me like you're getting your fingers back into that messy ol' Washington pie."

I tried to smile disarmingly. "Can't help it, I guess. Old instincts at work. I like to know who the players are. If I can help the senator, I will. And you know everything that's going on in Washington. The good, the bad, and the ugly. So I figured I'd pick your brain and get up to speed."

"All righty, then. Off the record, of course. Jackson is a rising star and getting more attention in the party these last two years. The Democrats are clearly grooming him for the future, in my opinion. He's got the entire package. Solid record. Strong family back home in Nebraska. Keeps his nose clean here in Washington, and no, I haven't invited him over. He's already on the fast track." She grinned.

"I'm impressed. What about his chief of staff, Jed Molinoff? What's your opinion of him?"

Samantha took another sip and reached for a fried oyster before answering. "He's your typical hyper-ambitious chief staffer who knows his star rises and falls with the congressman. He's made it a point to impress some of the senior representatives and even some senators, so he's getting kind of full of himself. He can also be a little prick from what I've heard. Likes to throw his so-called weight around and impress junior staffers."

"That kind of confirms my opinion of him. And Karen's."

Samantha signaled for another drink, then jiggled the ice cubes in her empty glass. "There was a rumor about Karen and Molinoff. I don't know if —"

"She told me about the affair. She was also breaking up with him the night that she was killed." I watched the pink concoction swirl in my glass. "That's what she was doing outside in her car that night, dammit. Calling all her Hill contacts to find another position. She was quitting Jackson's office because of Jed. And now that I've gotten a chance to see him in action, I'd have to agree with your description. Except, I'd make it stronger. He's a bastard. If it wasn't for Jed, Karen wouldn't have been outside when that vicious scum walked by looking for targets." I drained the glass.

Samantha watched me carefully. "Life's not fair, Molly. You and I know that better than most people. The good die young. And leave the rest of us to clean up the mess. Let it go."

I sank back into my chair as the waitress took my empty glass and provided Samantha with a replenished one. "You're right. And I wish I could let it go, but I can't. Jed Molinoff keeps doing things that set off my buzzer."

"Like what?"

"Well, for starters, I caught him coming out of Karen's apartment when I went back for her clothes. He didn't see me because I hid downstairs. The bastard was even talking to his wife on his cell while he was there."

"What do you think he was looking for?"

"Personal items and photos, probably. I saw him stuffing something into his jacket pocket, and the photos in Karen's desk were all messed up. I'm guessing he came to remove any link between Karen and himself. Suddenly remembering his wife and kids in Nebraska, no doubt." I gave a disgusted snort.

"That was pretty brazen but understandable, Molly. He's just covering his ass."

"Yeah, I know, but he's also been doing weird stuff at Jackson's office. One of Karen's staffer friends saw Jed rifling Karen's desk and copying files from her computer. When this girl said something to him, Jed had her reassigned to a lower-level job in Records."

"Nothing strange in that, Molly. Again, it was just cover-your-ass tactics."

"Yeah, I know. But he's also sent some creepy guy he just rehired to spy on the office."

"Creepy guy?"

I accepted the new Cosmo the waitress offered. "Some guy who got in trouble earlier for harshly berating a female staffer. Larry something." I took a large sip and felt the vodka fuel my righteous indignation.

"Larry Fillmore?" Samantha looked appalled. "Good Lord. That's not good for Jackson if Fillmore's skulking around the office."

Once again I was grateful for Samantha's rolodex memory and ability to sort gossip along with gospel. "That sounds like the name. Talk to me. What have you heard?"

Samantha took a drink, then licked the mint. "Larry Fillmore is a smarmy little ass-kisser who's bounced around from one Hill office to another. He's a razor-sharp staffer, but has zero people skills and his set point is on confrontation, according to the buzz. That's what usually causes his reassignments. Certainly not lack of brains. Rumor has it his former wife put a restraining order on him a few years ago. She was also a staffer, and apparently he kept showing up at her place after the divorce, harassing her. She finally left the Hill and left town. He's lucky she never charged him with anything, or he would have lost his job."

"Actually, he did lose his position in Jackson's office and was reassigned elsewhere. Apparently Karen caught him browbeating the female staffer and insisted Jed let him go. Now that Karen's gone, Jed's hired Larry again, according to Karen's friend. Jed claimed he needed Larry now that Karen was gone."

Samantha didn't say anything at first, but I could tell from her worried expression she was thinking about what I said.

"Well, Molly, now you've raised my curiosity too. I may ask some of my mice to keep track of Jackson's office and see what's going on."

"Mice?"

"It sounds so much better than spies, don't you think? They're simply good friends who're scattered about town, keeping their eyes and ears open. How else do you think I get all this information?"

"Your secret's safe with me."

"And now that you're back, you can keep

me apprised as to how the flamboyant Senator Russell is doing. Nothing confidential, you understand." She gave me a knowing smile. "Just keep your ears open at all those receptions and if anything gives your antennae a buzz, I'd like to hear about it. You used to have good instincts."

"Okay, anything that gives me a buzz, I'll pass along. As long as it doesn't compromise the senator, of course." Remembering something that had buzzed a few days ago, I added, "By the way, what do you know about the Epsilon Group? I've heard its name mentioned. Apparently some international speakers or some such."

"Well, that's an abrupt change from the tawdry Larry Fillmore and his ilk. Let's see, the Epsilon Group." Samantha closed her eyes, clearly calling up her mental data files. "Oh, yes, it's a high-level think tank that sponsors forums on international finance mostly. Lots of brainpower. Distinguished university professors and academics or officials of the international financial community, like finance ministers. And investment bankers, too. They come up with policy papers. But their main purpose is to craft financial initiatives that can be incorporated into legislation that can then be introduced into Congress and the European

Union. Apparently some filthy-rich old investment banker in New York funded it years before he died."

"Whoa," I said in wide-eyed admiration, then held up my glass. "That's even more than I got from Senator Baker and he's been going to their seminars."

"I'm only as good as my sources." She raised her glass in turn. "To my mice."

"Squeak, squeak."

"Now, enough about official Washington. Let's get back to finding *you* some companionship. Male companionship, that is. I think it's time you got off the bench and back into the game."

I sank into my chair, laughing. Letting the vodka float take me. "Good lord, Samantha, I'm surrounded every day. You forget that Russell is still entertaining Congress, region by region. Believe me, I'm up to my neck in meeting people. And making new friends." I flashed her my meet-the-client smile, which only made Samantha laugh.

"I know the senator is still working his way through Congress. That's a lot of receptions, and a lot of men. So, tell me truthfully, Molly, there must have been someone you've met recently who got your attention. If not, then I'm going to check your pulse."

"Nope, no one," I lied, glancing to the

side before I took another large sip.

Samantha fixed me with her eagle's gaze. "I saw that."

I widened my eyes as innocently as possible, given the vodka. "What?"

"Don't try to lie, Molly. I saw that look. You look to the left every time you lie."

I do? I didn't know that. Not good. "I'm not lying," I protested feebly.

"You met someone, didn't you?"

"No, I didn't . . ." Glancing to the left again. *Oh, damn.* Blame it on the vodka. I guess I couldn't drink and lie at the same time.

Samantha set her julep glass on the table with a thump. *"Mendacity!* All around me is mendacity," she proclaimed in a melodramatic mezzo-soprano. A couple turned their heads from a nearby table.

I had to laugh. "Well, if you're going to quote Tennessee Williams, I guess I'll have to tell the truth." I took another large drink and threw caution, and all attempt at mendacity, to the winds. "Yes, I've met someone, but he's just an old friend from high school. We've gone to dinner a couple of times and he took me sightseeing. And we've gone running along the canal a few times. That's all."

"Old friend from high school, hmmmm."

Samantha closed her eyes. "I vaguely recall your telling me about some good-looking guy who had a motorcycle."

Again, I marveled at Samantha's memory. "I can't believe you remember all that."

Samantha grinned. "I also remember you were dying to finally get into a co-ed school in your senior year. I don't know how you endured that girls' school for so long. At least the nuns at Saint Matthews in Washington let us girls and boys be together."

I had to laugh. "And I remember some of the trouble you got into with those nuns."

Samantha examined me closely, her eyes not missing anything. "Let's get back to you and this old flame from the past. How did you two get together? Had you been keeping in touch with each other or something?"

"No, he tracked me down after seeing a charming photo of me in that rag, the *D.C. Dirt.* We went out for coffee and caught up. End of story."

"I'd say it was the beginning, Molly. If you'll let it. Tell me about him. What's he been doing all these years?"

"Serving his country as a career Marine. He went off to Vietnam right after high school. Stayed in and became an officer. Retired a few years ago. Lives here in Washington."

Samantha's expression softened. "I like him already."

"I figured you would. He's a good guy. And right now, we're just friends. And I'd like to keep it that way. I need friends right now, Samantha. My world has turned upside down these last few months. I'm still trying to adjust to it all."

My pitch for sympathy seemed to work. Samantha relented. "I understand, sugar. Friends are what help us get through the tough times. I know how much I depend on mine. My guys. I depend on them to talk sense to me when I need it and escort me to the theatre when I need that." She gave a rueful smile. "And I just lost one of my dearest sweetest guys last month. That's why I was still out of town when you arrived and when Karen died. I was still mourning for my dear Sol."

Sol Karpinsky. "I was so sorry to hear about his death," I said. "It's a huge loss to the Senate. He was the last old lion. The watchdog."

"God rest his soul. He'd been doing much better after his last heart attack. Then, suddenly, he was gone." She swirled the julep before she drank. "I still miss him."

"I'd forgotten you and he had, had . . ."

"You can say it. We had an affair before

251

he was divorced, but I wasn't the reason."

"I'd forgotten the details. Boy, I also forgot that you can drink and still be sober. How do you do that, Miss Thing?"

She gave me a devilish smile. "You never could hold your liquor, Molly. Don't you remember some of the scrapes I had to rescue you from?"

Memories floated up through the vodka. "Good God, you're right."

"And my beloved Beauregard taught me how to drink with the best and still hold my own. My Bojangles. Bless his heart and soul. Here's to you, Beau." She raised her glass.

I followed suit, finishing off my Cosmo. "To Beau. And bless his taste in jewelry." I glanced to the diamonds, rubies, and sapphires that adorned several of Samantha's fingers.

"That's why I called him Bojangles."

"Bling, bling."

"Oh, and sugar, please let me know if you need money. I don't want you doing without in this town. No need. You're closer to me than some of my own kin."

"That's sweet, Samantha, but I think I'll be okay now."

"Well, just keep it in mind. Thanks to my late daddy and my sweet Beauregard, I've got more money than God. And even I can't spend it all."

I laughed so hard I barely noticed the waitress serve our fresh lobster and scallops entrée. "Oh my God, Samantha. I didn't know how much I'd missed talking to you until now. Maybe if I'd had you around for advice, I wouldn't have made so many mistakes over the years."

Samantha took another large sip. "We all fall down, sugar. What's important is that we keep gettin' back up again. And, incidentally, I saw that photo in the *Dirt,* and I thought it was cute as the dickens. And your wardrobe is lookin' a whole lot better now." She gave a low chuckle.

"You know who wrote that little knife job? Diedre Turner from my old girls' school, St. Mary's. Apparently she's a part-time gossip columnist for that rag."

Samantha gave a dismissive snort. "That little pissant? Phooey. She's gone after everyone in town. Trying to make a name for herself. She's aimed some of her little arrows at me. Ignore her."

"She's got an acid pen, so watch out. She might get wind of your finishing school," I teased.

This time Samantha threw back her head and let out her trademark sultry low laugh.

"Oh, sugar, what could she possibly say about me that hasn't already been said?"

THIRTEEN

I drank my coffee while I looked out the bay windows of my sunny kitchen at the people walking by the townhouse. Some hurried, briefcases in hand. Others strolled, dogs on leashes. Young mothers pushed babies and toddlers in fancy strollers that didn't exist when I pushed my little girls along these streets.

My cell phone rang on the table and I glanced at my watch. 7:35. Couldn't be Peter. He knew I'd be in the office in ten minutes. I saw Celeste's name on the screen.

"Hey, Celeste. Are you at work already?"

"No, I'm not. I just got off the Metro and thought I'd call before I reached the office. I wanted to update you on the latest searches and stuff."

"Oh, good. What did you find?"

"There were several emails that mentioned Epsilon. Some that referred to recent contributions to Congressman Jackson's election fund. And another to a charity that Jackson sponsors back in Nebraska. It provides scholarships for low-income students."

"Did everything look okay to you?"

"I haven't searched all the emails yet, but nothing has made my little buzzer go off yet. Which makes me feel better, to tell you the truth. I was afraid you'd found something fishy about the group."

"No, not at all. I've asked several of my Hill contacts, and the Epsilon Group seems to be exactly what it purports to be. A policy group that concentrates on international financial issues. At least that's what their speakers seem to address from what I've heard."

"There were several emails from Jed announcing Epsilon Group forums on different issues. And there were also a couple of emails about legislation and policy papers. Apparently Jackson has included a couple of their policy points in some legislation he's working on in subcommittee."

"That's interesting. So, Jackson has been going to their forums, too, I guess."

"I guess. I'll keep copying all of those emails onto flash drives so I can mail them to you when I'm finished. I want you to have them."

There was an anxious quality to Celeste's

voice that reached out. I couldn't miss it. "Is that creepy guy, Larry Fillmore, still spying on everybody?"

"Yeah, he is, the bastard. He's really pissing me off, too. I told him yesterday to stop hanging over me. He just stood there and smirked at me, like he didn't care."

That gave me a bad feeling, especially after what Samantha said about Fillmore. "Listen, Celeste, I don't want you to get into any trouble on my account. You don't have to do any more searches for me. I think we've established nothing illegal or underhanded is going on in Jackson's office. Jed may be a son of a bitch, but he doesn't seem to be breaking the law."

"That's okay, Molly. I want to finish those files. No matter what Creepy Larry does. I swear, he's even calling my home phone and leaving hang-up calls. Leaves them on the answering machine."

"Whoa, Celeste. Are you sure it's him?"

"No, I'm not," she exhaled a loud breath. "But who else would be calling me three times a day? The caller ID says 'out of area' for the phone number. I figure it's gotta be him. Well, it's not gonna work. He's not going to threaten me like he did that junior staffer. She was the one he targeted when Karen caught him in the act. And he got really mad when Karen told him to back off."

"He sounds like a real piece of work."

"Oh, he is. He likes to intimidate women with his 'look.' He's got these dark eyes that glare at you. Dark hair, pale skin. Like I said, really creepy. But he didn't intimidate Karen, not even when he threatened her."

"Tell me about that again. What did he say exactly?"

"When Jed finally told him he was being reassigned, Larry was furious. He slammed around the office, throwing his stuff into a briefcase. Then, he stomped over to Karen's desk and told her 'she'd be sorry.' "

Now I really felt uneasy. "You know, Celeste, I'm beginning to wish you didn't work in that office. The atmosphere there has deteriorated, badly it seems."

"Don't worry about me, Molly. Jed used to intimidate me, but he doesn't anymore. I've seen him for the weakling he is. And those emails show that Karen was the one feeding him most of the policy information and data. He acts like he knows everything, and he doesn't. It's just show. I think that's why Jed has that attack dog, Larry, around. To scare away anyone who might threaten him."

"Well, forgive me for sounding like a

mom, but it sounds like you're in a snake pit there. And I think you should look for a transfer out."

"We'll see. I've actually gotten used to it here in Records. It's quieter and less hectic, I'll say that." Her voice sounded lighter, like she was trying to make a joke. "Listen, I'm in front of my building so I'd better go inside and get to work. Talk to you later, Molly."

"Take care, Celeste," I said as she clicked off.

Tossing the rest of my coffee down the sink, I grabbed my over-the-shoulder briefcase and headed out. Time for me to get to my office, too. Maybe the fast walk to Senator Russell's mansion would help dispel the uneasiness I felt about Celeste.

Maybe I *was* being a mom. Then again, maybe my antennae were more acute than hers. Maybe I should call Samantha and ask her to find something more on this Larry Fillmore. Alert her mice.

Closing my front door, I noticed the enormous tabby cat sunning himself beside my flowerbeds again. "Good morning, Striped Kitty," I'd taken to calling him. "Leave the birds alone," I warned as I raced down the steps.

Striped Kitty meowed in reply, which

probably translated to, "No promises." Predators. They were everywhere.

I bent over the railing overlooking a stretch of the C&O Canal. Water was pouring overtop one of the locks.

More out of breath than usual after my run, I vowed that one of these days I'd be able to talk and run and not break my stride. Of course, running with Danny meant I'd already ramped it up. The way my heart was pounding right now, I figured my cardio workout was on maximum.

"You okay?" he asked as he stretched out one long muscular leg, then the other.

I followed suit and stretched, noticing Danny had a healthy sheen. I was dripping. "Why do I get the feeling you're slumming when you're working out with me? You barely broke a sweat. Look at you. And I'm beat."

"You'll be okay. You're getting faster. I can tell."

"Flattery, flattery." I bent upside down with my palms flat on the ground between my legs.

"You just got all caught up in talking about this Celeste and all the weird stuff happening with her." He grabbed his wrists and stretched both arms behind himself.

How could anybody look that good in a worn-out tee shirt and shorts? All muscle. "Property of U.S. Marine Corps" was stamped across his olive green chest. Well, *semper fi.* I just hoped I looked halfway decent. Of course, my tongue was probably hanging out as far as the one on my Rolling Stones tee shirt.

"Be honest, Danny. Do I sound crazy?"

"No, you don't sound crazy. But I'm not sure about this Celeste. Listening to your description, she does sound a little paranoid. Who knows why Molinoff transferred her? Maybe her work was unsatisfactory. And her story about this Larry guy skulking around her office, spying on her. I gotta tell you," he said, shaking his head. "That does sound pretty off-base."

He unzipped the small pack he carried on his back and offered me a clean towel, which I took gratefully. "Well, I ran the longer version past an old friend of mine —"

"There's a longer version?"

"*Yes.*" I flicked the towel at him. He caught it mid-swat, his hand moving so fast I barely saw it. "I ran it past an old friend who has her finger on Washington's pulse. She knows everybody in Washington and everything they're up to, good or bad. And she confirmed this Larry Fillmore was a bad actor. He's gotten into trouble in several Hill offices. Likes to intimidate women."

Danny arched a brow. "Really. Well, that changes the whole picture."

"Doesn't it now? Apparently this Larry guy threatened Karen after she insisted that Jed transfer him. He told Karen she'd be 'sorry.' Then, as soon as Karen died, Jed Molinoff rehired him to spy on the office staff."

"This Larry guy is the one who keeps prowling around Celeste?"

"Yeah. It sounds like Molinoff wants to drive Celeste out of the office and is using this Larry to do it. I think she needs to change positions, the sooner the better. Transfer to another Hill office like Karen was going to. But it sounds like Celeste is digging in her heels, refusing to be pushed out."

Danny motioned me toward 31st Street, heading up the hill to the main drag, M Street. "Is she still doing those email searches for you?"

"Yes, even though she hasn't found anything incriminating. I told her she didn't need to do them anymore. I don't want her to get into any more trouble, in case they're checking on her. She says she's covering her search tracks, whatever that means."

"It means she's a clever girl. Let's hope she's clever enough to stay out of trouble. Because it sounds like that Larry guy is looking for anything he can find to get her in trouble with Molinoff."

"You know, it makes no sense that Jed Molinoff would act this way. Why would he care if a staffer was reading those emails? They weren't confidential. From what Celeste said, there's nothing in any of those emails Molinoff wouldn't want known. They sound like ordinary business, even the ones about the Epsilon Group. Other policy groups try to influence legislation and make political contributions."

"What was that group again?"

"It's a high-level policy think tank called the Epsilon Group. Emphasis on international finance. They give a lot of speeches around the country." An idea came to me as I stepped around a large sidewalk planter full of tulips. "I was going to attend one of their presentations next week. Would you like to come with me? It's at Dumbarton Oaks on Tuesday. It'll be a pretty setting at least, even if the speech is dry."

Danny grinned. "Are you asking me on a date?"

"Yeah, I guess I am."

"Only if we can have dinner afterwards. If it's like most of those affairs, it'll be mediocre wines and dry appetizers. International finance or no, we can do better than that."

He paused right below the busy intersection of M Street and 31st. Reaching into his small pack again, he withdrew two small water bottles, offering me one. I gratefully accepted and drained it while watching the crowds walk by.

It was Friday night and everyone was out, heading to restaurants and cafes. And they looked way better than Danny and I did in our sweaty workout clothes and our healthy sheens. Even the tourists were starting to stare at us.

"I'm sorry I messed up your plans for tonight. You probably had another great café already reserved, and then I called and asked you to go running instead."

"That's okay. The café will wait." He drained his bottle. "Besides, it sounded like you needed to talk."

"Well, you're right about that. Running always helps me sort through things when I'm worrying. And it helped to bounce this stuff off you, too. You're a good sounding board."

"Anytime, Molly." Then he motioned me through the tourists and locals and headed toward the curb, arm outstretched. He signaled a taxi. "C'mon, let's go to dinner."

I stared at him perplexed. "We can't go to a restaurant looking like this."

"Sure we can. We're having dinner with the tourists along the Mall. Burgers and brats from a truck, cold drinks, ice cream on a stick. Gourmet fare." He motioned an approaching taxi to a stop in front of us.

"Well, at least we'll fit in," I said with a laugh as he opened the door.

"When's the last time you ate hot dogs on the Mall, Molly?" he asked, climbing in after me.

"It's been years."

"Okay. Let's start where most of the tourists are. Lots of food trucks there. Washington Monument, please," he said to the cabbie.

"She's persistent, I'll say that," Larry Fillmore said into his cell phone as he drove through early evening traffic on Pennsylvania Avenue. "And cleverer than most."

"Too clever," the man's deep voice replied. "And she's much too curious. We don't want her stumbling across information she shouldn't. Especially since we think she's talking."

"What're you going to do?" Larry paused

265

at a traffic signal. The gleaming white Capitol building lay straight ahead, the tip of the Pennsylvania Avenue arrow.

"First, we need to find out exactly how much she knows. And who she's talking to. Then we'll turn up the heat."

Larry continued down the avenue. "Let me know what you want me to do."

"Count on it," the man said before he clicked off.

FOURTEEN

I let my gaze drift over the beauty of Dumbarton Oaks gardens while I sipped my wine. They were as lovely as I remembered. Towering oak trees shaded the manicured grounds. Dave and I had attended a reception here for one of the organizations he supported. It was a fundraiser for the nonprofit's scholarship fund.

"That last mushroom canapé was about as dry as Ambassador Holmberg's speech," Danny observed beside me.

"I think I've heard as much as I can stand about global financial initiatives." I sipped the mediocre Chardonnay.

"Holmberg did make some good points," Danny added. "Developing nations' populations and competition for global natural resources. That's a ticking time bomb."

"I agree. But I could have absorbed more if he wasn't such a monotone." I leaned against the stone balustrade that bordered the stairway where we stood overlooking the gardens.

Danny frowned at his wineglass. "We can definitely do better."

"Well, at least we look better than we did the other night at the Mall."

"You're forgetting Sunday's brunch. Thanks again for inviting me to your cousin's. I take it I was brought over for family inspection."

I grinned. "You might say that. And you impressed the locals, which is definitely a plus."

"I aim to please."

I was about to follow up on that comment, but my eye caught a familiar face among the crowds below. Jed Molinoff. I pushed away from the balustrade, the better to watch him.

"Okay, Molly. You're tracking somebody. Who is it?"

"Jed Molinoff," I said, stepping around another couple who were admiring the view. "I spotted him walking across the lawn. I bet he's here because of Holmberg."

I looked around the clusters of people mingling below until I spotted Jed again. He was talking to a shorter bald man, gesturing and smiling. Then, with a nod, Jed was on the move again. Weaving his way toward a larger cluster of people that had formed around the evening's speaker, Ambassador Holmberg.

"There he is, moving in on Holmberg." I pointed as I started down the steps. Seeing Jed Molinoff was like waving a red flag in front of a bull. The anger and resentment I still felt for Karen's boss was never far below the surface.

Danny caught up with me as I hurried down the rest of the steps. "We're on a surveillance mission, I take it. Target Molinoff?"

"Yeah, I want to see who he talks to." I began to weave around the clusters of attendees who were chowing down on the dry appetizers like it was their last meal. Some people will eat anything.

"Just one question. Why?"

Pausing near the outer ring of people surrounding Jed and the Ambassador, I looked him straight in the eye. "I'm not really sure, Danny. Maybe because seeing Jed reminds me he's the reason Karen was outside in her car that night when a vicious thug came trolling for prey. He's partially responsible in my book, and I'm angry." I looked over the heads blocking my view of Jed and companions. "I'm also mad because he sent his office creep to spy on Celeste. Maybe I just want to turn the tables and spy on him. See how he likes being watched."

"That sounds more like surveil and harass. Sure you want to do that, Molly?"

Surveil and harass. That had a nice ring to it. "Yeah. I do. Let's see how spineless Jed handles being 'surveiled.' Is that the right word?"

"Close. Sounds like you don't care if you make him mad."

I gave a derisive snort. "Jed Molinoff's a coward. I scowled at him once at the senator's reception, and he hightailed it from the room. You should have seen him when Casey told him to back off with Karen. Jed took one look at Casey and went white as a sheet. In the words of my old friend, the Washington sage, he's a 'little prick.' "

Danny laughed softly. "Okay. I got the picture. Mission, surveil and harass. Target, spineless coward. May I make a tactical suggestion?" He pointed to the mezzanine behind us that jutted out right above where Ambassador Holmberg was holding forth with Jed and others. "We need to reclaim the high ground for this mission. Just a suggestion."

I glanced at the balcony. We'd have a great view of Jed and company and — more importantly — he'd have a great view of us watching him. Perfect.

"Excellent suggestion. I'll bet you've done this before."

"Once or twice."

"Okaaaay, lead the way, squad leader. Or whatever I call you."

"That'll work." He guided me by the elbow to the stairs where we stationed ourselves on the balcony.

Glancing over the crowd below, I saw that Jed had indeed sidled up beside Ambassador Holmberg, face showing rapt attention. Hanging on to every monotone word Holmberg uttered. Standing beside Jed in the packed circle was a shorter dark-haired man with a high forehead that was fast receding into his hairline. He'd be bald within a few years. He looked familiar. I searched through my memory for the pictures of congressional staff I'd perused online. That had to be Larry Fillmore. Dark hair, pale skin, intense expression.

"You've spotted someone else," Danny said as he stood beside me with his back to the crowd below. He leaned against the stone wall, watching me as I watched the crowd.

"How could you tell?" I said, still watching.

"Your line of sight shifted ever so slightly.

Who is it?"

"Gotta be Larry Fillmore, the creep who's bothering Celeste. He matches the photo I saw in the congressional staff directory."

Danny glanced over his shoulder, checking the crowd. "Good job, corporal."

"Did I just get a promotion? I thought the starting point was as a private."

He gave a mocking scowl. "You're in the Marines, not Army. Stick with me, and you'll move through the ranks. Field promotions."

Danny's joking manner made me laugh, which felt good. I noticed that the cluster of people around Holmberg started laughing too, so the ambassador must have made a joke. Jed threw back his head as he laughed, and in so doing, he looked up. Jed froze the moment his gaze landed on me. His smile crumbled.

"Target acquired," I said, as I glared down, watching with great pleasure as Jed's face drained of color.

I lifted my glass toward Jed, then flipped the remaining wine into the planter below in a contemptuous gesture. Jed blinked and backed away from the ambassador.

"That's right. Run away, you coward."

I noticed Larry Fillmore ease away from the ambassador as well, following after Jed.

Watching Jed confer with Larry Fillmore, I crossed my arms and kept staring at him with a scornful expression. I must have looked for all the world like a scolding wife spotting her errant husband with another woman.

Danny glanced over his shoulder and chuckled deep in his throat. "You can let up on him now, Molly. He's in retreat."

"No way. I got him on the run. He's calling for backup."

Larry Fillmore glanced my way. I glared back, noticing Fillmore didn't even blink. He simply smirked up at me. His expression did change, however, when Danny looked their way. Fillmore and Jed both scuttled away like sewer rats.

"Mission accomplished," Danny announced. "Spineless coward fled the field, tail between his legs. That's one helluva scowl you've got there, corporal. Weapons grade. I think I'd better promote you before you turn it on me."

Once again, Danny's humor caused the tension of the last few moments to evaporate. I felt myself relax as I laughed and leaned against the stone balustrade. "Boy, I never knew it was this easy to advance in rank. I should have joined the Marines rather than wasting my weapons-grade scowl on politicians all these years."

"Feel better?"

I released a huge sigh and glanced at Ambassador Holmberg mingling with the crowd below, still holding forth. "Yeah, I do. I know that sounds petty, but I can't help it. I wanted Jed to know what I think of him."

Danny was looking at me with a smile as he leaned against the balustrade. "I think he got your message loud and clear."

"Thanks for going along with me on this mission. Weird as it was."

"I'll ride shotgun for you anytime, Molly. I've had some moments or two of vengeance myself. Now that the mission is accomplished, what do you say we ditch this place and head to a real restaurant? There's a place in Adams-Morgan I want to show you. I think you'll . . ."

I didn't hear Danny's restaurant description. In fact, I missed everything after "shotgun." I'd caught sight of Larry Fillmore leading a tall broad-shouldered man up to Ambassador Holmberg. No need for the congressional online directory. This face I remembered. I'd never been able to forget it no matter how hard I'd tried. Long-buried memories seared through me, burning as hot as yesteryear. I sank into the flames until Danny's voice called me back.

"Molly? Are you there?"

I snapped awake and the past slithered back into the bushes. "Uh, sorry . . ." My gaze darted from Danny back to the scene below.

Danny studied me for a long minute before speaking. "The last time someone looked at me like that, he had a knife in his hand."

I kept staring below, unable to stop.

"Who the hell is that, Molly? I figure it's gotta be the older silver-haired guy talking with Fillmore and the ambassador."

I took a deep breath before answering. "Congressman Edward Ryker of Montana."

Danny stared below. "So that's Ryker? He's been here forever. Over thirty years, I think."

"Thirty-two."

"Isn't he chairman of the House Financial Services Committee?"

I watched Ryker smile his oily smile and grab Holmberg's elbow as they all laughed. Fillmore laughed, too.

"Yes, the Ranking Majority Member." I paused, wondering how to phrase what I had to say next, then decided to just spit it out. "And the man responsible for my husband's death. He may not have fired the bullet into Dave's brain, but he might as well have."

This time, Danny studied me for only a second. "You're going to have to explain that to me on the way to dinner. Let's get out of here." He extended his arm and I took it, then turned my back on the reminders of my past and walked away.

Danny poured the remaining Pinot Noir into my glass, then his own. "So there was never any way to prove Ryker was taking bribes."

"Never." I ran my finger around the rim of my wineglass. "Ryker was careful not to leave any traceable connection to the mining companies. No phone messages. No letters. There was never proof, only allegations. Rumors. Some former employees were brave enough to talk to Dave, but they were afraid to go public." I took another big sip. "Dave confronted Ryker in the House corridor once, and that really pissed him off. Dave said there was steam coming out of Ryker's ears. Of course, that was the final straw for Ryker. After that confrontation, the newspaper attacks picked up. The Colorado papers ran articles practically every week. All of it smears and innuendoes and lies against Dave."

Some of those memory fragments floated past my eyes, and I brushed them away. "They insinuated Dave took bribes and payoffs for his votes. Lies, all of it. David Grayson never sold his vote for anything or anyone. Ryker paid that Grand Junction developer to lie. Gossip had it he retired from real estate two years after Dave's death." I ran my fingernail down the linen tablecloth seam. "Of course, after Dave's death there was this orgy of apologies and soul-searching in the newspapers, hand-wringing over whether their accusations had led to his despair and suicide. *Bastards.*" I flicked a crumb of French bread from the tablecloth. "Of course, the opposition kept spewing out their lies, emboldened by Dave's suicide. They said it 'proved' his guilt."

No matter how hard I tried, I couldn't keep my feelings from showing on my face. I deliberately hadn't let these thoughts and memories course though me for years. They had a power of their own and had kept me in their thrall years ago. Too long. It had taken concentrated effort to break their hold. I didn't want to go under again.

"That must have been hard. Listening to all that."

I didn't look up. I knew what Danny was

doing. He was watching me intently, listening and barely saying a word. "Ohhhhhh, yeah."

"You wanted to fight back, didn't you?"

That question surprised me, and I glanced up. Disarmed by his perceptiveness, I answered honestly. "It still shows, huh?" I shook my head. "Damn."

"I've been there, Molly, so I recognize it."

"I wanted Dave to fight back in the press. Name names. Hit Ryker where it would hurt."

"That's because you're a fighter, Molly, like your father."

"Damn right." I allowed some of the forgotten passion of yesteryear to fill my voice. "Ryker was the one covering up his corruption. Dave had refused to go along with Ryker's lead on the House committee on mineral resources once he discovered Ryker was being paid off by the mining industry execs. They wanted to insert language into the bills that gave them preferential drilling rights. Unfortunately, Dave couldn't go to the press without any proof. I understood that. What I couldn't understand was why he didn't try to counter those malicious lies Ryker spread in the Colorado newspapers. He kept saying his record would speak for itself. But that just played into Ryker's hands. He saw Dave's actions as weakness, and he went in for the kill."

Danny was quiet for a moment. "Some people aren't fighters, Molly. They don't have the killer instinct."

I sipped my wine, letting the velvety-smooth finish roll on my tongue. I stared out the window onto Connecticut Avenue, watching traffic pass by. "Dave was smart and passionate about helping others. There wasn't a dishonest or deceptive bone in his body. Bringing him to Washington was like leading a lamb to the slaughter. I've come to see that now. I guess my old friend is right. She says the good die young and leave the rest of us to clean up the mess."

Danny gave a crooked smile and watched me sip my wine for a minute. Then he asked softly, "Have you forgiven him yet?"

Whoa. Danny's perceptiveness was downright spooky. But since I'd had a fair amount of Pinot Noir with only soup and salad to soak it up, I looked at him, completely open.

"You mean for killing himself or for not fighting back?"

"Both."

I stared out into traffic once again. "I tried to. I really did. I learned how to release the anger years ago, otherwise I would have exploded. And I learned to channel most of it into fighting for the causes Dave and I both believed in. Education and the environment. I really thought most of it was gone until last month when Karen died." I let my eyes focus on the red lights changing at the intersection. "But it came surging back. You got to see a sample tonight." I sent him an apologetic smile. "Sorry about that."

"No apologies necessary. Anger is an old friend. Or enemy, depending how you look at it."

I held up my wineglass. "To old enemies and old friends."

Danny clinked my glass with his. "Whatever the hell that means."

I took a deep drink of the luscious smooth red. "Well, for one thing, it means I was right to be suspicious of Jed Molinoff. If his assistant is cozying up to Ryker, then there's something going on. Ryker doesn't come out and ooze his oily charm for nothing. If he's laughing and talking with Ambassador Holmberg, then you bet there's a reason. Ryker is chairman of the Financial Services Committee. So there are millions of reasons why he could be interested. And they all have dollar signs on them."

Danny looked skeptical. "Maybe Ryker was there to hear Holmberg speak, like the rest of us."

"Maybe." I swirled the remaining wine in my glass. "But a leopard doesn't change his spots. Ryker's spots have gotten bigger over the years. Rumors have his personal fortune growing at a healthy rate."

"Rumors?"

I was about to repeat some of them when my cell phone jangled in my purse. Checking my watch as I dug it out, I wondered who would be calling me after ten o'clock at night.

Celeste's name flashed on the screen.

"Hey, Celeste, is everything all right?"

"No, Molly, it's not." Traffic sounded in the background. "Could you meet me, please? I'm over at that coffee shop in Foggy Bottom where we met last time."

"Sure, sure, I'll come over right now. What's happening?"

"Somebody came into my apartment tonight when I went out for my run. I tell you, Molly, it scared the hell out of me." Her voice was higher than usual.

A cold ball formed in the pit of my stomach. "Someone got into your apartment? Are you sure?" Danny looked over his coffee cup, his concern evident.

"Absolutely. When I came back from my run, several desk drawers where my computer sits were hanging open and so were

281

drawers in my dining room bureau and in my bedroom. Whoever that freak is, he even went through my closets! My dresses were all pushed back, and the medicine cabinet in the bathroom was wide open. *Freak!*"

I looked at Danny while I repeated. "He went through your desk and your bedroom, too? My God, Celeste, it sounds like some sicko."

I watched Danny's expression change. He took out his pen and wrote on his napkin.

"Whoever it was, it means he had to be watching me to know exactly when I left for my workout."

Danny handed me the napkin with the word "Message" written on it. "Maybe it's a message, Celeste. If so, that's scary. You need to leave Jackson's office now —"

"To hell with that office, Molly, I'm leaving *town!* Tonight. I packed up my suitcase, my briefcase, and laptop, and all my files, and I got the hell out of that apartment. I'm not staying around while Jed and his goon stalk me."

"Where are you going?"

"My aunt left me her house on the Eastern Shore when she died several months ago. It's been closed up for nearly a year, but I have the key. I plan to hole up there until I can find another job. Maybe in Washington, maybe not. I've had it with this stuff. But I wanted to give you these data files before I go. I'm sorry to be calling so late. Do you think you can come over, please? I want to get on the road before midnight, if I can."

"Sure, Celeste. I'll be right over. Stay inside the coffee shop. I'll be there as soon as I can."

I caught Danny's concerned expression as I closed my phone. "I know what you're thinking, and I'm thinking the same thing. It's way weird —"

"Nope, what I'm thinking is I'll drive you over and stay in my car to keep watch in case this guy followed her." He signaled for the check.

"So, you believe her story?"

"Hell, yes. Someone sent Celeste a message tonight. Whoever is behind this, it looks like they want her out of Congressman Jackson's office."

I ordered some black coffee while Danny signed the check.

Celeste bent over her large takeout coffee. "I have a feeling that guy came in before and didn't find what he was looking for. That's why he came back."

"What do you mean?" I asked, hunched over another cup of coffee. I wasn't going to be able to sleep tonight anyway.

Celeste looked up at me with her clear gaze. "I never leave any search files on my laptop. I put everything that's important or sensitive on flash drives, including those email search files. And I always carry those flash drives with me. I throw them into my purse or briefcase. The only time I don't have them physically with me is when I run outside around my apartment in Capitol Hill. So, I figure Jed's goon watched me long enough to learn my schedule, then he came in and found the flash drives lying beside my laptop."

"Are any of them missing? Did he take anything?"

She shook her head. "No. All of them are there, but they were moved around, my cell phone, too. I think that guy deliberately moved everything and opened drawers and stuff to let me know he had been there and could come back again. He did it to scare me." She shuddered.

That cold hand in my stomach squeezed tighter, and another emotion surfaced. *Guilt.* It was my fault Celeste was in this mess.

"Celeste, I'm so sorry I got you involved in all this. If I hadn't asked you to do those email searches, you never would have gotten on Jed's or Larry's radar screen."

"That's not true, Molly," she countered. "Remember, this all started when I saw Jed searching Karen's computer files and began asking questions. Don't feel bad. I got on Jed's radar screen all by myself."

"Promise me you'll start sending out those job inquiries."

"Believe me, I plan to once I'm away from Washington and safe on the Eastern Shore."

"Email me and let me know where you are and how you're doing, okay?"

"Don't worry, I will." Celeste checked her watch. "I'd better head out now, so I won't be driving too late." She grabbed her coffee and stood; she was still wearing her workout clothes.

Feeling a maternal surge suddenly, I rose and gave Celeste a big hug. A "mom" hug. She squeezed back. "Take care of yourself, Celeste, please. And keep in touch with me, okay? I want to hear from you."

"I will, Molly, I promise. Oh, I almost forgot." She reached into her jacket pocket and brought out two of the portable data storage units or flash drives. They were no bigger than key chains. "These are the files I've already searched. I'll mail you the last one when I finish with it this week."

I dropped both of them into my purse. "Thank you, Celeste, for everything you've done. And don't think that Jed Molinoff and his goon squad are going to get away with threatening staffers. I'm going to spread the word that Larry Fillmore is up to his old tricks," I vowed.

Celeste found a small smile. "Thanks, Molly. I've already emailed Jackson's office my notice of resignation, so they can believe they've successfully run me out of town if they want to. I don't care anymore."

I walked with Celeste out to her car parked in front of the coffee shop. Glimpsing Danny still in his car across the street, I waited for Celeste to rev her engine before giving her a good-bye wave. She waved once more, then pulled out into the steady flow of nighttime D.C. traffic.

I stared after her until she turned the corner, then I walked across the street. Danny was standing beside his car, holding my door open.

"You okay?" was all he asked.

I looked him in the eye and let him read my thoughts. I was a long way from okay.

FIFTEEN

His cell phone rang as he exited the parking garage. He checked the screen and walked away from the pedestrians crowding the downtown street, office workers hurrying to their jobs.

"What's next?" he asked, watching tourists pass by, fanny packs and water bottles at the ready.

"When can you leave for the Bay?" Raymond asked.

"I can be there tonight."

"That's fine. Just let me know when you're in place."

"Roger that." He clicked off, then edged around a line of tourists who waited to load a nearby sightseeing bus.

"Step away from that coffeepot, Peter, I plan to drain it." I marched into the Russell kitchen, two huge coffee mugs in hand.

Peter looked at me with feigned shock.

"Good God, Molly. If you drink all that, we'll have to scrape you off the ceiling before the reception."

"Have to, Peter," I said, filling first one mug then the other with Luisa's dark brew. "I didn't get much sleep last night."

Peter looked at me with a devilish smile. "Would that lack of sleep have anything to do with your increasingly busy social life? Household gossip has it that you've been seeing a retired military officer. I believe Luisa refers to him as 'the colonel.' "

I took a large drink of strong coffee before taking the bait. No way was I up to bantering with Peter without caffeine. A lot of caffeine. "Household gossip, huh? I had no idea I'd fallen into a nest of busybodies."

"That's a non-answer if ever I heard one," Peter teased. "Boy, that relationship must be heating up."

"Relax, Peter. We're old friends from high school. And we spend our time sightseeing around the city or running along the canal."

Peter looked doubtful. "Luisa is going to be very disappointed to hear this."

"Luisa's a matchmaker at heart. She'll find someone else to set up. How about you? You've landed in single-guy heaven, Peter. Girls outnumber guys in Washington by five to one at least."

He gave me a wink. "Good maneuver, Molly. Switched to offense."

I saluted him with my mug before taking another drink. "C'mon, Peter. Girls must be throwing themselves in your path. Why don't you grab one?"

"I do, occasionally." He acknowledged with that deceptively boyish smile of his. "But spare time is a rare commodity around here, as you know."

"Amen. And for the record, my sleep deprivation was caused by worry. I've kind of adopted one of Karen's friends from the office, and she's going through a hard time right now." I deliberately made it sound like my attentions were maternal.

It worked. Peter nodded. "Once a mom, always a mom, right, Molly? Well, you tell her that working on Capitol Hill is exciting, but it also takes its toll on you."

"That's about what I told her. Some can handle the pressure, others can't. And it's okay to head home for a break, too."

Peter checked his watch. "I have to head over to the Hill, so I'll see you this evening with the Western delegations. Old-home week." He drained his coffee as he headed for the door.

I accompanied him into the hallway. "I confess that I'm looking forward to this reception. I figure the entire Colorado Democratic contingent will head straight for me. Some will whine, others will cajole. It should be fun."

Peter cackled. "Looks like we've corrupted you entirely; you sound like an Independent."

"Blame it on my naturally contrarian nature asserting itself. I've never liked someone telling me what to do and whom to vote for. If the Democrats start to annoy me, I'll go over and talk to the Republicans. That'll drive them nuts."

"You are bad, Molly. See you tonight." He sped down the hallway to Albert's waiting car outside.

I finished off the first mug as I walked to my office. Emails and phone calls were waiting for me. Instead of returning to the computer's blinking cursor, however, I stood in the doorway and started on the second mug.

There was no exaggeration in what I told Peter. I had been up most of last night, pacing around my living room in the dark, just the television screen's filtered light flickering on the walls. I barely noticed. My mind was consumed with everything that Celeste had told me earlier that evening.

Jed had sent someone to stalk Celeste,

then break into her apartment. Deliberately invading her privacy, leaving multiple signs a prowler was there. Surely Molinoff wouldn't resort to such tactics because she was checking emails. Was it because she'd dared to question his rehiring of Larry Fillmore? Or was it because Celeste knew about Jed's affair with Karen? That *had* to be it, I decided. Jed needed to protect his squeaky-clean family image so his star could continue to rise alongside Congressman Jackson's. Meanwhile, I agreed with Danny's assessment. Jed was sending a message to Celeste: *Back off!*

That thought angered me. Cowardly Jed probably sent Larry the creep to do the dirty work. Larry was more than a bad actor. According to Samantha, his record on the Hill was rife with office confrontations with young women. Did Molinoff think he could unleash his attack dog at will? We'd see about that.

I slipped my cell phone from my pocket and punched in Samantha's number. After several rings her voice mail came on. "Hey, Samantha, Molly here. I wanted to ask a favor. Could you ask your network of mice to see what else is out there concerning Larry Fillmore? He's up to his old tricks, targeting a friend of Karen's in Jackson's office. Frightened her out of town in fact. Tell your mice to spread the word. And while they're at it, see if they can find someone who knew him personally. Or maybe knew his ex-wife. I want to know if Larry has an even darker side. You know, like violent behavior in the past. Throw some light on it. Fillmore shouldn't get away with scaring talented staffers out of town. You can chalk this up to my being a mom. Thanks, Samantha. I really appreciate it."

I clicked off and continued down the hallway, mind still churning. Maybe a few minutes in the mansion gardens would be calming. I pushed open the glass doors and stood on the patio, admiring the well-tended flowerbeds and shrubbery balanced throughout the garden. Elegance and symmetry.

"Pretty, isn't it?" Casey's voice sounded behind me.

"It surely is," I agreed as Casey walked over to unlock the back gate. I heard the distinct sound of the caterer's truck coming down the mansion driveway. Sure enough, the red and white truck appeared. Checking my watch, I waited until Casey rejoined me on the steps. "Aren't they a little early? Usually they don't show up until noon."

"The senator is pulling out all the stops for this reception. Colorado delegation will be here." He gave me a smile. "I have a feeling you won't be happy when you see the bills."

"Thanks for the warning. At least I'll know to sit down when I open the mail."

The caterer's staff started unloading cartons, trays, and metal storage units, rolling them toward the side door where Luisa stood waiting. The kitchen was Luisa's domain, and no one trespassed without her permission. Caterers included.

Casey and I stood watching the parade as several familiar faces passed by, giving us a wave. Unfamiliar faces also passed by, pushing carts and carrying trays. Different nationalities. A miniature global tour of nations. I noticed Casey scrutinizing each and every one of them as they walked to the kitchen. A stray thought wiggled from the back of my brain.

"I notice your checking out the staff, Casey. I'm curious. Do the caterers use the same kitchen staff each time or do they hire from a central pool or something?"

Casey didn't take his eyes off the parade as he answered. "I wish they used the same ones each time. It would sure make my job easier. But, no, they've told me they use a large employment agency that provides temporary kitchen hires, just like most caterers in town."

"So those agencies do the ID checks on their employees?"

Casey snorted. "I wish. Realistically, there's so much demand in Washington, they're hard-pressed to find enough workers. Most of them are foreign-born and barely speak English, if at all. This is a good way for them to earn money, because there's always a need. And given the senator's decision to entertain half of Washington, there's no way the caterers could have complied without temp hires."

"I think the official term is 'undocumented workers,' " I said with a wry smile.

"I'm afraid so."

I paused, trying to phrase my next question. "Tell me, Casey, did the police ever question the caterers or kitchen staff the night of Karen's death?"

Casey gave me a quizzical look. "Yes, I was with Lieutenant Schroeder when he questioned the two women who own the business and their kitchen staff. They were too busy running things inside to notice anything happening outside."

I nodded. "I imagine they would be. But I was more curious about the others. Those temp workers we've been talking about. I've noticed they come and go, back and forth from the kitchen to the caterers' trucks, to the living and dining rooms and garden, and outside to the trash bins. And I've noticed one or two taking a smoke break outside as well." I shrugged. "I was just wondering if one of them saw anything that night. Anything at all. Karen's car was parked down this street. Maybe one of them saw something or someone."

Casey pondered what I said. I could tell he was surprised by my question and even more surprised that I'd pointed out a potential source of information that might have been overlooked. Undocumented workers had become almost invisible in our urban environments. They were everywhere and nowhere.

"That's a good point. The temp workers were long gone when Schroeder and his boys were asking questions. Let me ask the caterers and see if they remember their repeat hires. I know I've been able to recognize several faces today already. In fact, tonight would be a great time to ask questions. The senator has doubled his orders for this reception, so there're twice as many workers in the kitchen as usual." He paused for a moment. "Now you've got me curious, Molly. I'll start asking questions and see what I find out."

"Thank you, Casey. I really appreciate that. We may not find out anything, but at least we asked. That'll make me feel better."

He peered at me again. "There's little chance of ever catching the scum who killed your niece, you know that, don't you? Even if one of these folks saw something, we'd never be able to get them to testify or even give a statement. At the mere mention of the police, they'd disappear back into the shadows."

"I know, but at least I'll feel like I did something. I guess I'm still frustrated the police have nothing to go on. And I keep wondering if somebody somewhere saw something that night. Something, anything that might help find the killer."

"I just wish I'd been outside when that guy appeared on the scene. He never would have approached Karen's car if he spotted security."

"Don't beat yourself up. I've done a number on myself too. I was feeling guilty that Karen was making phone calls outside, rather than going home first. I'd asked her to come home with me to spend the weekend with my cousins in Virginia. But my friends pointed out that Karen would have stayed at the reception with or without me. Her entire office was here."

Casey eyed me. "Don't forget, her boss Jed Molinoff was the real reason your niece was still outside."

Hearing Casey mention Jed gave me an opening. "Can I tell you something in confidence? Something that I've only told Danny, your former commanding officer, retired Colonel DiMateo."

Casey finally cracked a smile. "He was Lieutenant DiMateo when I knew him."

"Did you guys actually call him 'Double D'?"

"We called him Lieutenant. 'Double D' was strictly amongst ourselves."

I couldn't resist. "What's it stand for? Other than the double initials?"

"Off the record? Damned Dangerous. He was scary brave, but we'd follow him anywhere."

Damned Dangerous. I'd have to ask Danny about that. "Okay, then, off the record. I've been contacted by Celeste, one of Karen's friends in the congressman's office, and she alerted me to some of Jed's strange behaviors since Karen's death. He rehired a guy, Larry Fillmore, that Karen had insisted he fire earlier because of bad behavior. When Celeste asked Jed about it, he got mad and demoted her to the Records office. Then this guy, Larry, started bothering her at work. I checked out this guy with a Washington source, and she said he's got a history of being transferred from offices, often for problems with female staffers."

At that point, Casey's expression changed from skepticism to interest. "That's easy enough to check."

"I already did. Apparently his ex-wife also filed a restraining order on him a few years ago. Over a week ago, Celeste started getting hang-up phone calls on her answering machine every day. But last night, everything got kicked up another notch. Celeste called and said she came back from her evening workout run and found that someone had been in her apartment. And whoever it was deliberately left signs of his entry. Drawers open, things moved around on her desk. She thinks he was checking her computer data files, too."

Casey's expression had hardened. "How credible is this girl? Do you think she's a head case?"

"I believe her. As I said, an old friend with impeccable connections validated Larry Fillmore's tawdry history, and we've both seen Jed's erratic behavior in action. Danny was with me last night, and he thought the break-in could be a message to Celeste to stop asking questions."

"That's possible. But it's more likely she was vandalized by some random sicko who likes to paw through women's underwear. Tell me, how's this Celeste taking it? She must be pretty spooked."

"Yeah, she was. Celeste packed her bags last night and headed out of town. And she's quit her job in Jackson's office. We met at a coffee shop so she could say good-bye." I didn't mention the data storage drives.

Casey peered at me. "Where're you going with this, Molly?"

"I'm not sure. All I know is my antennae have been buzzing on Jed Molinoff for the past few weeks. Ever since I saw him coming out of Karen's apartment after her death. He rifled her desk and took some photos."

His eyebrows raised. "Do you think he broke in?"

"He obviously had a key. Karen told me they were having an affair, so I'm betting he went back to eliminate any traces. To keep the wife and kids back home in Nebraska from finding out."

Casey gave a wry smile. "Well, that's the most logical explanation."

"I was ready to write off Jed's behavior as

299

cheating-spouse panic until Celeste called. Her story makes me wonder if something else is going on with Jed Molinoff. If so, I want to find out what it is."

"How do you propose doing that?"

Casey's skeptical expression had returned. So I tried to appear disarming. "Well, I'm not sure. I've exhausted all my gossip and search sources. So, I guess I've got to find some more." I gave him a sideways smile. "You've worked in security and law enforcement. Any suggestions?"

Casey smiled knowingly. "If you're asking if I do surveillance work, the answer is 'not anymore.' You can burn out on that pretty quickly. And I wouldn't advise you to start snooping around, either. Especially not on a congressional chief of staff."

"Don't worry, Casey. I wasn't planning on peeping in windows. I'll stick to asking questions."

Casey's BlackBerry sounded and he motioned to me as he stepped away to answer. "Later, Molly."

I needed to return to my office and get back to work. My cell phone was on my desk, fairly quivering with messages, no doubt. As was my computer email inbox. Swishing the last of the coffee in my mug, I decided that a third mug would be necessary this morning. Peter was right. They would have to scrape me off the ceiling before the Western delegation arrived tonight.

Sixteen

"Molly, your father is rolling in his grave right now, you know that, don't you?" a long-time Democratic party staffer rebuked. "How can you betray your father's principles like that? You should be working for the Democrats!"

Only the better-quality Sauvignon Blanc allowed me to moderate my response to the irate Denver Democrat. "I haven't betrayed any of my father's principles, Carl, and you know it. Senator Russell may be an Independent, but he's picked up Robert Malone's mantle and run with it. You guys dropped it in the dirt in that last campaign. All that partisan bickering between Democrats and Republicans, I could barely watch the news. It was all I could do to drag myself to the polls in November."

The old-line Democrat blinked at me, surprised by my sharp response. I drained the glass, glad that I'd only had one so far.

Figuring I'd better redeem myself for the senator's sake if nothing else, I gave him my brightest campaign smile. "Believe it or not, Carl, we're all batting for the same team. Helping Coloradoans, right? That's why I'm here. And I know you are too."

Carl frowned petulantly. "Still, you should be on *our* team, Molly. It's just not right. It's . . ."

He struggled for some other words that might convince me. Trouble was, I'd had a lifetime of listening to words. They were no longer enough. I needed action now. I wasn't sure when that shift had taken place inside, but I could feel it. Whether or not Russell would be able to deliver more than words, time would tell. The front door opened both ways.

I was about to maneuver the disappointed Dem to the bar so I could hopefully escape when Peter came striding toward us. Rescue was at hand. I caught his eye and gave my please-take-this-guy look.

I'd been verbally flogged by every Colorado Democrat for the past two hours. All that saved me was escaping to the buffet tables. I'd be dieting for two days after tonight's binge. But it was the only way to keep my former colleagues mellowed. Democrats were easy that way. Feed them and show them the bar. Republicans were trickier.

"Good to see you, Carl. I figured I'd better run interference before you convinced Molly to jump the fence again. Pardon me for gloating." He did a poor job of concealing his glee.

"He was pitching hard," I jumped in before Carl could start another tirade. "I'm sure you gentlemen will excuse me for a few minutes."

I was about to make a dash for freedom when Peter placed his hand on my arm. "Casey wants to see you. He's in the kitchen hallway."

Peter returned to mollifying the Denver Democrat while I skirted around the edge of the living room, hoping no other Westerner would drag me into another heated conversation. Holding my empty glass in front of me, I looked like just another thirsty political staffer headed to the bar.

I spotted Casey down the corridor that lead toward the kitchen. "Peter said you wanted to see me."

Inside the kitchen the catering staff was busily moving into dessert mode, loading trays and plates. Silverware clanking, glass dishes clinking together. The aroma of coffee filled the air as the giant urns started revving up the brew.

Casey bent his head closer as two workers passed by, trays in hand. "Michelle and Natalie pointed out some of the temp workers they've had these past two months, and I got one of the other workers to help me ask questions. And believe it or not, one guy remembered seeing a woman sitting in her car when he was taking a smoking break outside."

My heart skipped a beat. "Did he see anything else? Did he see someone come up to the car?"

Casey met my anxious gaze with a steady one. "As a matter of fact, he did see a guy come up to the car and talk to the woman, then get inside the car. And he recognized the man because he'd seen him at the reception."

"What!"

Casey's gaze hardened. "It was Jed Molinoff. The temp worker said he recognized him as the same guy I had to calm down at the party. He also saw Molinoff leave Karen's car after a few minutes and walk down Q Street."

I stared back at Casey, momentarily speechless. Meanwhile, my heart pounded so hard I could barely breathe. Anger started to rise. "Dammit to hell . . ." I whispered.

"Your antennae were right on, Molly. That son of a bitch Molinoff doubled back around the corner and returned to Karen's car. He was the last one to see your niece alive, and he's been hiding it all this time. We've got to tell Schroeder about this."

I glanced over my shoulder. "Where is this guy? What's his name?"

"Forget about it, Molly. He's pretty spooked already. There's no way he'll stay here long enough to talk to the police. He's about ready to jump ship right now. Sweating buckets when we questioned him."

"Then how can Schroeder confront Jed if he doesn't have a witness?"

"Let's leave that to Schroeder, okay?" Casey recommended. "He's an old pro. He can put pressure on Jed and see if he cracks. Maybe he'll admit he went to see Karen. And who knows? Maybe he saw someone lurking about in the area when he left. Maybe."

"And maybe not. Maybe all Jed Molinoff did was keep Karen from finishing her phone calls. That's why she was still sitting in the car when that thug walked by. *Bastard.*" I looked Casey in the eye. "I *knew* Jed was responsible for Karen's death. I could feel it."

"That's stretching it, Molly."

"It's his fault she was in her car so late. She was calling to find another staff job. Maybe she'd already found one. If Jed hadn't shown up to harangue her again, she would have been out of that car and gone."

"You don't know that for sure."

"I don't have to know it. I can *feel* it."

Casey watched me. "Let Schroeder handle this, Molly."

I pulled my BlackBerry from my pocket and flipped to my directory. "What's your cell number, Casey?"

He paused for a second, then rattled off the local number. "Can I ask you a favor, Molly?"

"Sure."

"I can tell you're mad as hell, but make me a promise, would you? Don't do anything without checking with either Danny or me, okay?"

I could live with that. "Deal."

The taxi had barely pulled away from the sidewalk in front of Russell's mansion before I dialed Celeste's cell number. I didn't care if it was nearly eleven at night.

Her voice sounded anxious when she answered after three rings. "Molly? Is everything all right?"

"Yeah, Celeste. Everything's okay," I lied. "I just wanted to check how you were doing."

"Did you get my email this morning?"

"Yeah I did, but I wanted to hear your voice. Just being a mom, I guess."

"Thanks, Molly," I could hear her smile. "That feels good. There's no way I can tell my mom about this stuff. She never wanted me to come to Washington anyway."

"Your mom's a smart woman. Maybe a trip home wouldn't be a bad idea, Celeste."

"Yeah, I might do that. After I figure out this job situation. Then, I'll know what I'm doing. Right now, I'm actually enjoying being here on the Bay. My aunt's house was all closed up and covered in dust. But it's a block from the beach, so I take long walks every morning and at sunset too. It's really peaceful."

I could picture her sitting on a porch, staring out at Chesapeake Bay. Peaceful. I could use some of that myself.

"Well, that makes me feel better, Celeste. Listen, you stay in touch, okay? I'll look for an email every morning, otherwise, I'll be checking in on you." I made sure my tone was warm and maternal.

"I will, I promise. But feel free to call me anytime. I can always use a little mothering." She actually laughed.

"I'll do that. Now you get back to planning your next career move, okay?"

"Will do. Talk to you later."

I clicked off, still feeling unsettled despite the cheerful tone in Celeste's voice.

The taxicab pulled up in front of my house. Light shone from every window. After Celeste's home break-in episode, I decided I no longer wanted to come home to a pitch-black house at night. I paid the driver and exited the cab, still clutching my cell phone. There was another call I wanted to make.

Racing up the steps, I dug out my house key while searching through my directory in the dim light of the streetlamp. Once the front door closed behind me, I paused only a moment before punching in Danny's number.

He answered on the third ring. "Molly, are you all right?"

"No, I'm not. I want to rip out Jed Molinoff's throat."

"What happened?"

"I asked Casey to question some of the kitchen staff about the night Karen died, and one of them saw Jed get into her car late that night. After Casey showed him the door."

There was a pause before Danny replied. "Are you still at the senator's or at home?"

"I'm at home. I'm sorry to be calling so late, but I need some tactical advice. I've been living on caffeine and canapés and no sleep since yesterday, and I'm getting madder and madder by the minute. I need to bounce all this off someone who's still rational before I decide how to confront that bastard."

"I'll be right over. Can I make a suggestion?"

"Please," I said, letting my anxiety show.

"Don't drink any more coffee."

"Sanity must be resurfacing, because I'm feeling majorly guilty about calling you so late," I said as Danny stepped into the foyer. I noticed he had a bottle of wine in his hand. Dressed casually, he looked amazingly relaxed considering it was after midnight.

"No problem. I said you could use me as a sounding board anytime, and I meant it."

"You might change your mind after tonight," I said as he followed me into the living room.

Danny held up the bottle. "First, the wine. Then you can start the debriefing. That's an order, corporal."

I found a smile for the first time in the

last two hours. "It is, huh? Okay, Squad Leader, follow me." Beckoning him to the kitchen, I pointed to the cabinets. "Corkscrew's in that second drawer." Opening another oak cabinet, I found the wineglasses Nan had loaned me until I could retrieve my own things from Colorado.

Danny popped the cork then proceeded to pour the rich, dark red into both glasses.

"No breathing?"

"No time tonight. This is twenty-year-old reserve Cabernet. I figured it would do the trick."

Now I *really* felt guilty. "Twenty years? Danny, you shouldn't waste it. I'll be pacing the floor and ranting."

"Believe me, it won't be wasted. You need some sleep before you do anything. Especially pay a visit to Molinoff." He handed me a full glass. Then raised his in salute. "Do you want to pace here or in the living room? I'm going to get comfortable. Rant when ready."

Danny headed back to the living room, slipped off his leather jacket, and settled at the end of the sofa. I inhaled the rich aroma and took a sip, letting the velvety smooth taste of blackberries and cherries roll on my tongue. Luscious.

"Ohhh, this is too good . . ." I said, as I wandered after him.

"I'm waiting for the floor show. You promised pacing and ranting. You better get to it before the Cabernet goes to work."

I took another sip, deeper this time as I began a slow ramble around the living room. "I knew Jed Molinoff was hiding something. I could feel it. Turns out he lied to the police. He never mentioned going back to Karen's car after he left the reception. Casey plans to call Schroeder. The police have to question Jed again. He was the last one to see Karen alive."

"Exactly what did the kitchen worker see?"

"He saw Jed walk up to Karen's car and get inside while she was making phone calls."

"Did he see anything else?"

I nodded as I passed the bookshelves. "After a few minutes, Jed left the car and walked down the street. *Bastard.* If he hadn't shown up to delay Karen, she would have been out of her car when that vicious scum went trolling for prey."

"Let the police handle it, Molly."

I took another deep drink while I circled the room. Past the sofa, around the antique secretary, past the bookcases again. "But the police can't prove anything. Casey said the kitchen worker was ready to jump ship. They're all undocumented workers. You know how it works. He'll go to ground. No way he'll testify against Jed. So Schroeder can only push Jed so far without a witness." I turned and repeated another lap of the room, Danny watching me, sipping his wine. "There's something Jed's not saying, Danny. About Karen's death. I can feel it."

"What do you think it is?"

Taking another large drink, I felt the velvet seep inside my veins, bringing its warmth. Relaxing warmth. I continued my path. "I think Jed saw something that night. Who knows? Maybe he passed the killer on the sidewalk and is afraid to admit it."

"Why wouldn't he admit it?"

I paced beside the windows. "Because if he did, then Jed would expose himself and his affair with Karen. Especially if he had to give a statement to the police. No way would that stay a secret. It would get back to Nebraska and the wife and kids. And boom — squeaky-clean image shot to hell."

"That makes sense," Danny said, taking another sip.

I circled the living room again and again, slower each time, stewing over Jed, sipping Cabernet. "I knew he was hiding something. I knew it. I knew it," I chanted softly. "I'm not going to let him get away with it."

"Get away with what?"

More pacing, slower. "Hiding his involvement. Not telling the truth. He's got to tell the police. I'm going to make sure he does."

"How do you plan to do that, Molly?"

I stopped pacing and suddenly felt very tired. Cessation of movement. I stared at Danny, who was watching me carefully. "I'm gonna make him."

Danny patted the sofa. "Sit down and tell me how."

I settled on the other end of the sofa, letting the cushions envelop me. Sinking back into the soft cushions' embrace, I took another sip of the seductive velvet.

"I'm gonna tell him somebody saw him get into Karen's car."

"What happens when he says 'prove it'?"

I slipped off my heels and let them fall to the carpet, then snuggled even deeper into the cushions. Taking a large sip, I pondered what Danny just said. But my thoughts were coming slower, not racing as they had been since yesterday. I took another sip of Cabernet as I searched for ideas, but no new ideas came. My eyelids felt heavier.

I lay my head back. "Haven't figured that out yet." I saw Danny through my eyelashes.

"You can figure it out tomorrow."

"Tomorrow . . ." I repeated. I wasn't sure, but I thought I saw Danny reach over and take the glass from my hand as my eyelids closed.

SEVENTEEN

It was the sound of birds singing that woke me up. Morning birdsong. I opened my eyes and found myself still curled up on the sofa, but I was covered by an afghan that was usually across the back of a stuffed chair.

Danny was still at the other end of the sofa, lying back on the cushions, his leather jacket over him. He'd kept watch over me all night.

Glancing at the clock on the bookcase, I focused on the time. 6:10. Still early. Sleep tugged at me, but the other part of my brain was already waking up. Maybe I could just slip away quietly, go upstairs to shower . . .

As if he detected my slight movement, Danny woke up. He looked over and gave me a crooked smile. "Go back to sleep, Molly. It's early yet."

"Can't. I looked at the clock. That's the kiss of death for sleep. Besides, guilt is seeping in again. You wound up babysitting me the entire night."

"It was easy. Remember the twenty-year-old Cabernet?"

I laughed softly. "How could I forget? Man, that stuff is powerful."

"Yeah, it is." He tossed his jacket over the coffee table and sat up and stretched.

So did I. "Listen, let me take you out to breakfast. Without that Cabernet I'd probably still be pacing. Thanks to you, I had a restful night."

"You've got a deal. There's a great little French café on M Street. Best French bread in town. Coffee's good too,"

"Think it'll be open this early?"

"Positive."

I grabbed my shoes. "Let me take a fast shower and change so I can go to the office directly. There's orange juice in the fridge."

I pulled the fat croissant apart, letting the buttery flakes fall on the plate. The familiar rich taste never disappointed. And black raspberry jam, to die for. Calories, be damned. I took a big sip from the jumbo bowl-sized cup of coffee.

"You were sweet to stay last night."

"I wanted to make sure you got some sleep before you made any decisions. You look a lot better this morning. Not as frazzled." He popped a jam-laden bite of croissant into his mouth.

"Frazzled. That's being kind," I admitted. "But you're right. I do feel better."

Danny took a drink of black coffee. "Do me a favor, will you? Give me a call before you head out on Mission Molinoff."

I quirked a smile at him. "You want to ride shotgun again?"

"Oh, yeah."

I nodded and made him the same promise I'd made Casey. "Deal."

Casey leaned in the doorway to my office, his red-rimmed eyes indicated he hadn't had much sleep either. "You doing okay, Molly?"

I looked up over my computer and leaned back into my cushioned desk chair. "Yeah, I am. Thanks to Danny. He brought over a bottle of reserve Cabernet so I could have a good night's sleep. Bless him." I left out the part of Danny watching over me all night. No need to add to household gossip.

Casey's tired face smiled ever so slightly. "I'm glad to hear that. You looked pretty damn mad last night. I was worried what you might do."

I reached for my coffee mug. "I'm still damn mad, Casey. I just haven't figured out what to do yet." That was a half-truth. I already knew what I planned to do, but I was still working out the details.

"Danny give you any advice?"

"Oh, yeah. He made me promise he could ride shotgun if I decide to pay Molinoff a visit."

I saw Casey visibly relax. "That makes me feel a whole lot better. When are you planning to do this?"

"I'm still deciding," I hedged, knowing he could tell. "By the way, did you tell Lieutenant Schroeder?"

"Yeah, and he was not happy to hear that Molinoff was holding back."

"Is he going to question Jed again?"

Casey shrugged. "He'll probably give him a call, see if he can coax any more information out of him. Let's face it, with no witness, there's not much Schroeder can do."

"That's the problem," I said, tapping my fingernail against the rim of the china mug.

"I know you want to confront Molinoff and get in his face, but it won't be worth the effort or the aggravation. He's been working for politicians for years. He can lie twenty ways till Sunday. You'll never get him to admit anything."

"You may be right." I stared out through the curtains lifting in the breeze. The late

April warmth was inviting, calling me outside. "But maybe I can get in his head while I'm getting in his face. You know, throw the fear of God into him." I sent him a wry smile.

"Good luck with that. Meanwhile, I'll need you to hold down the fort for the rest of the day," Casey said as he stepped into the hall. "I'll be doing chauffeur duty all day and tonight probably. Ferrying media types and publicity firms out to Dulles Airport. Senator Russell is inviting them on his own green-energy tour back in Colorado. Wind and solar."

"Why isn't Albert driving?"

"He and Luisa are taking this weekend off and visiting their daughter and grand-children back in Colorado, so I'll be drop-ping them off at Dulles too." He gave a wave as he headed toward the foyer. "Just lock up when you leave, Molly. I'll come by and check late tonight after I finish driving."

"Take care, Casey. At least you can use the Dulles Access Road."

"Amen to that," he called down the hall.

I returned to checking my email, sipping coffee as I answered messages. In the midst of one email, a beep sounded and a mes-sage from Peter's BlackBerry flashed onto my screen.

"Molly. I left a mailer on my desk with Russell's replies to Congressman Jackson's inquiries about the western states' energy consortium. Please call the congressman's office and have one of their people pick it up. I forgot to drop it off this morning. Thanks. Have a great weekend."

I read the email again, taking my time as I sipped my coffee. Then I read it again. An idea sprang up. I let the various elements play through my head several times, sorting through it all, as I went to refill my coffee mug. My high heels echoed on the floors of the empty house. By the time I returned to my office with another steaming mug, I'd made my decision.

Settling in my upholstered chair, I checked my BlackBerry directory for Congressman Jackson's office number.

"What's up?" Danny answered on the second ring.

"Ready for Mission Molinoff?"

"I can be. You've got something planned, Molly. I can hear it in your voice."

"Russell and all of the house staff, including Casey, are off to Dulles. Even Casey will be gone for hours. Peter asked me to get a package to Congressman Jackson's office. So instead of asking for a courier, I called

321

and said Russell's 'staff' had some questions. I asked if Jed could come over."

Danny paused. "That's a fine line you're skating."

"I know, but it's technically correct. I am part of Russell's staff, but they'll automatically think it's Peter who's got the questions."

"When's this going to happen?"

"The receptionist called me back and said the congressman's chief of staff would be over sometime after five."

"Okay, I'll be there by four. Just in case Molinoff's early."

"Don't hold your breath."

I watched from the side hallway as Danny escorted Jed Molinoff to the outside gardens. Emerging from my viewing post, I met Danny as he walked back down the hallway. The thick mailer tight in my hand, I smoothed the skirt of my fuchsia red suit. Red always made me feel good.

"You ready, corporal?" Danny eyed me.

"Oh, yeah," I said, quickening my pace down the hall, Danny on my right.

I stepped out onto the patio and spotted Jed Molinoff pretending to admire the flowerbeds. He turned at the sound of my footsteps coming down the steps. I took no small delight in seeing the various emotions flash across Jed's face. Surprise, then apprehension, with a hint of fear.

"Where's Peter Brewster? I'm supposed to meet with him," Molinoff demanded as I approached.

Danny stopped at the bottom of the steps. The better to block any quick exit, no doubt.

"Peter had to return to Colorado this weekend," I said, tapping the mailer in my hand. "He asked me to give you this." I handed it over.

Jed didn't even bother to conceal his annoyance. "You mean you called me away from the Hill for a delivery? We could have sent an intern." Jed snatched the mailer from my hand. "This is a farce."

He started to walk away, until I stepped into his path, my hand up. "Not yet, Jed. I have some questions."

Molinoff shot me a scornful look. "I'm not answering any questions. I'm leaving."

Suddenly Danny appeared by my side, blocking Jed's exit. "Ms. Malone has some questions. So why don't you settle down and answer them. It shouldn't take more than a few minutes." His voice was low and didn't sound overtly threatening, but there was a tone of *"Better do what I say."*

Molinoff looked up at Danny and immediately retreated to the flowerbeds. "Okaaaay, I can tell you've got something on your mind, so why don't you just spit it out, *Ms.* Malone."

"Has that police detective, Lieutenant Schroeder, called you to ask more questions?" I asked, folding my arms.

Apprehension showed briefly on his face, then was replaced with his mask. "I don't know what you're talking about."

"If not, he will. Especially since our security guard found out one of the kitchen workers saw you getting into Karen's car the night she died."

Molinoff blanched, and panic darted through his eyes for a second before he ducked his head and cleared his throat. "Look, Ms. Malone, I know you're still mourning your niece's death, but I swear to you, I had nothing to do with Karen's death. It was a horrible tragedy." He looked back, and I saw the scorn was gone. I had to give him credit. His expression appeared sincere.

"Oh, yes you did, Jed. You saw something that night, didn't you? Was it the killer? Did you see some guy walk by her car after you left her alone and defenseless?"

Molinoff's eyes widened, real fear this

time. "No! I swear to you, I didn't see anyone!"

"You have to tell the truth, Jed. Our security said the detective was not happy to learn you didn't tell him the whole truth the first time he questioned you. You were the last person to see Karen alive, admit it."

Jed glanced away, twisting the mailer in his hand. "I'm not admitting anything. You have no proof anyway. Who is this kitchen worker? Some illegal?" He looked back, scorn returning to his face. On the offensive again. "I know what you're up to. You've got some twisted vendetta against me because Karen and I had an affair, that's all. And now you're trying to implicate me in her death. Well, it won't work. You've got nothing on me. No credible witness. Nothing. I'm not listening to any more of this bullshit."

He started to walk the other direction. Danny immediately went to intercept him, until I reached for his arm to hold him back. Danny gave me a questioning look.

"Either you go to the police, or I go to the press," I called out as Jed raced up the steps to the patio door.

Jed halted his escape and turned. Gone was the bravado I'd just witnessed. Wiped away in an instant. "What are you talking about?"

"If you won't do the right thing and admit what you know to the police, then I'll alert the media and tell them I have a statement concerning my niece's violent and tragic death." I caught Jed's nervous gaze and held it as I walked up the steps slowly. "Once the reporters and the television crews are in place, I'll tell them the real reason my brilliant and accomplished niece was killed by a roaming mugger that night."

"What do you mean?"

I paused at the top of the steps. "Ohhhhh, it'll make a great story. Perfect for the tabloid-TV news shows. Sex and scandal. Red meat for the press. Congressional staffer who's trying to end a tawdry affair is hounded by her rejected ex-lover at a reception. Hiding out in her car, she falls prey to a ruthless mugger who kills his victims."

Jed's face went whiter than before. "But that's not true!"

"Ohhhhh, but it is. And we do have witnesses to your intimidation and argument with Karen. The security guard who had to restrain you, the senator's chauffeur who showed Karen to her car, and me. I saw it all. Credible witnesses, each and every one of us."

I stepped toward him, not breaking my gaze. "The press will eat it up. You'll lead the sleaze news reports for days. Not just here in Washington, but in Nebraska, too. How do you think this will play in Omaha? Think the folks back home will understand? How about your wife and kids, Jed? You've been pretty good about forgetting them, haven't you?"

Jed started backing away from me, so I moved forward. "Have you ever been hounded by the press, Jed? I have. It was over twenty years ago, but I can still remember the sickening feeling. Seeing that mass of cameras waiting outside my house, and reporters yelling questions in my face. I remember how scared my little girls were whenever they saw those crowds. They started to cry every time." Watching Jed's lower lip start to tremble, I waited a second, then asked. "How old are your children, Jed?"

He stared at me, clearly frightened. "You wouldn't."

I observed him for a minute, watched desperation and panic dart across his face. "Yes, I would. Even if it costs me my job. I'm going to do everything I can to find Karen's killer. No matter what it takes. The press doesn't scare me. So I have nothing to lose. But you do. Think about it, Jed."

His mouth opened, like he was going to say something, but no words came out.

"Help the police find Karen's killer. And you'll never hear from me again."

With that, I walked toward the patio door. Pausing on the threshold, I turned to Danny, who was watching intently. "Could you please show Mr. Molinoff out?"

Jed set the glass back on the coffee table. His hand shook so much, the whiskey spilled on his trousers. "Are you still there?" he asked, wishing his voice hadn't cracked.

"I'm here," the deep male voice came over the cell phone. "What else did she say?"

"Just that she wasn't scared of the press. They'd come after her before and she'd do whatever it takes to find Karen's killer. Jesus, she's *gotta* be crazy! I mean, she's a crazy woman. You should have seen her."

"Crazy like a fox."

Jed didn't like the sound of that. "What do you mean?"

"Go back to your normal routine, Jed, as if that conversation never happened."

"So I shouldn't talk to the police, right?"

"Not unless we tell you to."

He felt a little better, hearing that. "You're

right. She's bluffing. I figured she was. Right?"

"Why don't you go back to Omaha and spend the weekend with your family? That'll make you feel better." The deep voice had a warm, reassuring tone.

"If you think so." Somehow Jed didn't feel reassured.

The click on the other end of the line was the only answer.

EIGHTEEN

He stared at the screen of his cell phone, scrolling through the text message instructions. *Time to wrap it up.* Glancing at the boats bobbing out in the bay in the morning sun, he sipped his beer, then returned the phone to his zippered jacket pocket.

Samantha rattled the ice cubes in her square-cut crystal glass. "Lord, Molly, a week and a half ago you said you were trying to fly beneath the radar. And now you've faced off with Jackson's chief of staff. What is up with you?"

I pushed the glider on Samantha's screened porch into another gentle arcing swing. "So much for keeping a low profile, huh?"

Sipping my vodka and orange juice, I admired Samantha's McLean, Virginia, garden. All lush and green symmetry, hedges bordering English-style flowerbeds. Neat and orderly. Not the same artistic flair of Nan's and Deb's gardens, with wildflowers mixed in with roses, and perennials cheek by jowl with bright-colored annuals pushing forward for attention. Samantha's garden was the only thing old-fashioned and subdued about her.

"Well, off the record, I'm not sorry you confronted him. Hearing this sorry tale makes me mad all over again about losing Karen. All because Molinoff was an obnoxious s.o.b." She reached over and poured herself more aged bourbon from the crystal decanter on the white wicker table beside her.

I pushed the glider again and watched dusk creep at the edges of the garden. Mimosa trees with their fragrant yellow and pink fluffy blossoms and cherry trees bursting into bloom. April was a heady month in Virginia, rich and redolent with blossoms. Flowering dogwoods, pink and white, snowy white apple blossoms, and crab apples pink as bubblegum. And everywhere you looked, azaleas — crimson, violet, fuchsia, rose pink, white, coral, lavender — scattered all over the city.

"What are you gonna do if he calls your bluff?" Samantha eyed me over her glass.

"It's not a bluff. I'll call the newspapers

and the TV stations."

"Good God, Molly, are you sure you want to expose yourself to that sordid mess again?" Samantha looked like she'd bitten into a sour apple.

"I have to, Samantha. It's the only way I can force Jed to talk to the police. He saw something, or he knows something. I'm sure of it. You should have seen his face when I confronted him. He looked petrified."

"With good reason. His career will be over after the press gets hold of him. And so will yours. Have you thought about that? I mean, *really* thought about it?"

"That's all I thought about the last two days while I was driving."

"I can't believe you drove the Blue Ridge Parkway down and back this weekend." She shook her head before taking a drink. "You're crazier than a bedbug, girl."

I smiled at Samantha. Old friends kept you honest. "Well, it was the closest I could get to my mountains back home in Colorado. The Shenandoah aren't the Rockies, but they're pretty and peaceful. And I needed some mountains to help me think."

"And these mountains helped you decide to throw away this great new job you've landed with the senator? I think you should let me take you to the beach next time you want to think." She sipped her bourbon, and a slow smile formed. "I bet you were playing the Stones the whole way down the parkway."

I rested my head on the back of the cushions. "Ohhhhh, yeah. And Clapton and Seger. Grace Slick. The whole bunch."

She chuckled over her glass. "You haven't changed a bit."

"Rock 'n' roll forever," I said with an unrepentant grin.

A serious expression wiped away Samantha's smile. "What do you plan to do about your mother?"

I closed my eyes and pushed the glider. "Can't handle more than one crisis at a time. Ask me that again after I've gotten some justice for Karen."

Samantha gave a genteel snort. "Sugar, you know better than that. You don't look to Washington for justice. That's in the movies, not real life. What's your Marine escort and running partner say about this strategy?"

"Not much, actually. After Jed left, we went out to some rooftop café overlooking the city. I can't even remember the name. My mind was still swirling. We sat and stared out at the lights and didn't say much. Picked at the food. Danny was good enough to give me the space I needed."

"Well, be careful with that 'I need some space' line. Or you'll turn around one day, and he'll be gone, and you'll have nothing left but space."

I laughed softly. "Well, let's see how it goes. He left on business this weekend, so if he doesn't call me when he returns, then I'll know I scared him away."

"I don't know what I'm gonna do with you, Molly." She took a deep drink. "What sort of business? Consulting, I imagine."

"Of course. Logistics and tactics or tactical logistics or some such. Stuff you don't know and couldn't talk about even if you did."

"The usual. Have you told your family about any of this?"

"Not yet. I'll give them a heads-up before I call in the hounds of the press. They can head for the shore. Lie low, until the dust settles."

Samantha simply wagged her head, not saying anything. Meanwhile, my own mention of the sea shore caused another worrisome subject to push back onto my radar screen.

I hadn't heard from Celeste since early Friday morning when she'd sent an email. After Saturday came and went and still no email, I waited until today when I had stopped along the parkway for lunch. I called Celeste's cell phone but got no answer, just her recorded message. I'd called twice since then and got the same result. No answer.

"By the way, I heard from some of my sources. One of them was close with Larry Fillmore's wife. It seems she would occasionally come to the office with facial bruises, which she tried to explain away." Samantha's voice hardened with obvious contempt. "So, it looks like that bastard Larry Fillmore has a violent streak after all."

I pushed the glider, letting the unsettled feeling gnaw my stomach again. "God, I'm glad Celeste quit her job and left Washington."

Samantha fell quiet for several moments. "When's the last time you ate?" she said at last, pulling me out of my concern.

"Lunch somewhere along the parkway. Can't remember where."

"Well, why don't we raid my freezer and see what the caterer left."

"Who've you been entertaining?"

"No one lately. The caterer supplies me with home-cooked meals that I keep whenever I'm not dining out, which is most of the time." She drained her glass again and pointed to mine. "Would you like me to freshen that up for you?"

"Absolutely. I depend on you to have a full bar."

Samantha grinned as she leaned back on the floral cushions on the white wicker summer furniture. "That vodka was my sweet Sol's favorite." Her smile faded. "I miss him still. He was the closest friend I'd had since Beau died."

"The Senate is poorer for his loss," I said, raising my glass. "To Sol Karpinsky. Thanks, Sol, for watching out for the taxpayers for as long as you did. Or tried to." I tossed down the rest of my screwdriver.

"I still miss you, Sol," Samantha said, raising her glass.

I toyed with the words that played on my tongue. Vodka was encouraging me to spit them out. "You know, Miss Thing, I heard some rumors about Karpinsky. Any truth that he was out with you the night before he died?"

"All true. We were here at the house having a private catered dinner."

"Good God, Samantha. Don't tell me you were . . . ." I gestured, looking for words.

"Servicing the senator?" She arched a brow. "No, I was not. Rumors are wrong on that one. Sol wanted to talk, and he needed a sounding board. That's my strong suit, Molly, you know that. He was all wound up about some banking bill, kept talking about irregularities, whatever. Sol wanted to schedule hearings, but he never got the chance. That great big heart of his gave out." She wagged her head, then drained her glass.

Now it was my turn to rattle the ice cubes in my empty glass. "Well, there are worse ways to go than dying in your sleep. Better than some awful lingering disease."

"Amen to that."

NINETEEN

Hurrying up the sidewalk on Q Street, I tried to search my cell phone directory and keep from tripping over the uneven brick walkway at the same time. Tree roots caused miniature hills and valleys to push up on Georgetown brick sidewalks. The unwary were often sent sprawling.

I'd overslept this morning. No doubt due to my post-midnight return from Samantha's. I'd fallen into bed last night and sank into a deep sleep. Caused probably by the accumulated sleep deficit I'd been working around for the past few days. Catching up all at once had its drawbacks. When I finally awoke, it was only ten minutes before I usually left for the Russell mansion. New land speed records were set for showering, and I had no idea if my makeup was on straight since I did it while trying to dress at the same time.

Punching in the Russell phone number, I

waited for Luisa to pick up with her cheery hello. "Luisa, this is Molly and I'm racing up Q Street right now. Overslept. I hope there are no emergencies or anything."

"Relax, Molly. We're all moving a little slower. Except the senator, of course." She chuckled. "He left for the Hill at seven thirty."

I crossed another intersection. "That man is superhuman, I swear he is. Hey, how was your family visit? Grandkids doing okay?"

"Growing like weeds. I have some new photos of the little one. I'll bring them in with your coffee."

"Luisa, you're a lifesaver. See you in a few minutes."

I clicked off and was about to drop the phone into my jacket pocket when I remembered another call. I punched in Celeste's number. After six rings, Celeste's voice mail message came on once again. I stopped in the middle of the sidewalk, pondering whether to leave yet another message and decided against it. I'd left two messages already.

Why wasn't she answering her phone? I picked up my pace. I hadn't heard from Celeste since Friday morning's email. Today was Monday. She knew I wanted her to stay in touch and she had promised she would.

Why hadn't she?

Passing the brick walls surrounding the mansion grounds, I hurried to the front gate. Maybe I could find a spare moment and search that congressional directory again. See what other contact information was listed for Celeste. As I entered the mansion foyer, Luisa was walking toward me with a full mug of coffee in her hand.

"Take a deep breath, Molly. You're going to need that along with the coffee. I opened your office door and saw the message light blinking like crazy. It's Monday."

"Monday, all day," I said with a groan, then took a big drink of caffeine.

"Did you mail it?" Raymond's voice came over the phone.

He paused outside the coffee shop and sipped his latte before answering. "In the mail this morning. It should be delivered tomorrow." A shaft of bright sunshine reflected off the polished hood of a nearby limo parked along Pennsylvania Avenue. He slipped his sunglasses from his jacket pocket as he walked. "You want me to stand by?"

"No, this one will be handled differently."

"I can't wait to find out."

"We'll be in touch. And they said to tell you 'good work.' "

He passed a group of tee-shirted school children, heading out on a day of sightseeing. "I aim to please."

"Hey, Casey," I called from my doorway. "How did your shuttle service turn out? All charges accounted for?"

"Just barely. I didn't make it back to the city till nearly midnight Friday." He paused in the hallway and took a swig of coffee before answering. What would any of us do without caffeine?

"Any more in Luisa's coffeepot?" I dangled my empty mug as I fell in step with him down the long hallway.

"Fresh five minutes ago."

"Music to my ears. I'm trying to wade through a mountain of emails and messages. And I feel like I'm falling behind because more messages keep coming in."

"Don't you love Mondays?"

I toyed with what I was about to say, then simply spit it out. "Well, at least it's distracting me from worrying because a friend's cell phone is still going to voice mail when she promised to stay in touch with me. I'm beginning to wonder if something's wrong. Maybe there's a connection problem with the cell towers on the Eastern Shore."

Casey looked at me quizzically. "Who're

we talking about here?"

"Celeste Allard. She's that staffer in Karen's office who got in trouble with Molinoff when she asked too many questions." I beelined for the coffeepot on the spotless granite kitchen counter.

Casey stood in the kitchen doorway, sipping his coffee. "Didn't you say she'd left town?"

"Yeah, but I made her promise to stay in touch. She'd been emailing me every morning and I talked with her a couple of times, but I haven't heard a thing since Friday. No emails, no calls." I lifted the filled mug and sniffed the deep rich aroma. Ahhhhh. Let the harsh burn slide down my throat. "I've called several times since Sunday, and all I get is voice mail. Maybe I'm being too much of a mom, but I'm starting to worry."

Casey tapped his mug, clearly thinking. "You know, there are some normal explanations, Molly. She could have simply lost her cell phone. People do that all the time. Drive off with it on the hood of their car. Leave it on restaurant tables."

Strolling back to the doorway, I took another deep drink of coffee. "But what about the emails? Even if she lost her phone, she could still email."

"Not if she left town," Casey said with a

smile as we headed down the hallway again. "Think about it. Maybe she went to visit a friend. Or her family."

I paused in front of my office doorway. What Casey said made sense. "So, you think I'm overreacting?"

"I think you nailed it when you said you were being too much of a mom. You've kind of adopted this girl, so now you're worrying about her. Give it another few days." He lifted his mug to me before heading down the hallway toward the front door.

Maybe he was right. Maybe I was being too much of a mom and worrying about Celeste like she was my own daughter. I settled at my desk chair again and clicked on one of my accounting spreadsheets. Lose myself in the numbers for another few days.

The recorded music track playing through the Georgetown Shops mall was distant enough to be unrecognizable. It sounded vaguely like Billy Joel, but I couldn't tell. Walking past the food court, the aroma of pizza wafted through the air and my stomach growled. I deliberately turned away. Coffee instead. Then I could go home and scavenge my freezer for dinner. Unfortunately, there were no gourmet catered dishes awaiting me. Maybe a spinach soufflé if I was lucky.

Rounding the corner of the upscale vertical shopping mall situated right in the middle of busy Georgetown, I noticed an Italian restaurant whose bar jutted out into the walkway. I could grab a diet cola, then head for home.

I'd walked down to the canal-side mall to get some exercise. Unfortunately, I'd forgotten how brick sidewalks and high heels do not go together for long distances. Of course, I hadn't planned on doing more than a couple of errands. Then I noticed the great sale at the sports store on running shoes and well, there I was, several packages over my arm. It was definitely taxi time for the trip back to my townhouse.

Grabbing an empty bar stool, I ordered a cola to go and entertained myself watching the local evening news on the flat-screen television above the bar. The male newscaster was interviewing a D.C. resident who was trying to organize a local charity.

"Keep the change," I told the bartender when he brought my plastic cup and was about to leave when a female newswoman's voice caught my attention. Glancing to the screen again, I was startled to see Celeste's photo. Her owlish eyes stared out behind her glasses, which could not disguise her youthful face.

"More tragedy has struck the office of Nebraska Congressman Randall Jackson. Several weeks ago, one of the congressman's top staffers, Karen Grayson, was shot and killed in a brutal mugging turned murder in Georgetown. Now, we've just learned that another of the congressman's staffers has died in a gas explosion in the Eastern Shore community of Deale, Maryland. Celeste Allard, who'd worked for the congressman for five years, was killed when the house her family owned went up in flames Saturday. Fire department investigators think the fire started in the kitchen, probably due to fumes escaping from the gas stove, which ignited nearby candles. When asked for comment, one of Congressman Jackson's staff did mention that Ms. Allard had been depressed lately and had exhibited erratic behavior. So police are considering the possibility that her death could be a suicide."

The woman's voice went up an octave as she smiled brightly into the cameras. "And now, here's Bernie with the weather."

I stared as the image of Celeste disappeared from the screen, replaced by a large map of the Washington metro region, a smiling meteorologist standing beside.

A cold hand reached inside my gut and

squeezed hard. I pushed away from the bar stool and bolted down the winding mall corridor, heading for the canal exit. *Outside.* I had to get outside.

I drained my second glass of wine and held it up for the waiter at the harbor-front café.

He scurried over to my umbrella-shaded patio table. "Another Fat Bastard, ma'am?"

"Please. And more of those cheese things." He hastened off, and I scavenged the last morsel of cheese and baguette on the table while I watched the Potomac flowing peacefully past the Washington Harbor. I barely remembered how I wound up here. I'd stumbled out of the mall and wandered for blocks along the C&O Canal on the towpath. Then I started winding through the lower Georgetown streets leading to the condos and cafés that bordered the river until I came to Water Street and the newly developed harbor front. Danny and I had had dinner here only a couple of weeks ago.

I looked over my shoulder to the luxury condos that rose above and surrounded the cafés, coffee shops, and businesses that clustered below. Karen and I had breakfast at one of the upper-level cafés the day she died.

The wide river sparkled in the late afternoon sun. All manner of craft floated by, from kayaks to sleek yachts. Theodore Roosevelt Island wildlife refuge was to the right, the Lincoln Memorial and Kennedy Center were across the water straight ahead, and to the left was the once-notorious Watergate complex. It was a truly stunning view. When I was a child only flour mills, warehouses, and other industrial buildings enjoyed the same view that all of the café's patrons were enjoying right now.

"Here you go, ma'am," the college-aged waiter said, placing my refilled wineglass and the appetizers in front of me.

I reached for another cheesy bite, but it was too late. The rich French Chardonnay had beaten the cheese into my system with the first glass. I was buzzed, and I didn't care. At least I couldn't hear the accusatory voice in the back of my head.

Celeste is dead. And you're partly responsible. If you hadn't asked her to poke around in Molinoff's files, she wouldn't have gotten into trouble at her office. Celeste would have stayed here in Washington, and not gone to the Eastern Shore to some old closed-up house with a leaky gas stove.

I recognized Sober-and-Righteous's scolding tone and flinched inwardly. Sober was right. I should never have involved her in my quest to investigate Jed Molinoff. Celeste would be alive today if I hadn't.

Taking a big sip of the round fruity wine, I nibbled more cheese, letting Sober run roughshod over my conscience. A sleek yacht motored up to the harbor's dock, filled with partying couples making merry. The tourists passing by ogled the boating party and tried to discreetly snap photos.

Runners sped by as well as cyclists, despite the signs warning them to dismount and walk their bikes. Hopefully the strolling tourists would pay attention as they took in the gorgeous views. A collision was only a misstep away.

I glanced to the side and noticed one of the tourists, a man with a gray backpack, was aiming his camera in my direction. In my buzzed state, I lifted my glass as he clicked away.

The partying couples started dancing to a quiet salsa beat, martini glasses in hand. I sipped my wine and watched the tourists watching the boaters. Tourists feeding the pigeons. Tourists taking photos. Photos of the river. Of the views. Of the buildings behind me. Pretty pictures. I let myself enjoy the salsa beat. Then my cell phone jangled atop the table.

"Hey, Molly, how're you doing?" Danny asked.

I let his warm voice settle over me, joining the Chardonnay. "Not okay. Celeste's dead."

Danny was quiet for a second. "How?"

"Her house on the shore blew up. Gas explosion, the police say. They think the stove ignited it."

"Where are you?"

I took another sip. "I'm here at Washington Harbor trying to drown my guilt, drinking Fat Bastard and eating cheese. Where are you? Still away consulting?"

"Actually, I'm driving across Key Bridge right now. I was on the way to your house to see if you'd like to go out, but since you already are, I'll meet you there."

"Danny, you don't have to babysit me," I protested.

"I'm not. I'm coming to keep you company, that's all. See you in a few minutes."

He clicked off and I went back to watching the tourists watching the sights. The tourist with the backpack was gone.

"It's not your fault, Molly. You told me Celeste had already gotten into trouble with Molinoff for asking questions he didn't like. Plus she'd seen Karen and him together."

"Yeah, but I made it worse. I should never

have asked her to help." I nibbled the tasty fried calamari Danny had ordered.

"She called *you,* remember? She'd already been checking into Molinoff, confronting him about Fillmore. And that's what got her on his radar screen. Not you and your email searches."

I wagged my head. "I disagree. I think the email searches are what made Jed send the burglar."

"You don't know that. Look, you don't know what was going on in Celeste's life other than what she told you. Maybe that newscast was correct. Maybe she really did suffer from depression. Maybe this accident was really a suicide."

I toyed with the steak Danny had also ordered. "I hear you, but somehow I still feel responsible. Even if it doesn't make any sense. Even if it sounds crazy."

"I don't think it sounds crazy, Molly," Danny said, leaning both arms on the table. "I just think you've suffered another horrible loss of someone you care about. You admitted you'd adopted Celeste. And now she's gone. A little over a month ago, you lost your niece." His voice dropped. "Face it, you've had a helluva past few weeks. I don't think you're in any position to sit in judgment of yourself. You're simply trying to make your way through a really rough time."

I sliced into the filet and let the rich flavors melt in my mouth. Laden with cholesterol and fat, but damn, it was good. Danny's reasoning settled over me as I savored the beef. Maybe he was right. I didn't know anything about Celeste's private life. Maybe she had problems I wasn't aware of. None of us really knows what's going on inside someone else. Sober mumbled in the background but didn't contradict.

"Any idea if Molinoff went to the police yet?" he asked, sinking back in his chair. Shirtsleeves rolled up, tie off, jacket over the chair.

"Casey hasn't said a thing, and I'm certain he'd tell me if his detective friend had called with information."

Danny took a drink from his Scotch, then sliced into the filet. "So, what's your next move, Molly?"

I savored another bite while I let my mind shift from guilt back to the problem that I'd wrestled with the entire weekend. I took another bite, then sipped the black coffee I'd ordered for myself.

"I'll ask Casey tomorrow if he can check with Detective Schroeder. See if he's called

Jed yet. If he hasn't, then maybe that will spur him to do so. If he has called him, then I'll wait to hear if Jed gave any new information."

Danny paused, filet nearly to his mouth. "And if Jed hasn't complied?"

I sank back into the wire café chair, coffee cup in both hands while I stared out at the Potomac flowing past. "Then I'll have to explain my situation to Senator Russell and Peter and offer my resignation. I don't want my actions to reflect on people I've come to respect and care for."

Danny returned to his steak while I stared out at that lazy river. A tidal river. Whenever bad weather whipped the Atlantic nearby, storm surges swept up the river on its strong currents. The Potomac was used to stormy weather, be it political or meteorological.

Glancing at me with a crooked smile, Danny pointed to my plate. "Better finish that filet. You're going need your strength."

TWENTY

I spotted Casey heading toward the Russell kitchen. Taking a deep breath, I went down the hall after him. Better to get this process started. Delay would only eat away at my resolve. And right now, resolve and bravado were the only things I had keeping me on track.

"Casey, can I ask you something?" I said as I entered the kitchen. "Have you heard yet if Lieutenant Schroeder called Jed Molinoff? I was curious if he learned anything new."

Casey kept his eyes on the black stream of coffee filling his mug. "Matter of fact, I heard from Schroeder earlier this morning. He called Molinoff yesterday and tried to pry some more information out of him. But he didn't get anything new. Even when Schroeder asked him flat-out if he'd returned to Karen's car after leaving the reception."

"What'd he say? Did Schroeder give a hint?"

Casey shrugged. "Sounded like Molinoff stonewalled. Told Schroeder that the kitchen worker had to be mistaken." He walked toward me while he drank his coffee. "Sorry, Molly. I know how much you were counting on that."

You have no idea, I thought to myself, as I felt my gut squeeze. "Sorry is putting it mildly. Do you have a minute?" I beckoned him to the hallway again. "Let's go outside to the garden. Tonight the Pacific Northwest congressional delegations will descend on us, so this may be our last quiet minute."

"What's up, Molly?" he asked, following after me.

I stepped out onto the patio and stared out at the roses for a minute, then confessed. "This will probably be my last reception for the senator. I'll be handing in my resignation tomorrow."

No mistaking Casey's surprise. "Why? Has something happened? Is your mother all right?"

"No, she's fine and my family's fine. This is all me, Casey. My decision and mine alone."

"I'm listening."

"Last Friday I did meet with Jed Molinoff. He denied seeing Karen or anyone else on the streets. I knew he was lying, so I threatened him."

"With what?"

"I told him if he didn't tell the police what he knows, then I was going to the press. I promised that by the time I finished telling the story of their tawdry love affair, he'd be the king of sleaze on the television tabloid news."

"You didn't."

"Yeah, I did. And I meant every word. Jed went white as a sheet. He saw someone that night. I'm sure of it. But he won't confess unless I force him to."

"Was Danny with you?"

"He was the muscle that kept Jed from bolting."

Casey observed me for a long minute. "And that's why you're resigning?"

"I don't want my actions to reflect upon Senator Russell or any of you. So it would be best if I remove myself from the senator's staff beforehand, so you folks can have total denial that you knew anything."

"Damn, Molly."

"That about sums it up." I took a deep drink of my coffee, while I watched Casey dig his ringing BlackBerry from his coat pocket.

"When are you going to tell Peter?" he asked as he scanned the phone screen.

"After everyone leaves tonight."

Casey began backing away, phone to his ear. "Don't say anything yet, Molly."

I took my time walking back to my office at the end of the hallway, admiring the antique-filled rooms and surroundings I'd become accustomed to these last few weeks. Clearly, working for Senator John Russell had provided the most comfortable and lavish office setting I'd ever experienced. I would miss it. But not as much as I would miss the people who'd become my "office family." I was surprised how quickly I had assimilated into the Russell routine. Karen had been right. This was where I belonged. It was in my blood.

Who knows what kind of job I'd be able to land next. Probably not in Washington, and certainly not in politics. Not after I'd ratted out a congressional chief of staff. Speaking the truth was not necessarily considered a virtue in Washington.

I settled at my desk and reached for the mail that Luisa had placed beside the computer. Sorting through the usual letters, I noticed a larger manila envelope. It had a type-written mailing label addressed to me but no return address.

That got my attention. I turned the envelope over several times, checking for any powdery substances or anything else strange. Nothing was evident, so I used the letter opener to carefully slice the envelope open. There were photographs inside. Three 8 × 10 photos. I slid them from the envelope.

The photos appeared to have been taken at night because the light looked strange, harsh. The first showed a man standing beside a parked car, leaning over the driver's window. The next showed the man entering the front passenger side of the car. I stared at the photos, noticing the car's license plate. Karen's license plate. That was Karen's car.

Was that Jed? I wondered, scrutinizing the photos. Was that person in the driver's seat Karen? I flipped through to the last photo and stared at it. My heart raced. This photo had zoomed in closer so that I could definitely see Karen behind the wheel and Jed Molinoff in the passenger seat beside her. They appeared in the midst of conversation. No mistaking it.

Oh, my God. That *is* Karen with Jed beside her. Glimpsing the small print in the lower left corner of the photo revealed the date and time. 10:08, the night of her death. I checked the back of all three photos for more identifying marks. Nothing.

Who in the world would have taken photos of Karen and Jed that night? The clarity of the pictures was excellent, despite the harsher light. Whoever took these photos was a good photographer, that was obvious. But who would do that? Was there some voyeuristic neighbor who spied on the senator's guests whenever there was a party? Even if that were true, why would that photographer send the photos to *me?*

I studied the photos again. Here was proof that Jed Molinoff deliberately lied to police. He had gone to Karen's car after he left. Proof that the kitchen worker was telling the truth. The police would have reason to question Jed now. And he couldn't lie his way out of it.

"Caterers will be here around noon, Molly," Casey's voice sounded from the doorway.

I beckoned him inside my office. "You won't believe what I just received in the morning mail." I held out the photos.

Surprise registered on Casey's face immediately. "Who sent these to you?" he asked in a low voice.

"I haven't a clue. There was no return address and no markings." I showed him the empty envelope.

Casey examined it, holding the envelope up to the light. "Date and time on the photos. Proves Molinoff was in her car."

"Who would take these photos, Casey, and why would they send them to me?"

Casey handed them over. "I don't know, Molly. But it certainly saved you and your family a helluva lot of trouble." He peered at me. "No need to call in the press now."

"You're right," I replied, letting the realization settle over me. Somewhere deep inside my chest, a muscle relaxed. "But who would be taking photos? This photographer is a pro. And knows how to take night photos." I peered up at Casey. "Are there surveillance cameras in this neighborhood?"

Casey gave me a little smile. "Who knows? This is Washington, remember? There are diplomats, international businessmen, government officials, and all the regular politicians who people these neighborhoods. In addition to the Old Establishment types."

I studied the photos again. "That still doesn't answer the question why the photographer would send them to me."

Casey's BlackBerry sounded, and he backed away toward the door. "Just be glad he did."

There was a beep on my office phone

359

indicating a text message had arrived. Peter, advising me about tonight's reception. I slid the photos back into their envelope and was about to return to my computer screen. But first, I sent a text message of my own to Danny.

Danny's eyebrows shot up the moment he saw the photos. "Where's the envelope?"

I handed it over. "No markings, no return address. But whoever it was knew I worked for the senator and knew Karen was my niece. Why else would they send them?"

Danny held up the envelope, then scrutinized the photos again. "Well, whoever took them has done surveillance work because he knew exactly what kind of camera to use and how to capture these shots at night."

"I racked my brain all morning and afternoon trying to figure out who the photographer is, and the closest thing I can come up with is a 'voyeuristic neighbor' theory. They would know about Karen's death and that I work for the senator." I leaned back into my office chair and took a drink of lukewarm coffee.

Danny placed the photos back on my desk. "You know, it doesn't really matter who sent them. The question is, what are you going to do with them now?"

I stared at the photos beside my computer. That question had also been bouncing around my head in between working on Russell accounts. Clearly, I needed to turn them over to the police. But . . .

"I'm going to take them to Detective Schroeder. But first, I'm going to scan them into my computer. Then I'm going to send copies to Jed Molinoff and suggest he reconsider his refusal to cooperate with police."

"Giving him one last chance?"

"Let's see what he decides to do." I turned on the scanner at the far corner of my desk. Clicking on the icon that popped on my desktop screen, I started the copying process while I wrote a short and succinct email to Jed. Attaching all three photos to the message, I sent it through. Danny watched without a word.

Albert paused at the doorway. Spotting Danny, he broke into a smile. "Colonel, it's good to see you. Molly, if you two were planning on dinner, I can tell Peter you'll be a little late tonight."

"Call me Danny, please," Danny said, extending his hand to Albert. "And dinner sounds like a good idea. What about it, Molly?"

"Why not? Maybe I'll be able to stay away

from the buffet table then."

Albert retreated with a big grin. I could tell he couldn't wait to report to Luisa. "Okay, then, I'll let Peter know. See you later, Molly. Good to see you again, Col, uh, Danny."

Danny checked his watch. "Nearly five o'clock. We could leave now so you won't be late for the reception."

Just then, I heard the familiar beep of a message coming through on my BlackBerry. Scrolling down, I read the message to myself and stared at it for a second before reading it out loud.

"It's from Jed. 'Please talk to me before you go to police. My apartment tonight 10:00 p.m. 1137 New Hampshire Avenue, number 1410.' " I glanced up at Danny. "What do you think?"

"I think you got his attention."

"Did you send the email?"

"Y-yes, just now," Jed said, pressing the cell phone closer to his ear. The phone slipped against his damp cheek. He hated that the sound of the man's voice made him sweat.

"Go to your apartment straight from the office, Jed. I'll drop by around seven o'clock."

"You're coming to my place? But why?" He was unable to conceal his panic.

The deep voice paused. "We need to talk, Jed. We need to make plans."

Plans. Plans were good. He grasped at that. "O-okay. Seven o'clock. I'll be there."

"When are you two going over there?" Casey asked as he scanned the clusters of congressman and staffers crowding Senator Russell's reception.

A light rain earlier had sent everyone fleeing from the garden, and the Russell mansion was packed. Living room, dining room, hallways, and doorways to the patio for those who didn't mind the drizzle. Only the caterers' closed door kept them from wandering into the kitchen. I was glad I'd locked my office door.

I sipped the Pinot Blanc. "Danny's coming over about nine thirty. It sounds like Jed's building is near Washington Circle, so it shouldn't take long to get there."

"Don't let him talk you out of it, Molly."

"Not a chance."

"I'll be glad to take you to see Schroeder first thing tomorrow," Casey added before he returned to his routine prowling of the edges of the crowd.

"Sounds good." I sipped the tart, fresh

taste and returned to my own prowling of the perimeter. There were fewer familiar faces in this crowd tonight. Consequences of the last election turnover, no doubt. Fewer conversations meant more time to think, and my thoughts were still churning, wondering about the mystery photographer. *Who and why?*

Wandering the edges of the living room, I spied Aggie smoothly serving drinks, moving about the crowd in a pattern. Ryan had his tray filled with appetizers as usual. And Bud was at his regular spot at the bar, efficiently filling the glasses of politicians who clustered around the rim.

As I watched and sipped, a long-ago memory inched from the back of my mind. Something my father had once said about Georgetown cocktail parties. Another sip brought it forward and into focus. *The spy network.* That was it. My father told me years ago that CIA spooks regularly worked political parties in Georgetown — wherever influential politicians and government officials gathered. Waiters, servers, kitchen staff moved freely about the crowds — invisible. No one noticed them, so it was easy to eavesdrop and report back everything they overheard.

Remembering more clearly now, I pictured

my father shaking his head in wry amusement when he told the stories of colleagues who drank too much. Espionage professionals knew that it was easy for secrets to slip out wherever liquor was flowing. Influential congressmen, senators, ambassadors, and diplomats liked to think they were careful, but the truth was they frequently slipped — and didn't even remember.

Another thought wiggled forward as I watched Aggie efficiently working around clusters of congressman and staffers. Replenishing drinks, removing empty glasses, moving through the room, pausing at each group.

Aggie had been working these Georgetown parties for years. She'd worked for my parents' parties, Dave's and mine, and she was still working. That was a lot of politicians over the years. I recalled something Aggie said to me the first week I returned to Washington. A comment about her "Cuban boyfriend."

Aggie offered wines to a nearby group of chattering congressmen, then headed my way. "I've got one Pinot Blanc left, Molly."

"I'm good, Aggie. Thanks, anyway." A crazy idea had come into my head suddenly. "Can I ask you a question?"

"Sure." She settled into a comfortable

stance, tray on her shoulder.

"You've been working these political parties for a lifetime. Most of them in Georgetown, right?"

"Mostly. But I also work in other areas of the city, as well as Virginia and Maryland, too. Wherever the parties are." She cocked her head to the side. "What are you asking, Molly?"

I felt her warm gaze settle on me, and I tried to appear as innocent as possible. Always a struggle for me. "I was simply wondering if you knew if there are any surveillance cameras located along Georgetown streets or security groups watching the neighborhoods. You know, since there are so many diplomats and politicians living here and all that."

A slow smile started. "There are all sorts of groups that work Washington. You know that, Molly. They've always been here. I've heard it said there are more spies per square foot in Washington, D.C., than any other city in the world."

Since Aggie had opened that door, I decided to walk right through it. "My father told me that CIA spooks were all over Georgetown parties years ago."

Aggie kept her smile, but made no reply.

So, I decided what the hell. "Are you a

366

spook, Aggie?" I sent her an engaging smile of my own.

Aggie's eyes lit up. "Who, me? Do I look like a spy? They're all tall, dark, and handsome, aren't they?" she replied as she backed away into the congressional clusters once more.

I recognized a non-denial denial when I heard one. Finishing off my wine, I was about to resume my stroll when Luisa approached.

"The colonel is in the kitchen, Molly. He says not to hurry, he's early."

I glanced at my watch. 9:25. Time for the last act of today's bizarre drama to play itself out. I drained my glass and followed after Luisa.

TWENTY-ONE

The lobby of Jed's New Hampshire Avenue apartment building was about what I expected. A nice but not fancy condo with secured entry. Guests had to be buzzed in. Exiting the elevator at the fourteenth floor, Danny and I located Jed's apartment only a few feet down the hallway.

Danny raised his hand to knock, then paused, glancing back at me. "Ready?"

"Let's do it."

Not entirely sure why Jed wanted to see me, I figured he probably hoped to make one last attempt to convince me not to involve the police. Beg me not to reveal his involvement. Plead with me to think of his family.

But I was way past the point where whining, begging, or pleading could affect me. As for Jed's family, he should have thought of them himself. Before he began his affair with Karen. Jed Molinoff's conscience wasn't my concern. Catching Karen's killer was.

There was no answer to Danny's knock at first, then the door opened. Jed Molinoff stood in the opening, staring at us for a second. He looked haggard, and his eyes were red. "Come in, come in," he beckoned us inside with a choppy wave of his hand.

Following Jed into his living room, I glimpsed the gorgeous view of the city through the balcony door. A briefcase sat open, and papers were strewn across the dining room table in the corner. A nearly empty bottle of Scotch and half-filled glass sat on the coffee table.

Jed sank into the sofa and reached for his glass. "Sit down," he waved toward the nearby chairs.

"No, thanks, Jed. We won't be staying long," I said, watching him take a drink. I waited for him to say something else, but he didn't reply. He took another drink instead. "As I said in my email, I'll give you until tomorrow morning to go to the police and tell them what you know before I take the photos to Detective Schroeder."

Jed leaned forward, his arms resting on his legs as he stared at the glass in his hands. He didn't answer.

I waited for him to start to wheedle or

plead or even cry. But nothing. He just sat there. Finally I said, "Do you understand me, Jed?"

This time he nodded. "Yeah I'll go," he said in a soft voice.

His abrupt capitulation caught me off guard, and I just stood there, watching him for a moment. "You saw something, didn't you, Jed?"

Again, he didn't look up; he simply nodded. "Yeah. I saw a guy pass me on the sidewalk after I left the car." He took another drink. "Afraid to tell." This time he drained the glass and reached for the bottle.

Watching Jed pour another half-glass of Scotch, I glanced at Danny, whose face registered the same surprise I felt. Something had happened to reawaken Jed Molinoff's conscience. And for that, I was shocked and grateful. But I'd still be checking Detective Schroeder's office at noon tomorrow to see if Jed showed up as promised.

"That's a good decision, Jed," I offered. "It'll be better if you approach the police first."

Jed kept staring at the glass of Scotch. Then his voice came softly. "I'm sorry about Karen."

That took me aback, and I waited another

full minute in case he ventured another comment. When he didn't, I started backing away. Jed removed his cell phone from his pocket and was dialing. Danny and I headed to the door and let ourselves out.

We walked to the elevator without a word. As the elevator doors closed and the motor's hum started on the downward motion, we looked at each other.

"That was weird," Danny said.

"I confess, I never expected him to admit it quickly. I mean, he didn't plead with me once."

"You had him by the balls, Molly," Danny said with a wry smile as the doors opened onto the lobby once more. "Molinoff knew you weren't going to cut him any slack."

I shook my head, still surprised. "I guess."

Danny pushed the heavy glass entry door open. "I know a good coffee shop down the avenue. I could use some right now, but I'd advise you to get decaf."

I cupped both hands around my hot chocolate. "I'm still amazed how submissive Jed was. All confrontation gone." I took a sip of the rich chocolately milk. Hot and sweet.

Danny hunched over his empty cup. "Think about it. His political career is over. There's proof he lied to the police in a murder investigation. That's bad enough. But when the reason he lied comes out, that's it. He's road kill. And the press will eat it up."

Danny's dramatic description was brutal but on target. The media vultures that hovered in the trees, watching and waiting, would swoop down and remove all traces of Jed. They'd scour the pavement clean.

I stared through the coffee shop window beside us in silence. Several couples hurried along the sidewalk, talking animatedly. "His apology caught me by surprise."

"He owed you one. You're still taking those photos to the detective, right?"

Two guys ran past the window. I noticed a couple pointing down the street and talking to another couple. "Yeah. I'll go over at noon."

A siren's wail sounded in the distance then grew louder, coming closer. A police cruiser shot by. Two couples dressed in workout clothes ran past on the sidewalk outside. More people appeared across the street.

"Something's up," Danny observed, staring out the window.

A college-aged couple entered the shop then, and a man sitting at the table beside us called out to them. "Hey, what's with the sirens and cops?"

"A guy jumped out of a building down the street," the young man said, pointing in the direction where Danny and I had been. "Right off the balcony." He made a diving gesture with his hands. *Blam!"*

His girlfriend made a face. "It was *gross!"*

The guy shrugged before they headed to the counter. Danny and I glanced at each other, then bolted for the door.

TWENTY-TWO

I sat at my kitchen table, drinking my first mug of coffee for the day, while I stared at the newspaper headlines again. *Nebraska congressman's chief of staff leaps to death. Confesses in suicide note. Killed ex-lover to keep her from revealing illicit affair. Lied to police. Covered up involvement in Hill staffer's murder in Georgetown.* And on and on. I'd read every article over and over. I couldn't read another word.

The garish bold-face headlines and sidebar stories highlighted the soap-opera details of the tragic story and blew them out of proportion. Made the people involved into caricatures, not real human beings. And they called that "reporting."

But standing on the sidewalk last night outside Jed Molinoff's condo building, the details were all too real. Real people had died in this tragedy. Not cartoon caricatures nor tabloid newspaper creations. Karen was

374

killed. Now, Jed's family had lost a husband and a father. Even Celeste's accidental death wouldn't have occurred if she hadn't been forced to leave Washington. The losses kept mounting.

I pushed the paper away and went to stand by the window to finish my morning coffee. Enjoy the blooms on the new azaleas and lilacs I had planted. I needed some beauty to balance the ugliness.

Jed's confession shocked me. I couldn't believe the headline when I first read it. Never had that possibility entered my mind. *Jed?* Jed Molinoff was a weak and weasely coward, yes. But a killer? That picture wouldn't come into focus.

My cell phone rang and I recognized Danny's number flashing. "You've seen the paper, right?" he asked.

"Oh, yeah. And it's hard to believe. I never thought Jed could kill Karen. How could he do that?"

"Maybe he just snapped. Fear does strange things to us all. It twists and distorts. Last night we couldn't understand why Jed killed himself rather than confess he'd concealed information. Now, we know why. Molinoff was guilty of murder. And the thought of prison was too much. He panicked."

Danny's explanation made as much sense

as anything that had surfaced from the quagmire of my own mind.

"Did you sleep at all after I took you home?" he asked.

"Fitfully. Weird dreams kept waking me up."

"That's understandable. Last night was pretty traumatic. We were the last ones to see Jed alive."

"You know, there are other things that keep bothering me, darting in and out of my head like they did last night."

"What's bothering you, Molly?"

"Ohhhh, stuff like the gun. I remember Schroeder saying that the gun used to kill Karen was a 9mm Glock. Why would Jed buy a gun like that? It's . . . it's just weird."

"It sounds like he planned it to me. As for the gun, if he bought it on the underground market then he'd take whatever the dealer offered him. And dumping it in the Bay was the smartest way to get rid of it. No way it would be found."

I pictured Jed taking his cabin cruiser out into the normally tranquil waters of Chesapeake Bay. Tossing the gun overboard along with the memories of all those weekend trysts with Karen. Cold-hearted didn't come close.

"Yeah, you're right, I guess."

"Anything else on your mind?" Danny asked when I'd been quiet for a minute.

"Yeah. Why did he write his suicide note on the computer? It's the last thing anyone will see of him. Wouldn't he write a suicide note by hand?"

"I don't know. I've never tried to kill myself. Maybe he was so scared his hand was shaking."

"Maybe so." I drained the last of my coffee and checked my watch. "Gotta get to the office. I'll call you later."

"Better idea. Why don't we go out to dinner?"

That *was* a better idea. "Sounds good. Why don't you pick me up here around five thirty."

"Got it. I'll find a special place. Someplace quiet and peaceful."

I flipped off my phone, slipped on my fuschia red suit jacket, and headed out the door. Quiet and peaceful? I'm not sure I knew what that was anymore.

"Hey, Striped Kitty, don't you have a home?" I called to the huge tabby sunning himself on the bricks edging my upper flowerbed.

Kitty answered with his usual lazy meow, not bothering to move. Wherever he belonged, Striped Kitty had taken up residence beside the flowerbeds every day. He greeted me every late afternoon when I walked home from the Russell mansion.

I raced up the wrought iron steps and paused on my doorstep while I dug for my keys. A car door slammed nearby and Danny's voice called out. "Perfect timing."

"Hey, there. Let me check the mail and we can go," I said, slipping the key in the lock.

"No hurry. How'd everyone take the news?" Danny asked as he approached.

"Everyone was shocked. Senator Russell stopped by my office before he headed for the Hill. Peter was really shaken. He'd met Jed while working for a California congressman years ago. Albert and Luisa couldn't believe it. Casey, well, he's like you — cool, calm, and collected." I gave him a grin as he walked up the steps.

"Casey and I have just learned how to keep it from showing, that's all." Danny followed me inside the house.

His comment reminded me of something I'd thought about earlier today as I was trying to concentrate on emails and financial transactions while juggling phone calls and messages from acquaintances expressing their shock at hearing the news. Somewhere in the midst of all those condolences it occurred to me that I'd finally found closure on Karen's death.

Now, I could turn to the future and look ahead at last. *What lay ahead?* I wasn't entirely sure. But there was one intriguing possibility standing right in front of me. But first . . .

I bent to scoop up the mail that lay scattered around the hallway floor near the mail slot. "Casey volunteered to take the photos to Detective Schroeder for me so I could stay and handle all the messages of sympathy that poured in."

"See? You've only been here six weeks, and you've made friends already," he teased, fetching a larger envelope that had fallen to the side. "Here you go." He handed it to me.

I sorted through the letters in my hand as I walked down the hall. Reading the return address on the large envelope, I saw that it was from Celeste. I fingered the envelope and felt the small object inside. She said she'd mail me the last flash drive.

A chilly feeling rippled over my skin. It was spooky receiving mail from a person who had recently died so violently. But then several people had died violently lately. I tossed the package along with the letters onto my coffee table.

Danny leaned against the archway between the living room and hallway. "I've picked out a great place. Delicious food. Soft lights, private corner booths, superb wines."

I slipped off my red jacket and tossed it on a chair. The walk from the senator's house was hot. May was on our doorstep and ready to bring her bosom companions — heat and humidity. I unbuttoned the top two buttons of my white silk blouse as I strolled across the living room.

"Good food. That's a start. How's the coffee?"

"You gonna keep going with that, because it's starting to get interesting." He pointed to my blouse.

I returned Danny's devilish grin. "You didn't answer. How's the coffee?"

"You're distracting me. Coffee's good, but not as great as the wine."

"No wine for us tonight, Danny." I unbuttoned one cuff of my blouse and rolled the sleeve up to my elbow.

He stared at me. "You're kidding."

"Nope. Just food and coffee." I rolled up the other sleeve. "We have a lot of talking to do, so we'll keep eating and drinking coffee until they throw us out."

"Are you serious?"

"Absolutely. How late is that place open?"

"Late. What is it you want to talk about?"

I walked up to him, hands on hips, then looked into his eyes. "I want you to start with the day after high school graduation and start talking. I want to hear everything up to now. Where you've been, what you've done, everything."

"I thought we already did that the first time we talked."

"Bits and pieces. This time I want it all. Full disclosure."

He stared at me solemnly. "Believe me, you don't want to hear it all."

"Yeah, I do."

"Why?"

I held his gaze. "These last few weeks you've learned more about me than my oldest friends. You've seen me enraged, vengeful, protective, and everything in between. I'm feeling very exposed right now. If this relationship is going to continue, then I need to hear more from you."

Danny stared into my eyes for a full minute, and I let him see within. He glanced away for a second, then gave me a crooked smile. "Full disclosure, huh?"

"You got it, Squad Leader."

"That's gonna take a long time."

"We'll stay up all night if we have to. That's why no wine. No drinks. Just food and coffee. If that place throws us out, we'll find an all-night diner."

"You're relentless, you know that."

"It's one of my few virtues."

Danny laughed softly and proceeded to loosen his tie. Sliding it off, he shoved it into his jacket pocket. "Okay, corporal, grab your gear and let's go."

I went to retrieve my purse from the coffee table, and another memory shot from the back of my mind. An old memory. An old secret. It was time to reveal it. *Full disclosure.* I turned to join Danny at the door. He already had it open.

"You know I lied. To everyone," I said as I slowly walked across the room.

"Lied about what?" he asked, watching me.

"About coming back to Washington."

"What do you mean?"

I paused in front of him. "I told everyone that I'd never returned to Washington after Dave's death. Never set foot in the city. The closest I got was standing beside my father's grave in Arlington National Cemetery, looking across the Potomac." I stared out the open front door into the golden spring sunshine. "But that wasn't true. I did come back into the city. Just once. It was in 1985 after The Wall was placed near Lincoln Memorial. I went over one morning when I came home to see family. I told them I was going to check nursing homes for my father, but I drove across Memorial Bridge instead. It was April, and it was raining lightly. I started at one end of The Wall and went all the way around. Reading every name. Searching to see if yours was there." I looked back at Danny, saw the effect of my words on his face. "I needed to know."

Danny gazed at me for a long moment without saying a word. Then he reached over and placed his arm around my shoulders, pulling me beside him as we walked through the door. As we stepped outside into the late afternoon sunshine, he pressed his lips against my forehead in a warm kiss.

Raymond stood beside the expanse of windows that looked out over Washington. This high up, he could see Pennsylvania Avenue stretch from the Old Post Office all the way to the Capitol. The Mall and monuments lay spread out in the distance. Twilight was fast approaching, and several streetlights had already blinked into life. He sipped the thirty-year-old Scotch and savored its golden heat on his ragged throat.

"Smooth enough for you?" the man's deep voice sounded behind him.

"Ohhh, yeah." Raymond turned from the compelling view and rejoined his companion in the corner of the luxurious office. He sank into a buttery-soft black leather chair, then took another sweet sip of nectar.

"A case of the Scotch will be delivered to your door tomorrow." The silver-haired man held up his glass. "Congratulations, Raymond, on another excellent disposition. You've never let us down. We appreciate that." He took a sip of Scotch, flashing a large diamond and ruby ring.

Raymond lifted his glass, returning the toast. "And I appreciate the business, Spencer. To a successful partnership." He laughed softly until his cough kicked in.

"I have to admit I was worried about the Grayson girl. There wasn't the same time to plan as we did with the others. But it actually turned out to be the most ingenious yet. We managed to eliminate Grayson and remove a weak link at the same time." Spencer's deeply tanned face spread with a satisfied smile. "Molinoff had become unstable. Fillmore will be much better suited to our goals."

"You're sure Jackson will make Fillmore his chief of staff?"

"Absolutely. Jackson's so spooked at losing Jed and that little staffer, Allard, both within a few days, he grabbed on to Larry to stay afloat."

"It looks like all the pieces are falling into place." Raymond took another sip, then stared into his glass. "There's still one piece that might cause a problem."

"You mean the Grayson girl's aunt?" Spencer gave a dismissive wave. "She was only interested in finding her niece's killer. That's why we gave her Jed. He'd been clumsy enough to call attention to himself, so he was the logical solution to the uh, problem."

Raymond chuckled. "I'll bet Molinoff peed his pants when she emailed those photos of him in Grayson's car."

Spencer gave a little snort as he swirled the liquor in his glass. "Just about. Which only proved we made the right decision to eliminate him sooner rather than later. He was totally unreliable." Spencer took another drink, and ran his tongue over his upper lip.

"How'd you ever convince him to take the fall? Literally, I mean."

"I promised we'd take care of his wife and children with a sizable anonymous donation. Suicide would be far easier than spending life in prison, especially given today's prison population. Jed knew the photos would probably be enough to convict him. He also knew better than to try and squeal on us. His family would get nothing, and he'd still be behind bars where his life would be a living hell."

Raymond stared out into the office. "That staffer, Allard, was feeding information to the Malone woman. Copying emails for her before she died. What if Ms. Malone gets curious and starts asking questions?"

"She didn't see anything important, but we plan to keep an eye on her anyway. Just occasional monitoring. Oh, and thank your man for his photos. They're excellent."

"Well, let me know if you need any higher-level services," Raymond said with a low laugh, then took a sip before his cough started.

"Count on it," Spencer replied before draining his glass.

ABOUT THE AUTHOR

Maggie Sefton (Fort Collins, Colorado) is the author of the bestselling Knitting Mysteries (Penguin). Her books have spent several weeks on the Barnes and Noble bestseller list and the *New York Times* bestseller list.

The employees of Thorndike Press hope you have enjoyed this Large Print book. All our Thorndike, Wheeler, and Kennebec Large Print titles are designed for easy reading, and all our books are made to last. Other Thorndike Press Large Print books are available at your library, through selected bookstores, or directly from us.

For information about titles, please call:
  (800) 223-1244

or visit our Web site at:
  http://gale.cengage.com/thorndike

To share your comments, please write:
  Publisher
  Thorndike Press
  10 Water St., Suite 310
  Waterville, ME 04901